Jean Lorrain

Monsieur de Phocas

translated from the French
with an introduction and afterword
by Francis Amery

Dedalus / Hippocrene

Dedalus would like to thank The French Ministry of Foreign Affairs for its assistance in producing this translation.

Published in the UK by Dedalus Limited, Langford Lodge, St Judith's Lane, Sawtry, Cambs, PE17 5XE

UK ISBN 1 873982 15 1

Published in the USA by Hippocrene Books Inc, 171, Madison Avenue, New York, NY10016

US ISBN 0 7818 0210 5

Distributed in Canada by Marginal Distribution, Unit 103, 277, George Street North, Peterborough, Ontario, KJ9 3G9
Distributed in Australia & New Zealand by Peribo Pty Ltd, 26, Tepko Road, Terrey Hills, N.S.W.2084
Distributed in South Africa by William Waterman Publications, PO Box 5091, Rivonia 2128

Publishing History
First published in France in 1901
First published in England by Dedalus in 1994

Translation, introduction and afterword copyright © Francis Amery 1994

Typeset by Datix International Limited, Bungay, Suffolk
Printed in Finland by Wsoy

Decadence from Dedalus

Books in the Decadence from Dedalus series include:

Senso (and other stories) – Boito £6.99
The Child of Pleasure – D'Annunzio £7.99
The Triumph of Death – D'Annunzio £7.99
The Victim (L'Innocente) – D'Annunzio £7.99
Angels of Perversity – de Gourmont £6.99
The Dedalus Book of Roman Decadence – editor
G. Farrington £7.99
The Dedalus Book of German Decadence – editor
R. Furness (June 94) £8.99
La-Bas – J. K. Huysmans £7.99
Monsieur de Phocas –Lorrain £7.99
The Green Face – Meyrink £7.99
The Diary of a Chambermaid – Mirbeau £7.99
Torture Garden – Mirbeau £7.99
Le Calvaire – Mirbeau £7.99 (June 94)
Monsieur Venus – Rachilde £6.99
La Marquise de Sade – Rachilde £8.99 (August 94)
The Dedalus Book of Decadence – editor B. Stableford
£7.99
The Second Dedalus Book of Decadence – editor
B. Stableford £8.99

Decadent titles in the Dedalus European Classics series include:

Little Angel – Andreyev £4.95
The Red Laugh – Andreyev £4.95
Les Diaboliques – Barbey D'Aurevilly £6.99
The Cathedral –J. K. Huysmans £6.95
En Route – J. K. Huysmans £6.95

All these titles can be obtained from your local bookshop, **or by
post** from Dedalus by writing to:
*Dedalus Cash Sales, Langford Lodge, St Judith's Lane,
Sawtry, Cambs, PE17 5XE*
Please enclose a cheque to the value of the books ordered + £1
pp for the first book and 75p thereafter up to a maximum of
£4.75

INTRODUCTION

The life and Career of Jean Lorrain

Paul Alexandre Martin Duval was born on 9 August 1855 at Fécamp, a small seaside town in Normandy. He considered that he came from a good family, but it was not a noble one. His father, Amable Duval, was a ship-owner whose vessels were involved in trans-Atlantic trade; his paternal grandfather and great-grandfather had captained similar vessels. Like them he was fair-haired, a trait which he attributed to Viking blood.

In later life, when he had become Jean Lorrain because his father did not want the good name of Duval to be trailed through the mud of a literary career, his feelings about his ancestry were mixed – as, indeed, were his feelings about everything else. On the one hand he was prepared to be proud of the blond taint of 'barbarism', which set him apart from the effete snobs of Paris and made him – seen from one oblique angle – a better kind of man than they. On the other hand, like the scion of any family of *parvenus*, he was very conscious of the fact that he was not an aristocrat, and would never be fully accepted into the high social circles whose lifestyle and pretensions he desperately coveted. The fascinated loathing which he cultivated for the decadence of *fin de siècle* Paris has a good deal of envy and ardent desire in it; in the words of Hubert Juin, he 'loved his epoch to the point of detestation.'

Fécamp only came to life in the summer months, when the ships from America regularly entered and left the harbour. Young Paul enjoyed this time of year, and fully appreciated the romance of ships and faraway places, but the attractions of the shipping business itself were not obvious to him. He was, in any case, primarily his mother's child, and although his possessive, ever-anxious mother was the daughter of an engineer, she was far more interested in aesthetic matters. She also had literary connections; her elder sister had married one Eugène Mouton, a published author. She was Amable Duval's second wife – the first had died childless – and was eighteen years his junior; she does not appear to have been close to her husband, but she was very close to Paul, who was her only child.

Paul's love of fiction was fostered at an early age and fervently encouraged. He was exceptionally fond of fairy tales, fables and fantasies, particularly fascinated by the idealised princesses who were so often their central characters. In later life he was to write many such *contes* himself, the vast majority of them featuring exotic princesses; his most important collection of them was issued under the title *Princesses d'ivoire et d'ivresse* (1902). He was also very fond of charades, and loved dressing up in silks and velvets; he was fascinated, too, by the glamour of circuses.

The Maupassant family were neighbours of the Duvals – a cut above them socially although not obviously richer – and Paul was once allowed to visit when Hervé de Maupassant, who was two years older than he, was staying with his grandmother. Hervé's older brother, Guy, was also present, and consented to join in their games, although he took a certain delight in tormenting and frightening the two smaller boys.

Paul attended the Lycée du Prince-Impérial at Vanves 1864–9, and then spent an unhappy time with the Dominicans at Arcueil, which mainly served to confirm a contemptuous hatred for the clergy which was to last a lifetime. By this time he was something of an *enfant terrible*, who had discovered the perverse rewards of shocking people, and he had already become notorious in and around Fécamp. It was easy enough to violate the ultra-conventional expectations of the local provincial gentry, but Paul must have been acutely aware of the fact that no mere novice in the art of notoriety could possibly compete with the English exiles who had crossed the channel to avoid the fiercer strictures of Victorianism. The most famous of these was Algernon Swinburne, who had lived nearby for some years and still remained the perfect model of notoriety so far as Fécamp was concerned.

Paul was too young to have encountered Swinburne personally, but Guy de Maupassant had, and Edmond Goncourt – who was later to become Jean Lorrain's fast friend and father-figure – had also visited him. The exotically lurid décor of Swinburne's house, and the scandalous things which were rumoured to go on there were, however, common knowledge, and what Paul heard about them at second-hand had a strong influence on his notion of what true decadence was. He did encounter Lord Arthur Somerset, a colourful character in his own right, who was a great admirer of Oscar Wilde. Lord Arthur took an interest in young Paul and maintained a correspondence with him, sending him pictures by Walter Crane and Edward Burne-Jones by way of assisting his artistic education. One of Jean Lorrain's most striking early stories – the title-story of the collection *Sonyeuse* (1891) – is a fantasy somewhat reminiscent of Edgar Allan Poe, in which a young man from Fécamp encounters an exotic English exile, Lady Mordaunt, with bizarre consequences.

By far the most significant of Paul's adventures in and around Fécamp was, however, his brief liaison with Judith Gautier, who was the daughter of one of the central figures in the French Romantic movement, Théophile Gautier. He met her while she was on a seaside holiday in 1873. She was ten years older than he, still married to – but separated from – the writer Catulle Mendès. Mendès was then a leading light among the 'Parnassian' poets but was later to become a central figure in the Decadent movement, as much for his lifestyle as for his rather cynical prose fictions in that vein. Judith was not short of admirers – she had already met and enchanted Wagner – but she was at a loose end and took Paul temporarily in hand. To her the encounter was trivial – she made no mention of Paul

Duval or Jean Lorrain in her autobiography, although (the significance of this will become clear in due course) she gave accounts of her friendships with Robert de Montesquiou and Pierre Loti – but he was profoundly affected by it. It changed his life to such an extent that Edmond Goncourt was later to lament that it had been the ruination of him, and that everything which happened to him after Judith Gautier's intervention was a long-drawn-out process of moral and physical suicide. Goncourt seems, in fact, to have believed that Jean Lorrain's homosexuality was some kind of traumatic response to his doomed infatuation with Judith.

Lorrain always declared that Judith Gautier was the only woman, save for his mother, he ever loved – but he had a long series of close Platonic friendships with various women and became one of the many ardent worshippers of the actress Sarah Bernhardt. Paul's literary tastes were decisively shifted by Judith. She poured scorn on his admiration for the sentimental verses of Alfred de Musset – a taste which he associated thereafter with childish innocence – and offered him the gaudy exoticism of Charles Leconte de Lisle instead. She was herself a lover of the exotic, especially the Oriental; her most notable work was a lush novel of the East, *Le Dragon imperial* (1868; tr. as *The Imperial Dragon*) Paul had already written some poetry, but the love-poems which he dedicated to Judith, written in the mid-1870s and later included in *La Forêt bleue* (1883), were his first serious literary adventures.

Paul's military service was undertaken on a 'volontariat' basis, by which it was cut to one year in consideration of a payment. He spent his time in barracks at Saint-Germain-en-Laye & Rocquencourt. His father, deciding that he must be prepared for life in the real world, then sent him to study law. In the course of these studies, which extended from 1876 to 1878, he frequently travelled back and forth between Paris and Fécamp. The project was probably doomed from the start, but Paul's situation was complicated by health problems. He began to suffer from burning fevers and chest-pains, probably caused by tuberculosis. He would suffer recurrent bouts of this trouble for the rest of his life, but he was sufficiently robust to enjoy good health in between the bouts until the problems were compounded by other factors. The fevers themselves were both fierce and debilitating, sometimes bad enough to require injections of morphine, but he never became a habitual user of the drug. Morphine was then regarded as primarily a female indulgence – men were supposed to smoke their opium raw – and his characterization of 'morphinées' in his later fiction is savagely scornful. His feelings regarding his illness were typically mixed; he knew well enough that Swinburne had been a career invalid, and he insisted that his sickroom at Fécamp – to which he continually returned so that his mother could nurse him – was appropriately decorated.

It cannot have come as a surprise to Amable Duval when his son finally announced that he was giving up the law in favour of a literary career; he agreed readily enough to provide a modest allowance, on condition that Paul used a pseudonym. Paul and his mother leafed through a directory in search of something suitable, and were delighted with their choice. In 1880 Jean Lorrain set himself up in Montmartre, eager to launch imself into the Bohemian life.

This was the Montmartre of Toulouse-Lautrec, a world of cheap furnished rooms in which impoverished members of the literary *avant-garde* rubbed shoulders with cheap prostitutes and formed enthusiastic cliques in cafés. The café in which Jean Lorrain elected to spend most of his days was the Chat Noir. Paul Verlaine was known to drop in occasionally – and was later to launch the fad for 'Decadence' with a poem in *Le Chat Noir*, the periodical founded by the regulars – but the hard core of the group were then in the habit of describing themselves as 'Hydropathes' and 'Zutistes'. They included Jean Moréas and Jean Richepin. The Hydropathes were literary Satanists, great admirers of the historian Jean Michelet, whose curiously rhapsodic book *La Sorcière* (1862; tr. as *Satanism and*

Witchcraft) had hailed the witches burned in days of yore as heroic and virtuous antagonists of a tyrannical church. They were enthusiastic apologists for the Devil, and conscientiously re-worked the mythology of witches' sabbats and black masses. Many of the poems Lorrain wrote under this influence are reprinted in *Sang des dieux* (1882) and *La Forêt bleue*.

Sang des dieux, Lorrain's first book, had a frontispiece by Gustave Moreau. Lorrain met Moreau in 1880, and immediately became a devout admirer of his work. The two did not become friends – Moreau became a virtual recluse in his later years – but Lorrain visited the artist's studio in the Rue La Rochefoucauld, which was left to the state as a museum when Moreau died in 1898. Moreau's work revealed to Lorrain a whole world-view: a gorgeous symbolically-transfigured vision of a world dominated by lust and luxury (concepts which seem to be more closely related in French than in English, in the words *luxure* and *luxe*), where eroticism is inextricably linked with cruelty and death, placed in fabulously gaudy settings: a 'Sublime Sodom', as Lorrain's biographer Philippe Jullian put it. The hallucinatory world of Moreau's art is dominated by *femmes fatales* – Salomé, Helen of Troy, the Sirens – who are all, in some sense, incarnations of the same eternal person. In Flaubert's *La Tentation de Saint Antoine* (1874; tr. as *The Temptations of St Anthony*) – another favourite of the Hydropathes – the archetype of which all these other females are avatars is called Ennoïa; she features in person, of course, in Moreau's own versions of the saint's torments. In many different guises – including Astarté, the name of one of the many pagan deities demonised by the monotheistic followers of Jehovah – Ennoïa was to play a central role in Jean Lorrain's personal mythos, although 'she' had an understandable tendency to become androgynous or frankly masculine.

In 1883 Lorrain began to frequent the salon of Charles Buet, where he made three more highly significant acquaintances. The first of these was the novelist Jules-Amédée

Barbey d'Aurevilly, then in his seventies, whose most famous book was *Les Diaboliques* (1874; tr. as *The She-Devils*), a collection of misogynistic stories about women whose beautiful faces and manners conceal appalling depths of depravity. Barbey d'Aurevilly was the leading exponent of the philosophy of 'dandyism', which he had considerably tranformed after borrowing the initial inspiration from Beau Brummell, promoting it not merely as a dress-code or even a lifestyle, but as a whole way of being-in-the-world. The most significant partial convert to this creed had been Baudelaire – now long-dead – but the incarnate image of dandyism, who seemed to have come by the heritage naturally, was Comte Robert de Montesquiou, *the* 'man of the world'.

Lorrain became such a wholehearted convert to dandy-ism that Remy de Gourmont was later to describe him as 'the sole disciple of Barbey d'Aurevilly', but he was always working from a position of irreparable disadvantage. Many of those who were already dandies were of the opinion that one had to be born to the vocation, and that no matter how hard one tried to adopt the philosophy and the manners of a dandy, one could never really *become* one. Several of Lorrain's contemporaries were inclined to refer to him as 'the poor man's Montesquiou' and it is hardly surprising that Lorrain cultivated a deep loathing for the man. Throughout his career as a chronicler of the *fin de siècle* Lorrain sniped at Montesquiou, often viciously, but he could never win the undeclared war because Mon-tesquiou automatically adopted the perfect defence: he ignored Lorrain completely, refusing even to concede him the dignity of being noticed.

The second important acquaintance Lorrain made *chez* Charles Buet in 1883 was Joris-Karl Huysmans. Seven years older than Lorrain, Huysmans had made his name as a naturalist of the school of Zola, but his career was about to undergo a decisive sea-change. He was working on a highly original novel called *À rebours* (tr. as *Against the Grain* and *Against Nature*), which would be published the following year and would become one of the foundation-stones of the Decadent movement. Lorrain's fourth collection of poetry, *Les Griseries* (1887), consists of material explicitly inspired by *À rebours*. Lorrain and Huysmans had a good deal in common, including their interest in Satanism, and they became good friends – a friendship which endured rather better than most of Lorrain's associations, although it was weakened when Huysmans got religion shortly after publishing his classic novel of Satanism *Là-Bas* (1891; tr. under the same title). Long after that, Huysmans wrote to Lorrain in order to heap praise upon *Monsieur de Phocas* (1901), recognising both its close kinship with and its significant variations from *À rebours*.

The third, and by no means the least, of the friends Lorrain made through Buet was Marguerite Eymery, who called herself Rachilde. Her literary career was yet to begin in earnest, although she had already begun to cultivate the notoriety which shaped her reputation. Rachilde shared Lorrain's passionate fascination for masked balls, which were then in their last period of great fashionability, and he became her regular escort, enthusiastically competing with her in the outrageousness of his costumes. The fact that he was openly homosexual made the liaison all the more useful in terms of her self-publicity. Lorrain was also making a name for himself with the vicious reviews which he wrote for the *Courrier français*, a successor to *Le Chat Noir*, where he first cultivated the scathing rhetoric for which he became famous. He attacked Zola, Maupassant and – perhaps most vitriolically of all – Catulle Mendès, but he could be correspondingly enthusiastic about the things he liked, which included Elémir Bourges' pioneering Decadent novel *Le Crépuscule des dieux* (1883 and, Huysmans' *À rebours*. His article advertising Rachilde, 'Madame Salamandre' (1884), became her launching-pad, well in advance of the *succès de scandale* she was to achieve with *La Marquise de Sade* (1887) and *Monsieur Vénus* (1889). Lorrain and Rachilde drifted apart in the years following her marriage to Alfred Vallette, the somewhat staid founder and editor of the *Mercure de France* (of whose work Lorrain was scornful) but they remained on good terms and she treated him far better than some of his other female friends.

The firmest friend Lorrain made in Paris, however, was Edmond Goncourt, whom he met in 1885. Goncourt was thirty-three years older than Lorrain, but this did not inhibit their friendship; they remained close until Goncourt's death in 1896. Goncourt always wrote about Lorrain in warm but sad terms, lamenting the tragedy of his having somehow gone wrong in life. He took the younger man under his wing, perhaps seeing something in him that reminded him of his younger brother and collaborator Jules, who had died in 1870.

In 1886 Lorrain met Sarah Bernhardt for the first time, and became one of the most fervent of her many admirers. She was the central figure of the Parisian *monde*, and she held the key to social acceptance in the circles in which Lorrain desperately desired to move. Her attitude to him was, however, amused tolerance. She accepted his adoration, but like Judith Gautier before her she preferred the company of Pierre Loti and Robert de Montesquiou, his two *bêtes noires*. They were both as flamboyantly homosexual as Lorrain, but in the eyes of the world – or those people in it who really mattered – Lorrain could never match Loti for style or Montesquiou for breeding. Lorrain wrote several plays whose main parts were tailor-made for Sarah, but she refused to appear in any of them. He continued to be extremely enthusiatic about her work – especially when she played male roles, like de Musset's Lorenzaccio, the would-be saviour of Renaissance Florence, who dons a mask in order to charm and ultimately to murder the tyrant who threatens it – but his patience finally broke. In 1900, when she had one of her greatest triumphs in Edmond Rostand's *L'Aiglon*, Lorrain attacked it with all the fury he could muster. Later, though, he was to use her as a model for characters in two of his more sentimental novels: Nora Lerys in *Ellen* (1906) and Linda in *Le Tréteau* (1906).

13

Amable Duval died in 1886, leaving his heirs to discover that his financial affairs were, to say the least, not in good order. The estate had to be liquidated in order to pay off his debts – a process which soured Normandy in Lorrain's eyes, and increased the cynical hatred which he already had for all things bourgeois, epecially commerce and the law. Mercifully, his mother had kept complete control of her dowry, and was not impoverished – but the necessity for Lorrain to earn his own living was now acute. He threw himself into journalism with considerable determination, and increased his output of prose fiction considerably. He had published his first novel, *Les Lépillier* (1885), a year earlier, and followed it up with *Très Russe* (1886).

His fiction was destined to make him at least as many enemies as his journalism, and Guy de Maupassant was sufficiently incensed by resemblances between himself and one of the characters in *Très Russe* to send his seconds round to seek reparation from the author. No one knows what passed between them, but no duel actually took place. This was the first of several such incidents. In 1887 Lorrain did go to meet the journalist René Maizeroy, but both came away unscathed. In 1888 Paul Verlaine sent his seconds round after Lorrain had erroneously reported that he had been committed, but the matter went no further. The most famous of his duels was, however, still some way off.

In the short fiction which he now began to write so prolifically Lorrain frequently introduced homosexual themes. Lesbianism had long been fashionable as a literary theme thanks to Baudelaire – who intended at one point to attach the title *Les Lesbiennes* to the collection which became *Les Fleurs du Mal* (1857) – and Théophile Gautier's *Mademoiselle de Maupin* (1855) but male homosexuality was still hedged about with taboos. Lorrain was not entirely displeased by the shock-wave generated by his stories of this kind, and was happy to cash in on it, ultimately compiling a rich catalogue of brief stories detailing all manner of exotic fetishisms and perversions, but the reputation he cultivated left something to be desired. He would never be regarded as a writer of the first rank in his own country, and there was no possibility of his being translated into English. The work of making male homosexuality acceptable as a literary theme was left for Proust and Gide to do.

In 1887 Lorrain left Montmartre to install himself in an apartment in the Rue de Courty, which he was able to furnish according to his own calculatedly bizarre taste. The phantasmagorical aspects of this private world were considerably exaggerated by the fact that he had begun drinking ether. His motive for doing this was undoubtedly medicinal, and he was initially impressed by the sudden surge of vitality which a dose of the drug gave him when he was ill or exhausted; it was one of several 'cures' with which he attempted to combat his increasing periods of debilitation. Under the hallucinogenic influence of ether, though, his apartments soon came to seem literally and figuratively haunted. Those of his short stories which did not deal with sexual perversity were mostly supernatural, and his works in this vein became increasingly strange and horrific, more akin to the works of E. T. A. Hoffman than Poe; much of his best work is in this vein, and he wrote some very striking stories of bizarre apparitions and peculiar obsessions. He was later to write a self-conscious cycle of 'contes d'un buveur d'éther', which were included in *Sensations et souvenirs* (1895), but the effects of the drug can clearly be seen in the stories in his other collections, particularly *Buveurs d'âmes* (1893) and *Histoires de masques* (1900).

In 1888 Lorrain left the *Courrier* for *L'Evénement*, where he was given a regular column in which to extend his mordant literary criticism into a more general critique of contemporary Parisian society. He called his essays along these lines 'Pall-Malls', after the English weekly *Pall Mall Gazette*, which had been edited since 1883 by W. T. Stead. Stead was an odd combination of muck-raker and crusader, who became a role-model for many later journalists. Stead's exposés of the London brothels which specialised in flagellation and child prostitution caused a great sensation, which was magnified still further when he was condemned to a period of hard labour after buying a child from her mother in order to demonstrate how readily children were sold into prostitution. Lorrain's image of the English gentry seems to have been largely formed by Stead's lurid articles, and he set out to do similar disservice to his own countrymen. His political stance was a curious kind of 'right-wing anarchism' based on a scornful hatred of both capitalism and socialism. He was a nationalist through and through, despising the revolutionaries of 1789 for their bourgeois tendencies, but the fact that he became a diehard opponent of the Dreyfusards probably had far more to do with his long-standing dislike for Zola than any judgment of Dreyfus' culpability. (Lorrain was also outspokenly anti-Semitic, but that too might have been a by-product of his personal detestation of Judith Gautier's Jewish ex-husband.) Problems with obtaining payment for his work led him to quit *L' Evénement* in 1890 for the *Écho de Paris*, to which he was a prolific contributor – under various pseudonyms – until 1895, after which he worked mainly for *Le Journal*.

At the end of 1890 Lorrain left his haunted house in the Rue de Courty and moved to Auteuil. By this time his recurrent fevers were complicated by syphilis. Sarah Bernhardt, who did little else for him, at least referred him to a good physician: the celebrated chirurgeon Dr Pozzi, who was a colourful and well-known character in his own right. Pozzi told him to stop taking ether, advising him that his gut had become so badly ulcerated due to the effects of the drug that surgical intervention was necessary. Pozzi carried out the operation, removing a section of the small intestine, in 1893.

Despite his health problems Lorrain travelled to Spain and Algeria in 1892, the first of several expeditions abroad. He was joined in Auteuil by his mother, who lived with him until his death – a somewhat mixed blessing, given her extreme disapproval of his lifestyle, but a blessing nevertheless. He was now earning good money and was able to support her in style; he sent her to the very best couturiers and had her painted by the noted portraitist Antonio de La

Gandara (who also did the most striking portrait of Lorrain himself).

He formed several new friendships with women around this time. The first – and the one of which his mother most fervently disapproved, especially when rumours began to circulate about a possible marriage – was with the exotic Liane de Pougy, a performing artiste of sorts whose great ambition was to be the most fashionable and most expensive whore in Paris: a perfect *femme fatale*. Lorrain wrote 'pantomimes' for her, just as he composed songs for the more respectable pianist Yvette Guilbert, whom he met the following year. Between 1892 and 1896 Lorrain was also frequently in the company of Jeanne Jacquemin, an artist in pastels, who shared his intense fascination with the occult. Together they ventured into the 'Occult Underworld' recently made fashionable by *Là-Bas* 1891 and made highly visible by the self-styled Rosicrucian mage Josephin Péladan – also a prolific author of books railing against the Decadence of modern Paris. Jeanne Jacquemin's husband was a friend of Verlaine, and did not seem to mind the wayward lifestyle she adopted. She liked to pose as a notable figure in Decadent Paris – she claimed intimate acquaintance with Rodenbach and Remy de Gourmont – but tended to be jealously possessive, and Lorrain fell out with her before setting off on his second trip to Algiers. He did not see her again for some years, and she faded from the Paris scene; unfortunately, she neither forgot nor forgave him.

In 1896 Lorrain was probably the best-paid journalist in Paris, and he had reached the summit of his brief celebrity. It is rather ironic that he is best-remembered today for an incident which attracted little attention at the time but which now figures as an episode in the many biographies of Marcel Proust. Lorrain twice attacked Proust's first book, *Les Plaisirs et les jours* (1896; tr. as *Pleasures and Regrets*), the second time in an article published in January 1897. The slanders were no worse than Lorrain's customary stock-in-trade, but Proust sent his seconds to demand satisfaction and the two men met on 6 February, armed with pistols. Two shots were discharged harmlessly, and the two then shook hands.

Lorrain continued to make friends as well as enemies, particularly among the people he met in the home of Jean de Tinan, where Rachilde was a frequent fellow-guest. It was there that he made the acquaintance of Pierre Louÿs, whose lush erotic fantasy set in ancient Alexandria, *Aphrodite*, took Paris by storm in 1896. He also met the poet Henri de Régnier, who remained grateful for the help which Lorrain lent his career, the pioneering surrealist Alfred Jarry, and Colette, who seemed to like him far better than many of the women with whom he kept closer company. The circle dissipated when Tinan died, not long before Lorrain decided that he had to leave Paris for the sake of his health and remove his household to the balmier climes of Nice.

It is significant that Lorrain abandoned Paris at end of 1900. For ten years he had been the self-appointed chronicler of the *fin de siècle* and the scourge of Decadent Paris; a great deal of his rhetoric had drawn on the fact that the nineteenth century was winding down, approaching an end that was devoutly to be desired. He was very conscious of the extent to which that rhetoric would lose its force once the new century was born, and this consciousness was reinforced by the spectacular Exposition Universelle held in Paris in 1900. It was as if he had fallen out of fashion instantly, by prior appointment. He continued to write for *Le Journal*, but he now gave priority to a new endeavour: the writing of two novels which would provide a kind of retrospective summary of the Decadent Movement and the world which had given birth to it. Huysmans had begun the movement with *À rebours* and Lorrain set out to provide it with a fitting conclusion. The two novels in question were *Monsieur de Phocas* (1901) and *Le Vice errant* (1902). They were recognised as his masterpieces, but were not greeted with any great popular acclaim.

Things began to go badly wrong for Lorrain immediately after the two novels appeared in print. Jeanne Jacquemin, seemingly repentant of her colourful past, recognised herself in Mme de Charmaille, one of the characters in a *nouvelle* called 'Les Pelléastres', serialised in *Le Journal*. Lorrain had grafted attributes of his friends on to his fictional characters many times before – often unflatteringly, as in *Monsieur de Bougrelon* (1897), whose central character is a sharp caricature of Barbey d'Aurevilly – without any significant comeback, but Jeanne Jacquemin sued him for defamation of character. The case generated a great deal of bad publicity, and Lorrain was attacked from all sides by those who had once walked in fear of his sarcasm. The court – perhaps desirous of making an example of him, although it is unclear whose benefit they had in mind – required him to pay astonishingly high damages of 80,000 francs.

The settlement of this suit left Lorrain broke and vulnerable; he was soon to face a second lawsuit and – perhaps more seriously, in terms of his reputation – a formal charge of corrupting public morals by literary means, brought by a certain M. Greuling against *Monsieur de Phocas*. A similar charge had once been the making of Baudelaire's reputation, but in Lorrain's case it only served to illustrate how dramatically the tide had turned, and how ardently the people of twentieth century Paris desired to advertise that the nineteenth century was dead and gone. He was disappointed that hardly anyone came forward to speak in his defence (Colette was one exception), and particularly hurt by the fact that Huysmans remained silent.

Lorrain threw himself into his writing in order to pay the damages, and continued to produce work at a furious pace, but much of it was pure hackwork. *La Maison Philibert* (1904), a calculatedly scabrous novel about a brothel, is of some interest as a Decadent work, but the other novels of this period were much weaker. His health continued to deteriorate, and his tuberculosis returned in full force in 1905; he took various 'cures' in the spas of the Riviera, but they left him sicker than before. With typically grim irony he began signing his articles in *Le Journal* and *La Vie parisienne* 'Le Cadavre'. He was grateful to find, though, that he still had some admirers. In 1906 he met for the first time the Italian Decadent Gabriele D'Annunzio, who readily acknowledged him as a great influence, and he received a heart-warming letter of appreciation from the sculptor Rodin, whose work he had always admired and complimented.

On 12 June 1906 Lorrain returned to Paris to help organise an art exhibition and to involve himself in an adaptation for the opera of one of his contes, *La Princesse sous verre* (1896). He took the opportunity to see Pozzi, who called in several colleagues to second his opinion that Lorain's gut was so badly ulcerated that an operation could not help. Pozzi could only prescribe palliative measures, and it was in the course of following this prescription that Lorrain died. He was found unconscious in his bathroom on 28 June, having perforated his colon while giving himself an enema. He was removed to hospital and his mother hastened from Nice to sit with him, but he died without regaining consciousness two days later. A funeral was held in Paris at Saint-Ferdinand-des-Ternes before his body was taken to Fécamp for burial. Régnier was there, and La Gandara, and Paul Adam, and Colette, but Sarah Bernhardt did not come, and nor did Yvette Guilbert; Liane de Pougy sent a wreath.

MONSIEUR DE PHOCAS

THE LEGACY

Monsieur de Phocas. With a flick of my fingers I turned the card over and then back again; the name inscribed upon it was completely unknown to me.

In the absence of my manservant, who was at Versailles for a twenty-eight day stint in barracks, the cook had introduced the visitor. Monsieur de Phocas was in my study.

Grumbling, I rose from the armchair where I had been dozing – the day was so warm! – and went into my study, determined to send the unwelcome visitor away.

Monsieur de Phocas! Having opened the door unobtrusively, I paused on the threshold.

Monsieur de Phocas was a tall but frail young man of twenty-eight or thereabouts, whose crimped and short-cut brown hair surmounted an extraordinarily old and bloodless face. He was neatly dressed in a myrtle-green suit, and he sported a pale green silk cravat speckled with gold,

That finely-chiselled profile, the deliberate stiffness of the slim, elongated body, the arabesque quality – one might almost say the *tormented* arabesque quality – of that elegant figure . . . I was certain that I had seen it all before somewhere.

It seemed that Monsieur de Phocas was not yet aware of my presence – or was it that he did not deign to notice me? He stood lightly at ease beside my desk in a graceful pose. With the tip of his walking-stick – it was a malacca cane worth at least two hundred francs, with a head bizarrely carved from raw ivory, which immediately attracted my attention – he was turning the pages of a manuscript set down among the books and papers, scanning them negligently from on high.

The sheer impertinence of it was intolerably odious.

This manuscript – the pages of prose or verse which the tip of the cane was stirring – had been set down among my own notes and letters, in the privacy of my own home, by a curious and indifferent visitor! I was both indignant at the act and entranced by its audacity – for I like and admire audacity in all things, and in those persons who exhibit it. Already, though, my attention had been distracted. My eyes were caught by the greenish fire suddenly lit within the folds of his cravat by an enormous emerald, whose proud facets sparkled strangely. The gem itself was strange enough, made all the more so by virtue of the fact that its fine, polished facets seemed almost as if they had been modelled in pale wax. It was similar to those which can be seen, bearing the signature of Clouet or Porbus, in the gallery of the Louvre dedicated to the Valois.

It seemed that Monsieur de Phocas did not even suspect my presence. Relaxed and aristocratic, he continued rummaging among my papers from a distance. The sleeve of his jacket had ridden up a little, and I saw that he wore a thin platinum bracelet studded with opals around his right wrist.

That bracelet! I remembered now.

I had seen that frail, white, thoroughbred wrist before, and that narrow circlet of jewelled platinum. Yes, I had seen them, but on that occasion they had been working through the select jewel-cases of a prestigious artist, a master goldsmith and engraver. I had seen them *chez* Barruchini, in the shop of the metalworker who was believed to have run away from Florence and whose establishment, known only to lovers of his art, was hidden in the depths of the Rue Visconti – a curious and ancient courtyard in what is perhaps the narrowest of the streets of old Paris, where Balzac was once a printer.

Delicately pale and clear, like the hand of a princess or a courtesan, the hand which had been stripped of its glove by the Duc de Fréneuse – for I also knew his real name now – had glided that day with infinite slowness above a veritable heap of lapis-lazulis, sardonyxes, onyxes and cornelians, pierced here and there by topazes, amethysts and rubicelles. That hand, ungloved by the Duc de Fréneuse, had sometimes settled like a waxen bird, designating with a finger the selected gem . . .

The selected gem . . .

My memories of that day were so precise that I could even recall the sound of his voice, and the manner in which the Duc took leave of Barruchini, saying in a curt tone to the goldsmith: 'The item must be delivered to me within six days. You have only the inlaying to do now. I am counting on you, Barruchini, as you may count on me.'

It was a peacock of enamelled metal which he had come to order from the master engraver. He had come to select for himself the jewels to be displayed on the piece, which would be one more original to add to a vast collection. The fancies of the duc de Fréneuse could no longer be enumerated; they had become the stuff of legend.

More than that, the gentleman himself had become a legend in his own right: a legend unconsciously created at first, but which he had undertaken to cherish and maintain. Such fabulous tales were whispered concerning this young man – a millionaire five times over, scion of a great and well-connected family – who played no part in society, had no friends, showed off no mistresses, and routinely left Paris at the end of November in order to spend his winters in the Orient!

A profound mystery, thickened according to one's taste, enshrouded his life. Outside of two or three theatrical premières which mobilised all Paris in the spring, the pale and tall young man whose figure was so straight and whose face was so world-weary was never encountered. At one time he had kept a racing stable, and had enjoyed considerable success as a breeder, but he had abruptly ceased to attend the meetings; he had sold his horses and his stud-farm. After deserting the boudoirs of young women he had for a short time defected to the salons of the suburbs, but these had only briefly retained his interest before he made a clean break and disappeared completely.

Nowadays, Fréneuse was a virtual stranger in his own

land. In the spring, however, when some sensational acrobat, male or female, was advertised to appear at the Olympia, the circus or the Folies Bergère, it sometimes happened that one would encounter Fréneuse every evening of the week – and that strange insistence would became a new pretext for stories, a new source of hypotheses, and of such copious gossip that everyone would know about it. Then Fréneuse would suddenly immerse himself again, retreating into silence. One would hear that he had set out once more for London or Smyrna, for the Balearics or Naples, perhaps for Palermo or Corfu – no one would be any the wiser, until the day came when someone at the club might report having met him on the quay, at the home of an antiquary, at the establishment of some dealer in precious stones in the Rue de Lille or some numismatist in the Rue Bonaparte, seated most attentively at a table, magnifying glass in hand, before some twelfth-century intaglio or some collectible cameo.

Fréneuse kept in his apartment in the Rue de Varenne an entire private museum of precious stones, celebrated among collectors and merchants alike. He had also, it was said, brought back from the Orient – from the souks of Tunis and the bazaars of Smyrna – a veritable treasuretrove of antique jewellery, precious tapestries, rare weapons and deadly poisons; but Fréneuse had no friends, and few visitors were ever admitted to the family apartment-house. His only intercourse was with merchants or other collectors like himself; among these, the master engraver Barruchini was perhaps the only one who was ever allowed to cross his threshold in the Rue de Varenne. The rest of the world was politely shown the door.

'One would be deranged by the opium fumes,' said the world, by way of revenge – and that was the most anodyne of the stories which were put about regarding the Comte de Fréneuse, so vindictively was the handsome young man despised by the great society of idlers and good-for-nothings. This man, it was said, had brought back with him all the vices of the Orient.

And it was the Duc de Fréneuse that I now had in my home, negligently rifling through my papers with the tip of his cane! It was Fréneuse and his legends – his mysterious past, his equivocal present and his even darker future – who had entered into my house under a false name.

He lifted his eyes, perceiving me at last. After a polite inclination of his head, he made a gesture as though to reassemble the pages scattered on my table.

'Firstly,' he said, as if he had read my thoughts, 'I must ask you to excuse me, monsieur, for introducing myself into your home under a false name, but that name is now my own. The Duc de Fréneuse is dead; there is no longer anyone but Monsieur de Phocas. Besides, I am on the brink of departing for a long absence. I am exiling myself from France, perhaps forever. This journey is the last one remaining to me; I have come to an important decision. All this undoubtedly matters little to you – and yet, given that I have taken the trouble to come to see you, perhaps it does matter a little.'

He gestured his refusal of the seat which I offered him, and likewise demanded that I let him continue.

'You know Barruchini. You have written an unforgetta-ble tribute to the engraver and his artistry – unforgettable for me at least, since it is their author that I chose to visit today. It was in the *Revue de Lutèce*. You have understood, and described in poetic terms, the multitudinous and turbid glimmers which constitute the prismatic art of that goldsmith-magician. Oh, what a mute and ever-changing fire sleeps within his jewels, what minute details of animals or flowers are set by him in the depths of gems! You have elegantly sung the praises of that golden flora, which is at once Byzantine, Egyptian and Renaissance! You have grasped the coralline quality of those submarine jewels – yes, submarine, for it is as if the almost-cerulean bloom of beryls, peridots, opals and pale sapphires, the colour of seaweeds and waves, has rested for a long time at the bottom of the sea. Like the rings of Solomon or the cups of the king of Thule, they belong to the caskets of cities engulfed by the sea; the daughter of the king of Ys must have worn such jewels when she delivered the keys of the lock-gates to the Demon . . .

'Oh, the Barruchini necklaces, those rills of blue and green stones, those over-weighty bracelets encrusted wih opals! Gustave Moreau has decked the nude bodies of his damned princesses with them. They are the jewellery of Cleopatra and Salomé. They are also the jewellery of legend, the jewellery of moonlight and evening:

'*And that which took place in times most ancient.*'

'That is the formula, as you have written, which springs to the lips when one confronts these glazed fruits, these flowers of polished stone set in gold. It is of Egypt and of the divided Roman Empire especially that these jewels of Memphis and Byzantium make one dream, but perhaps they remind one even more of the city of the king of Ys and its submerged lock-gates.

'You see that I know my authors. Now, no one has suffered more than myself from the morbid attraction of these jewels; and, sick unto death – seeing that I am being carried away by their translucent glaucous poison – it is you in whom I now wish to confide, monsieur: you, who have understood their sumptuous and dangerous magic well enough to communicate to others its thrill and its malaise.

'You alone can understand me. You alone can indulgently recognise the affinity which attracted me to you. The Duc de Fréneuse was merely an eccentric, monsieur; for all others save yourself, Monsieur de Phocas would be a madman. I mentioned just now the name of the city of Ys and the Demon which caused that city to be engulfed: the Demon of Lust, which seduced the daughter of the king. Such curses have the power to extend across the centuries. I tell you that this Demon is within me. A veritable Demon tortures and haunts me, and has done ever since my adolescence. Who knows – perhaps it was already in me when I was merely a child? Even though I may seem to you to be deluded, monsieur, I have suffered for many years the effects of a certain blue and green *something*.

'Whether it is the gleam of a gem or a gaze that I lust after – worse, that I am *bewitched* by – I am *possessed* by a certain glaucous transparence. It is like a hunger in me. I search for this gleam – in vain! – in the irises of eyes and the transparency of gemstones, but no human eye possesses it. Occasionally, I have detected it in the empty orbit of a statue's eye or beneath the painted eyelids of a portrait, but it has only been a decoy: the brightness is always extinguished, having scarcely been glimpsed.

I am above all else a lover of the past. Do you want me to tell you how the showcases of Barruchini have exasperated my illness? I have seen emerging and springing forth from his jewels that gaze which I seek. It is the gaze of Dahgut, the daughter of the king of Ys. It is also the gaze of Salomé. Above all, it is the limpid green clarity of the gaze of Astarté: that Astarté who is the Demon of Lust and also the Demon of the Sea . . .'

He paused, doubtless observing alarm in my features, and went on: 'Yes, agreed: I am a visionary, and what visions I have! Pray that you might be spared such torture, for I suffer so much from them that they will surely kill me. Yes, it is because of these visions and their horrible counsel, because of the whispers heaped upon me in my nightmares, that I am leaving Paris, leaving France, and leaving ancient Europe, which no longer has the power to contain such things . . .

'Will I escape them even in Asia?

'That night still . . . but I am abusing your hospitality. This is what I have come to ask of you, monsieur. I am going away, perhaps never to be seen again. I have consigned to these pages the first impressions of my illness: the unconscious temptations of a man of today, sunk in occultism and neurosis. Will you permit me to entrust these pages to you, and will you promise me to read them? I will send you the continuation of this first confession from

Asia, for which I shall shortly be embarking and where I wish to settle, in the hope that I might there find a remedy for my obsessions, for I need to cry out to someone the pangs of my anguish. I need to know that here in Europe there is someone who pities me, and would rejoice in my recovery if ever Heaven should grant it to me. Will you be that someone?'

I offered my hand to Monsieur de Phocas.

THE MANUSCRIPT

'And his hands – the lax gentleness of his icy handshake, his fingers gliding between yours like an escaping serpent! You haven't noticed his hands? They always made a singular impression on me . . . if you could call such an elusive embrace of a cold and fluid hand a handshake!'

'For me, it was the eyes which were particularly disquieting – those pale blue eyes, hard as diamond. They had such a frosty gleam they might have been made of lapis lazuli or steel, those eyes. And the stress of their regard! I, for one, was utterly disconcerted by them, every time he spoke to me at the club.'

'Yes, he is a rather bizarre fellow, like all his generation!'

'You know that he is at least forty?'

'Him! he looks twenty-eight.'

'Come on, have you never looked at him? His face is horribly old. I admit that the body has remained young – no one is more sveltely supple than he – but the face is ravaged. His complexion has the grey-brown tinge of an abominable lassitude, and as for the mouth! The thinness of his smile! That mouth has been tightened by the experience of a hundred years.'

'Opium ages people prematurely. Nothing brings the European down like the Orient.'

'Ah! He is an opium-smoker, then?'

'Without doubt. What other explanation could there be for the strange depressions and the frightful fatigues which overwhelm him so suddenly during these last five years. Sometimes, at the club, when he was on the point of departure, he would be compelled to stretch himself out and lie down for hours on end . . .'

'Hours?'

'Yes, long hours, lying inert and exhausted, as if his limbs were hanging loose. Look, de Mazel, you've known him for years – hasn't he been known to sleep for forty hours in two days?'

'Forty hours?'

'Certainly. He awoke at meal times, just to take nourishment, and afterwards fell again into his torpor. And Fréneuse had a strange horror of sleep; there was some abnormal phenomenon associated with it, some lesion of the brain or neurotic depression.'

'The troublesome cerebral anaemia which results from excessive debauchery. Another myth! I've never believed, myself, in the supposed debauchery of that poor gentleman. Such a frail chap, with such a delicate complexion! Quite frankly, there was no scope in him for debauchery.

'Pooh! About as much as Lorenzaccio!'

'You associate him with the Medicis! Lorenzaccio was a Florentine impassioned by rancour, a man of energy slowly brooding over his vengeance, caressing it as he might caress the blade of a dagger! There is not the slightest comparison to be drawn between Lorenzaccio and that gall-green, liverish creature Fréneuse. Fréneuse is an oddball, an idler, without any aim in life! If you ask me, he has smoked too much opium in the East, and that explains his somnolence, his morbid lethargies. It's the hazardous legacy of bad habits! He has been comprehensively undone; the heavy influence of poisonous opiates never ceases to oppress him. Besides which, his steel-blue eyes are surely the eyes of a smoker of opium. He carries the drunken burden of hemp in his veins. Opium is like syphilis ' – le Mazel released the word carelessly – 'it is a thing which stays for years and years in the blood, because the body is unable to purge itself. It must be absorbed, in the long run, by iodide.'

Then Chameroy spoke. 'You always put the blame on opium, but as I see it the case of Fréneuse is much more complicated. Him, an invalid? No – a character from the tales of Hoffmann! Have you never taken the trouble to look at him carefully? That pallor of decay; the twitching of his bony hands, more Japanese than chrysanthemums; the arabesque profile; that vampiric emaciation – has all of that never given you cause to reflect? In spite of his supple body and his callow face Fréneuse is a hundred thousand years old. That man has lived before, in ancient times, under the reigns of Heliogabalus, Alexander IV and the last of the Valois. What am I saying? That man is Henri III himself. I have in my library an edition of Ronsard – a rare edition, bound in pigskin with metal trimmings – which contains a portrait of Henri engraved on vellum. One of these nights I will bring the volume here to show you, and you may judge for yourselves. Apart from the ruff, the doublet and the earrings, you would believe that you were looking at the Duc de Fréneuse. As far as I'm concerned, his presence here inevitably makes me ill – and so long as he is present, there is such an oppression, such a heaviness . . . '

Such were the discussions stirred up by the departure of Fréneuse. The apartment-house in the Rue de Varenne and all its associated goods and chattels had been put up for sale, advertised two days in advance on page four of *Le Figaro* and *Le Temps*. Rumours, legends, hypotheses . . . it only required the name of Fréneuse to be pronounced, as if it were a kind of yeast, for the fermentation to begin: a vast brew of stupidities, falsehoods, presumptions . . . but for me there was nothing to be learned from these elegant and airy clubmen.

All the muffled whispers of the scandalmongers, all the rustlings of intrigued and mystified public opinion surrounding the true name of Monsieur de Phocas, had been going the rounds for ten years. And this was the man who had chosen me as a confidant! It was to me that he had offered, of his own free will, the honour or the shame of deciphering his life. I would have the opportunity to understand, at last, the enigma which he had consigned to the pages of his manuscript.

The manuscript was entirely written by his own hand, although in divers styles – for the handwriting of a man changes with his states of mind, and graphology bears witness, as a trait of the pen, to the fall of an honest man who becomes a rogue. I decided, one night, to read the pages entrusted to me: those which Monsieur de Phocas had read over so disdainfully while he spread them out on my table with the tip of his cane, reading out of the corners of his eyes beneath their darkened brows.

I transcribe these pages exactly as I found them, disordered and incoherent as to their dates – but I have taken leave to suppress a few whose contents are too audacious to be set in print at the present time.

At the begining, on the first page, there appears a quotation which is taken, with the supplementary note, from Swinburne's *Laus Veneris*:

> *There is a feverish famine in my veins . . .*
> . . . .
> *Sin, is it sin whereby men's souls are thrust*
> *Into the gulf? yet I had a good trust*
> *To save my soul before it slipped therein,*
> *Trod under by the fire-shod feet of lust.*

Oh, 'the sad hell where all sweet love hath end, all but the pain that never finisheth!'

After this there are four lines of De Musset taken from *Of what young girls dream*:

> *Ah! misfortune to him who allows Debauchery*
> *To fix her iron nail beneath his left breast!*
> *The heart of a virgin man is a profound vessel;*
> *The surface of the sea is calm when the blemish is on its bed.*

The personal inscriptions commence as follows:

8 April 1891
The obscenity of nostrils and mouths; the ignominious cupidity of smiles and women encountered in the street; the shifty baseness on every side, as of hyenas and wild beasts ready to bite: tradesmen in their shops and strollers on their pavements. How long must I suffer this? I have

suffered it before, as a child, when, descending by chance to the servant's quarters, I overheard in astonishment their vile gossip, tearing up my own kind with their lovely teeth.

This hostility to the entire race, this muted detestation of lynxes in human form, I must have rediscovered it later while at school. I had a repugnance and horror for all base instincts, but am I not myself instinctively violent and lewd, murderous and sensual? Am I any different, in essence, from the members of the riotous and murderous mob of a hundred years ago, who hurled the town sergeants into the Seine and cried, 'String up the aristos!' just as they shout 'Down with the army!' or 'Death to the Jews!' today?

30 October 1891

True beauty is only to be found in the faces of statues. Their immobility is a kind of existence very different from the grimaces of our features. It is as if a divine breath animates them sometimes – and then, how intense the gaze of their eyes becomes!

I have spent all day at the Louvre. The marble gaze of the *Antinous* still pursues me. With what softness and warmth – at the same time knowing and profound – its long-dead eyes settled upon me! For a moment, I believed that I perceived a green glimmer lurking there. If that bust belonged to me, I would mount emeralds in its eyes.

23 February 1893

Today I did something unworthy. I tried to get round a journalist I hardly know, in order to obtain from him a pass to attend an execution. I have even invited him to dinner. Yet the man bores me, and the sight of blood is repugnant to me – repugnant to such an extent that when I am at the dentist's, if I hear a cry in the next room, I almost faint and am quite taken ill.

A pass for the ceremony has been promised to me. Shall I actually go to this execution?

12 May 1893. Naples

I have been to see the most beautiful collection of precious stones. Oh, that museum! What delicate profiles and what deft delineations in the smaller cameos! The Greeks are more graceful – I know not what happy serenity enabled them to characterise divinity so well – but the Roman intaglios have such an intense ardour about them! In the setting of one ring there was an adorable laurel-crowned head, of some young Caesar or empress – Caligula, Otho, Messalina or Poppaea – whose expression was exhausted and possessive at the same time, so heart-rending and so weary that I will certainly dream about it tonight . . .

To dream! Such dreams certainly make life more worth living . . . and only dreams can do that for me.

13 July 1894

One encounters in the streets, late at night on the evenings of fêtes, the most strange and bizarre passers-by. Do these nights of popular celebration cause ancient and forgotten avatars to stir in the depths of the human soul? This evening, in the movement of the sweaty and excited crowd, I am certain that I passed between the masks of the liberated Bythinians and encountered the courtesans of the Roman decadence.

There emerged, this evening, from that swarming esplanade of Des Invalides – amid the crackle of fireworks, the shooting stars, the stink of frying, the hiccuping of drunkards and the reeking atmosphere of menageries – the wild effusions of one of Nero's festivals.

It was like the odour of a May evening on the *Basso-Porto* of Naples. It was easy to believe that the faces in that crowd were Sicilian.

29 November, of the same year

The gloomy and so very distant gaze of the *Antinous*; the ecstatic and ferocious, yet imploring, eyes of the Roman cameo. I have found them again, in a rather badly-executed pastel, signed with a woman's name – an unknown painter, but one to whom I would certainly give a commission, if I were sure that she could reproduce that strange expression.

And yet there is nothing to them! Two or three pastel crayons have been crushed in rendering that square, emaciated face with the enormous raking jawline, with the mouth voluptuously open and the nostrils flared, beneath a heavy crown of violets, with a poppy lodged behind the ear. The face is extraordinarily ugly, of a sad and cadaverous colour – but beneath the scarcely-raised eyelids there shines and slumbers a liquidity so very green: the dejected and depraved depths of an unsated soul; the doleful emerald of some fearful lust!

I would give anything to find that gaze.

18 December, of the same year

> *Asleep or waking is it? for her neck,*
> *Kissed over close, wears yet a purple speck*
> *Wherein the pained blood falters and goes out;*
> *Soft, and stung softly – fairer for a fleck.*
> Laus Veneris (Swinburne).

Oh, that wound inflicted on the beautiful neck of a woman, asleep and abandoned almost to death! The calmness of that body prostrated by pleasure! How that wound fascinated me! I would have loved to apply my lips to it, slowly and entirely sucking out the soul of that woman, and the blood as well! Then, that regular pulse would make me weak; the rhythm of her respiration, lifting up her throat, would fascinate me like the swinging of some nightmarish pendulum. I imagined the moment when my trembling hands would grip the sleeper by the throat – yes, by the throat – and squeeze it, until she breathed no more. I would have liked to strangle her, to murder her, to stop her breathing utterly and forever . . .

Ah, but she still breathes . . . !

I got up, with a cold sweat on my brow, confused by the soul of the assassin I had for ten seconds become. I should have tied my hands together, in order to prevent them placing themselves about her neck . . .

She slept on, and from her lips there came a slight odour of decay . . . that insipid odour which all human beings exhale when they are asleep.

Oh! how Anthony and the other saints of the Thébaïd were tempted by night, by soft and guilty nakedness, which came to them in the mirage of the desert. Oh, those errant figures of voluptuousness, which lightly brushed them behind and before, emanating waves of incense and perfumes even though they were evil spirits!

3 January 1895

I have slept with that woman again, and the temptation has returned – yes, the temptation to murder! How disgraceful it is!

I remember that as a child I liked to torture animals, I still recall the adventure of the two turtle-doves, which were once put into my hands to amuse me. Instinctively and unconsciously I suffocated them, by squeezing them too tightly. I have not forgotten that atrocious episode. I was only eight years old.

The palpitations of life have always filled me with a strange destructive rage. Now there have been two occasions when I was surprised by the idea of murder in association with love.

Might there be a second self lurking within me?

[The first manuscript concluded at this point.]

OPPRESSION

Undated.

The beauty of the twentieth century is the charm of the hospital, the grace of the cemetery, of consumption and emaciation. I admit that I have submitted to it all; worse, I have loved with all my heart.

The Opera rats of the *corps du ballet*; lilies of the *Rat mort*; frail *mondaines* with the muzzles of rodents . . .

In the course of my life I have had pre-pubescent ballerinas; emaciated duchesses, dolorous and forever tired, melomaniac and morphine-sodden; bankers' wives with eyes hollower than those of suburban streetwalkers; music-hall chorus girls who tip creosote into their Roederer when getting drunk . . .

I have even had the awkward androgynes, the unsexed dishes of the day of the *tables d'hôte* of Montmartre. Like any vulgar follower of fashion, like any member of the herd, I have made love to bony and improbably slender little girls, frightened and macabre, spiced with carbolic and peppered with chlorotic make-up.

Like an imbecile, I have believed in the mouths of prey and sacrificial victims. Like a simpleton, I have believed in the large lewd eyes of a ragged heap of sickly little creatures: alcoholic and cynical shopgirls and whores. The profundity of their eyes and the mystery of their mouths . . . the jewellers of some and the manicurists of others furnish them with *eaux de toilette*, with soaps and rouges. And Fanny the etheromaniac, rising every morning for a measured dose of cola and coca, does not put ether only on her handkerchief.

It is all fakery and self-advertisement – *truquage and battage*, as their vile argot has it. Their phosphorescent rottenness, their emaciated fervour, their Lesbian blight, their shop-sign vices set up to arouse their clients, to excite the perversity of young and old men alike in the sickness of perverse tastes! All of it can sparkle and catch fire only at the hour when the gas is lit in the corridors of the music-halls and the crude nickel-plated décor of the bars. Beneath the cerise three-ply collars of the night-prowlers, as beneath the bulging silks of the cyclist, the whole seductive display of passionate pallor, of knowing depravity, of exhausted and sensual anaemia – all the charm of spicy flowers celebrated in the writings of Paul Bourget and Maurice Barrès – is nothing but a role carefully learned and rehearsed a hundred times over. It is a chapter of the *Manchon de Francine* read over and over again, swotted up and acted out by ingenious barnstormers, fully conscious of the squalid salacity of the male of the species, and knowledgeable in the means of starting up the broken-down engines of their customers.

To think that I also have loved these maleficent and sick little beasts, these fake *Primaveras*, these discounted *Jocondes*, the whole hundred-franc stock-in-trade of Leonardos and Botticellis from the workshops of painters and the drinking-dens of aesthetes, these flowers mounted on a brass thread in Montparnasse and Levallois-Perret!

And the odious and tiresome travesty – the corsetted torso slapped on top of heron's legs, painful to behold, the ugly features primed by boulevard boxes, the fake Dresden of Nina Grandière retouched from a medicine bottle, complaining and spectral at the same time – of Mademoiselle Guilbert and her long black gloves! . . .

Have I now had enough of the horror of this nightmare! How have I been able to tolerate it for so long?

The fact is that I was then ignorant even of the nature of my sickness. It was latent in me, like a fire smouldering beneath the ashes. I have cherished it since . . . perhaps since early childhood, for it must always have been in me, although I did not know it!

Oh, that blue and green *something* which was revealed to me in inert depths of certain gems, and the even-more-inert depths of certain painted expressions – the plaintive emeralds of Barruchini's jewellery, and the eyes of certain portraits – I had not yet defined it. I had suffered so excessively from my inability to love almost all women because none of them truly had that expression.

Friday 3 April 1895
Evil prayers:

> *Your mouth is blessed, for it is adulterous,*
> *It tastes of fresh roses and the ancient earth,*
> *It has sucked the hidden juices of flowers and reeds;*
> *When it speaks, it sounds like the rustling of reeds in the*
> *   distance;*
> *And that ruby, impious with sensuality, all bloody and utterly*
> *   cold*
> *Is the final wound of Jesus upon the cross.*

Today, on Good Friday, a childish desire to recall the long-lost habit of piety took me to mass at Notre-Dame. I wanted to test the vigorous fire of my affliction – oh, if only I were able to extinguish it! – in the cool shadows of a church. While the Latin phrases rose and fell, chanted by the priest with the measured slowness of the knell, I dutifully followed the text in my book . . . but it was the horrible lines of Remy de Gourmont which fell from my lips like a series of caresses – like a series of sacrilegious caresses!

Your feet are blessed, for they are dishonest,
They have donned brothel-slippers and decorated stockings;
They have put their muffled heels on the shoulders of the poor;
They have trodden down the poorest, the purest and the gentlest.
And the amethyst mouth, which tightens the silken garter,
Is the last tremor of Jesus upon the cross.

The evening service dutifully mourned the death of Christ, but in the murmurous quietude of the chapel consecrated to the Tomb, I heard nothing but the evil antiphon of the poet . . .

Your eyes are blessed, for they are murderous,
They are full of phantoms, and the irony of chrysalids
Sleeps in them, as in the still water in the depths of green grottoes,
One sees sleeping beasts in the midst of blue and green anemones.

And it seemed that my flesh crawled with the gentleness of those glaucous things evoked by the verse. It was as if fingertips, like cut emeralds or fresh olives, were stroking the palm of my hand.

I had let my missal fall to the ground and I collapsed on my *prie-dieu*. I supported myself on my elbows, both arms hanging loose, hands unmoving and open at my sides . . . while fresh and round *things* were pouring from my head, dropping into my fingers.

The sensation was so unexpected, so finely pure and so deliciously light, that a shiver ran up my spine.

Had I, in a state of sensual hyperaesthesia, contrived to materialise upon my skin some occult contact with the eyes of my covetous desire? While the momentary interval of doubt remained, better to retain the sensation and to make it more fully mine, I lowered my eyelids. But the contact became more distinct, and the insistence of the caress made me look around. I wanted to see what it was.

A woman dressed in mourning – a woman still young beneath her widow's veils – was seated beside me. Her dangling rosary rested gently upon the fingers of my open palm.

Her eyelids were modestly lowered as she dangled the beads, but a smile played upon the slight arc of her mouth. Between her eyelashes, as between her rosy lips, there was an almost silvery glimmer of whiteness.

> *O dolorous sapphire of bitterness and fear!*
> *Sapphire, final expression of Jesus upon the cross,*

Tuesday 16 June 1895
I was at the Olympia yesterday evening. The ugliness of that room, the ugliness of the whole audience! The cos-

42

tumes! The disgrace of that sheet-metal pomp which constitutes the ideal outfit of modern man: all those stove-pipes
which enclose the legs, arms and torso of the clubman,
who is strangled meanwhile by a collar of white porcelain.
And the sadness: the greyness of all those faces, drained by
the poor hygiene of city life and the abuse of alcohol; all
the ravages of late nights and the anxieties of the rat race
imprinted in nervous tics on all those fat and flabby faces
. . . their pallor, the colour of lard! And in the boxes as in
the orchestra-stalls, beside the banal figures of the males,
the females glorying in their extravagance and their vanity!

There were the usual edifices of feathers, gauzes and
painted silks crushing frail necks and flattened bosoms;
narrow shoulders hunched up by enormous sleeves; everywhere the stiffened thinness of fashionable phthisis – or,
even worse, the artificial elephantiasis of fat wives, sculpted
in jet – and all displayed under the raw jets of the gaslight.

And while these marionettes smiled at one another, and
examined one another through their lorgnettes, onstage
there was the slow and supple deployment, the skilful play
of all the muscles of a marvellous human body.

Swaddled in a tight costume of pale silk, his bare flesh
spangled and sparkling wherever beads of perspiration
caught the electric light, an acrobat tumbled hither and
yon, arching his entire body. Then, righting himself
abruptly with a flourish of the hips, with his legs pointing
towards the wings, he imposed on the entire audience the
hallucinatory spectacle of a man transformed by rhythm,
with the supple grace of the closing of a fan.

I was in the circle box. In France, it is only permissible
to admire statues but tropical countries have no such
prejudices, and the emergent Oriental in me took full
account of the admirable proportions and the harmony of
the movements of the acrobat on the stage.

The Marquis de V . . . – whose falsetto voice and little
watery eyes I have always detested – was saying to me
with a wicked smile: 'Then again, the master gymnast
might break his neck at any moment. What he is doing

now is very dangerous, my dear, and the pleasure you take in his performance is the little frisson that danger affords you. Wouldn't it be thrilling, if his sweaty hand failed to grip the bar? The velocity acquired by his rotation about the bar would break his spine quite cleanly, and perhaps a little of the cervical matter might spurt out as far as this! It would be most sensational, and you would have a rare emotion to add to the field of your experience – for you collect emotions, don't you? What a pretty stew of terrors that man in tights stirs up in us!

'Admit that you almost wish that he will fall! Me too. Many others in the auditorium are in the same state of attention and anguish. That is the horrible instinct of a crowd confronted with a spectacle which awakens in it the ideas of lust and death. Those two agreeable companions always travel together! Take it from me that at the very same moment – see, the man is now holding on to the bar by his fingertips alone – at the very same moment, a good number of the women in these boxes are ardently lusting after that man, not so much for his beauty as for the danger he courts.'

The voice subtly changed its tone, suddenly becoming more interested. 'You have singularly pale eyes this evening, my dear Fréneuse. You ought to give up bromides and take valerian instead. You have a charming and curious soul, but you must take command of its changes. You are too ardently and too obviously covetous, this evening, of the death – or at least the fall – of that man.'

I did not reply. The Marquis de V . . . was quite right. The madness of murder had taken hold of me again; the spectacle had me in its hallucinatory grip. Straitened by a penetrating and delirious anguish, I yearned for that man to fall.

There are appalling depths of cruelty within me.

THE EYES

Undated

The eyes! They teach us all the mysteries of love, for love is neither in the flesh, nor in the soul; love is is the eyes which glance, which caress, which experience all the nuances of sensations and ecstasies; in the eyes where the desires are magnified and idealised. Oh! to live the life of the eyes, in which terrestrial forms are obliterated and annulled; to laugh, to sing, to weep with the eyes, to admire oneself in the eyes, to drown oneself like Narcissus at the spring.

Charles Vellay.

Yes, to drown oneself like Narcissus at the spring; there would be joy in that. The madness of the eyes is the lure of the abyss. Sirens lurk in the dark depths of the pupils as they lurk at the bottom of the sea, that I know for sure – but I have never encountered them, and I am searching still for the profound and plaintive gazes in whose depths I might be able, like Hamlet redeemed, to drown the Ophelia of my desire.

The world has the same effect on me as a sea of sand. Oh, the wastelands of warm congealed ash, where nothing can slake my thirst for humid and glaucous eyes! Truly, there are days when I suffer excessively. Mine is the agony of a nomad lost in the desert.

I have never read anything which echoes my soul and my suffering more closely than the work of Charles Vellay.

. . . I have passed years searching in the eyes for that which other men cannot see. Slowly and painfully I have discovered in everyone the limitless frissons which extend eternally in the irises of eyes. I have devoted my soul to the pursuit of mystery, and now my eyes are no longer my own: they have been enraptured,

little by little, by all the gazes of other eyes. Today they are no more than a mirror reflecting all those stolen gazes, which only come to life in a complex existence agitated by unknown sensations — and that is my immortality; for I shall not die. My eyes will live, because they are not mine, because I have formed them out of all eyes, with all their tears and all their laughter, and I will survive the sloughing of my body because I have all souls in my eyes.

All souls in his eyes . . .

But this man is a poet; he creates that which he sees, and what a mockery these souls are! Where there is nothing but instinct, nervous tics and the batting of eyelashes he has seen regrets born of dreams and desires. There is nothing to be found in human eyes, and that is their terrifying and dolorous enigma, their abominable and delusive charm. There is nothing but that which we put there ourselves. That is why honest gazes are only to be found in portraits.

The faded and weary eyes of martyrs, expressions tortured by ecstasy, imploring and suffering eyes, some resigned, others desperate . . . the gazes of saints, mendicants and princesses in exile, with pardoning smiles . . . the gazes of the possessed, the chosen and the hysterical . . . and sometimes of little girls, the eyes of Ophelia and Canidia, the eyes of virgins and witches . . . as you live in the museums, what eternal life, dolorous and intense, shines out of you! Like precious stones enshrined between the painted eyelids of masterpieces, you disturb us across time and across space, receivers of the dream which created you!

You have souls, but they are those of the artists who wished you into being, and I am delivered to despair and mortification because I have drunk the draught of poison congealed in the irises of your eyes.

The eyes of portraits ought to be plucked out.

November 1896
There are also eyes in the transparency of gems, antique gems above all: the turbid and milky cabochons which

46

decorate certain sacred caskets and the reliquaries of embalmed saints, such as one sees among the treasures of cathedrals in Sicily and Germany.

And the treasure of St Mark's in Venice. That includes, as I remember it, the goblet of some Doge, entirely embossed in translucent enamel, from whose depths the centuries watch you.

13 November 1896

Eyes! There is such beauty in them! There are blues like mountain lakes, greens like ocean waves; they can capture the milkiness of absinthe, all the greys of agate and all the clarities of water. I have even found some in Provence so profoundly warm and calm that they recalled an August night at sea . . . but none that human eyes had ever looked upon.

The prettiest eyes I ever saw were those of Willie Stephenson, the mime-artist of the Atheneum, who is nowadays in the theatre. They were flowery eyes – 'flowery' is exactly the right word – so very fresh and gentle, and so restless, they were like two blue flowers floating on water. She was a strange and captivating girl – or so, at least, I believed. She was certainly very expensive. It usually required four or five men to keep her, but the fancy took me of having her all to myself for a while. She was so delicately white, like the white of a sword-lily, with her spindly arms, her narrow hips, her flat belly and her little pert breasts. It was the anatomy of a mere child, belied by a very fine face: the perfectly-shaped angelic oval of a peeress where two huge, candid, disquieting, wild eyes trembled like two luminous flowers. They were modest, frightened eyes – the eyes of a bitch at bay . . .

And the adorable dark circles around those eyes! The pastel blue of their silky eyelids! How well those eyes suited that frail and perennially weary body! In truth, I believe that I have loved no others. They were beseeching during the transports of the bed, and in the extremity of passion . . . and then too, the wonderful slenderness of that

47

neck, so beautifully designed for the axe! Anne Boleyn must have had such a lean and satined nape beneath the smoky gold of her tresses.

Hers was a beauty of the scaffold whose fragility called forth the viol and violence: a bruised beauty which awoke murderous instincts in me. Lying beside her, I dreamed at times of those anaemic and gentle figures – gentle and perhaps impertinent – who were the victims of the Revolution: those tall and handsome aristocratic women that the Carriers and the Fouquier-Tinvilles transported, still all atremble with lust, to the drowning-pool or to the guillotine.

Willie re-emphasized that frail end-of-the-eighteenth-century beauty by means of her instinctive feel for costume and finery. In gauzes and buckrams, muslin shawls and long sheaths of striped Pekin, shimmering dresses of tea-rose or straw-coloured watered silk, that blonde fragility ripened again: 'The English school or the Trianon?' her pout enquired as I entered her room.

Playful candour and aristocratic authority; Willie was the last of the royal courtesans – but she got drunk like a stable-lad and hung around with prostitutes in the drinking-dens of Montmartre. That pink mouth cursed and swore like a coachman's. Once, when she thought I was in London, although a resurgence of my sickness had set me to prowling in the suburbs, I surprised her at the Point-du-Jour. Yes, in a cheap dance-hall, ensconced in the company of some red-faced dancer from the Moulin-Rouge, buying rounds of warm wine for a gang of pimps.

Oh, the cynical and muted alcohol-blue flame of Willie's eyes that day – her face suddenly aged by twenty years! The cynical and streetwise mask of the whore appeared in the suddenly crapulous crease of the mouth and the depravity of those beggar's eyes! Her very soul had risen to her face. But as the imprudent creature had around her neck a pearl necklace, worth forty thousand francs at the lowest estimate – the spolia opima of Berlin and St Petersburg – and given that the night falls quickly in winter, that we were in December, and that there was no one around, I took pity on her. Knowing the dangers which threatened her in that dive, I intervened in order to assist her departure.

Who knows? – perhaps I diverted the course of her destiny! That pearl necklace around the courtesan's neck invited and demanded the hands of a strangler . . .

As I was useful to Willie to the tune of ten thousand francs a month she became apologetic when I showed up, admitted to a sudden whim born of curiosity, and – suddenly wheedling – recovered the eyes of a little girl. But I had seen those whore's eyes. The spell was broken; I had the key to that particular puzzle. The fright that I relished in her eyes – their anguish and their disquiet – was the memory of the slums.

Cut-throats and burglars have similarly restless gazes.

Naples, 3 March 1897
These eyes undiscoverable beneath human eyelids, why do I see them in statues?

This morning, in the hall of the museum devoted to the excavations of Herculaneum, this blue and green *thing* from which I suffer – the plaintive and pale emerald which obsesses me – was clearly apparent to me in eyes of metal, in the burnished silver eyes of great bronze statues blackened by lava, which had been rendered into the semblance of infernal goddesses. There is, among others, a mounted Nero whose blind eyes are terrifying – but it is not in their orbits that I have rediscovered the gaze. Ranged against the walls there were huge Venuses draped in Greek skirts, like funereal Muses: huge Venuses of bronze, leprously calcined in places, whose eyes were fulgurant, splendidly empty, in their masks of black metal.

It was in the dizziness of those vacant and fixed pupils that I suddenly caught sight of the gaze.

30 April 1897
The eyes of listening men. It is the same with those who speak, most of all when they speak solicitously. They are

all watchful, forever on the lookout, but they have no expression at all.

The man of today is no longer a believer, and that is why he no longer has any expression.

In the final analysis, I have to agree with the priest. Modern eyes? There is no more soul in them; they no longer look up to Heaven. Even the best are preoccupied with the immediate. Base covetousness, petty self-interest, cupidity, vanity, prejudice, loose appetites and muted envy: these are the abominations crawling in today's expressions. We have the souls of notaries and cooks. There is nothing beneath our eyelids but the reflections of balance-sheets and the minutes of meetings; we no longer even have the yellow gleam of the old weighers of gold. That is the reason why the eyes of portraits in museums are so hallucinatory; they reflect prayers and tortures, regret and remorse. The eyes are the source of tears, but when the source is tainted the eyes are leaden; only the Faith can make them live, but its dead ashes cannot be reignited. We march with our eyes fixed on our shoes; our expressions are the colour of mud. When eyes appear beautiful to us, it is because they harbour the splendour of deception, because they recall to mind some portrait, some gaze glimpsed in the museum, or because they regret the Past.

Willie had a knowing gaze: the eyes of women always lie.

May 1897
Jacques Tramsel was just leaving my apartment.

'Have you seen the new dancer at the Folies?' he said to me.

'No.'

'Well, you must go to see her.'

'Oh! What kind of girl is she?'

'A Greek.'

'From Lesbos?'

'No. Joking apart, she says that she comes from a good Greek family. I believe her to be an Oriental jewess, a Levantine for certain, but she has an admirable body, a suppleness ... she is a great living flower which dances, perhaps a little monstrous in her anatomy but not in a way which will displease you. Honestly, she is two girls in one: her torso is that of an acrobat, supple, lean and muscular, but her hips and buttocks are quite extraordinary. She is the Callipygian Venus herself – Venus Anadyomene, if you prefer. Octave Uzanne – for she has fascinated literary men – has even described her as a Venus of the reign of Alcibiades. The thing is that she is at one and the same time Aphrodite and Ganymede, Astarté and Hylas.'

'Astarté! And her eyes, what are her eyes like?'

'Very beautiful – eyes which have looked long upon the sea.'

Eyes which have looked long upon the sea! Oh, the clear and distant eyes of sailors: the salt-water eyes of Bretons; the still-water eyes of mariners; the well-water eyes of Celts; the dreaming and infinitely transparent eyes of those who dwell beside rivers and lakes; the eyes which one sometimes rediscovers in the mountains, in the Tyrol and in the Pyrenees ... eyes in which there are skies, vast expanses, dawns and twilights contemplated at length upon the open seas, the mountains or the plains ... eyes into which have passed, and in which remain, so many horizons! Have I not encountered such eyes already, in my dreams?

I now understand the reason for my long, leisurely walks along the quays and in the harbours.

Eyes which have looked long upon the sea! I must go to see this girl dance.

IZÉ KRANILE

June 1897

A great flower which dances . . .

Tramsel was right: the girl is a tall calyx of flesh moving strangely on bulging casket-like hips – for I have been to see this Izé Kranile dance. (Izé Kranile is a very pretty name, if it is her own - one never knows with these creatures!)

In spite of her beautiful torso and the distracting curve of her breast, this Izé is certainly very stupid and very impudent, more maladroit in her flirtations than any girl I have seen in the corps de ballet. I am sorely annoyed with her, for no one in whom I have taken an interest has ever put her foot in it so comprehensively – and yet she had everything she needed to please me!

She was both straight and crooked. It as as if her bust was seated upon a heavy divided rump, like a ripe fruit: a guilty outcrop of lust. Her legs were slender, the knees round. Her form seemed abnormal, unexpected, almost arabesque in the perennial advancement of her taut and bulging breasts, sprung forth from her body as though to meet desire. In the contortions of her hips and the abrupt reversals of her whole torso she seemed suddenly darkened, like a huge flower in the rain. This Kranile, with the sharp oval of her flattened face, her stormy eyes and her triangular smile, was surely that creature of perdition execrated by the prophets: the eternally impure beast; the little girl wickedly and unconsciously perverse, who could crush the marrow of men and stir up desire in decrepit monarchs – Salomé!

Salomé! It was the immortal image of the Salomé of Gustave Moreau and Gustave Flaubert that was immediately evoked in me, the night when Kranile sprang forth upon the stage, thrown forward like a ball and rebounding likewise, the nudity of her bewitching body aggravated by her black veils.

Against a set of desolate scenery, amid spectral crags and livid mountains of ash, beneath the funereal daylight of slopes illuminated in blue, she personified the spirit of the witches' sabbat. Morbid and voluptuous, sometimes with extenuated grace and infinite lassitude, she seemed to carry the burden of a criminal beauty, a beauty charged with all the sins of the multitude. She fell again and again upon her pliant legs, and as she outlined the symbolic gestures of her two beautiful dead arms she seemed to be towing them behind her. Then, the vertigo of the abyss took hold of her again, and like one possessed she stood on point, holding herself fully erect from top to toe, like a spike of flesh and shadows. Her arms, weighed down just a few moments earlier, became menacing, demoniac, and audacious. Twisting like a screw, she whirled around, like a winnowing-machine — no, like a great lily stirred by a storm-wind. Clownish and macabre, a nacreous gleam showed between her lips . . . oh, that cruel and sardonic smile, and the two deep pools of her terrible eyes!

Izé Kranile!

The curtain had hardly been lowered before I was in her dressing-room. I was introduced to her by Pierre Forie, the impressionist painter who produces a new portrait every year, and has virtually appointed himself a public showman of such women.

With a rare immodesty, Izé received us while she was still fuming with powder and perspiration.

She was removing her costume. The bundle of black satin trimmed with tulle and jet which had, five minutes before, made her into a flower with petals of shadow, now lay like a mere rag on a chair. With her throat bare, all warm and moist, Kranile sat like a boy and spread out her arms so that her dresser, kneeling before her, might laboriously slide off the silk mesh that had stuck to the skin . . .

The time Forie required to pronounce my name was sufficient for the dancer to throw a shawl over her shoulders. Without getting up, she turned her damp and narrow face towards me.

'I shan't offer you my hand,' she said, 'I'm too wet. Sit down, messieurs, if you wish.' And, with a smile just for me: 'I know your name, monsieur; you're the man with the precious stones, the collector of rare gems. I've always wanted to see them – it's been my ambition ever since I arrived in Paris. Is it possible?'

She turned towards me the head of a depraved urchin: a witch's head, which had once again become cynical and Levantine. But gleaming beneath her heavy eyelids were two sharp grey eyes: two eyes of audacious agate, full of promises and caresses; two eyes which had certainly never looked long upon the sea, no matter what Tramsel had said, but two unexpected eyes of a kind I had never encountered elsewhere!

The heady odour of the dressing-room was almost suffocating: the odour of sex, of make-up, of sweat, of velveteen, and of a wild beast too! Izé Kranile was not free that evening; she coquettishly declined my invitation to supper and – with a whole heap of promises in her eye and her smile – escorted us to the door of her dressing-room, dabbing at her breasts with a towel . . .

Her eyes! It was her eyes that had been described to me. It was that description that had brought me to her, but it was not her eyes which haunted me that night; it was the acrid odour of her eau de toilette and her moist flesh, and the rusty stains in her armpits – the same bronze-hard rust-red as the hair on her head.

Izé Kranile!

Who knows? – perhaps she could have healed me, that one, if only she had wanted to. For a whole day – what am I saying? for forty-eight hours, the two full days of waiting before the evening fixed by her to dine with me – my obsession with eyes, the obsession which had been killing me for two years, consented to grant me a respite. I lived through those two days bound up in a unique desire to see again the little pink triangle of Izé's mouth, the flower of her delicate flesh immodestly opened over the short little teeth, the delicious design of her lips drawn back from a gleam of enamel ... and the odour, that strident and complex odour which emanated from her. Its persistence was almost a sickness, which nearly made me faint, but I delighted in it for two whole days: two days of glad escape from the persecution of the eyes; two days of liberation, at last, from the oppression of the dream, won by means of the imperious suggestion of that odour ...

But she did not want to heal me. She showed up that first evening so heavily made up, so gauchely dressed ... poor girl!

Since then, I have discovered a certain compassion for her, in thinking about the hopelessness of her ruses and of the pains which she must have taken in constructing the comedy of that awful evening. My god, what schemes and what stratagems! And with what result? I was annoyed with her for a whole month. She had so brutally squashed my embryonic desire! And the snare she tried to lay was so gross. To appeal to the jealousy of a man the moment one believes oneself to be desired is the strategy of a chorus girl in the music-hall – and yet Izé had danced at La Scala in Milan and at the Opera in Vienna. What pitiful lovers she must have entertained there!

What a lamentable adventure that dinner was! I cannot help smiling when I think of it. The comical figure of Forie, with his woeful eyes and his frightened manner, suffering the ballerina's unexpected fits of tenderness. Poor chap! She had hit upon the notion of feigning desperate love for Forie, in order to excite and arouse the great man. I was a great man, of course, because I owned the rare stones and had the income: that famous income, the well-known fortune, somewhat exaggerated and enlarged by fools and gossips; that ball-and-chain fortune which poisons my life wherever I am known; that fortune which I avoid – or, rather, whose legend I avoid – in travelling incognito in foreign lands for months on end. The Greek had conceived the idea of throwing herself at the head of poor Forie, of making much of him, of rubbing up against him like an amorous she-cat, and of stuffing him with kisses and caresses in my presence, beneath my very eyes. Her aim was to inflame me, to quicken and aggravate my desire.

What poverty of imagination! And how badly she misjudged me!

In fairness, she had probably been told that I was a man of a certain kind: a sadist, athirst for violent and complex sensations; a man of bizarre tastes, those which are sometimes called 'refined'. I know that I have that reputation, carefully cultivated by my friends, or those who pose as friends. In the houses where they dine, they recount indiscretions regarding me over dessert; it is something which ensures further invitations. Then again, journalists often solicit the honour of being introduced to me, of visiting my collection, of describing the interior of my apartments – and Izé was certainly acquainted with journalists!

She had probably been tipped off in some bar, over the absinthe, or by the gossip in the Neapolitan, while the crowds were leaving some première.

In any case, she played her part and she threw herself into it; it was touching, in a way. But the pair of them were utterly ridiculous. Forie defended himself – very embarrassed, because I had invited him – but Izé was dead set on wrapping him up . . . playing to the gallery.

It began with squeezings of the hand and touches of the knee under the table. They eventually progressed to kisses: kisses on the neck; kisses on the mouth, while eating. Forie choked on them, actually gagging with the arms of the gentle child about his neck and her lips on his! Forie became apoplectic; somewhat weakened by his resistance, she nevertheless clung stubbornly to her plan. She forced herself on his mouth whether he liked it or not: a mouthful of *filet portugaise*, on the tail of a lobster; kisses *à la sauce crevette* and kisses *à la mayonaisse*. It was sufficiently distasteful to to give the painter a very long face!

During dessert, she installed herself on his knees and delicately put strawberries into his mouth. She made him drink champagne from her glass, dipping her tongue in it beforehand. To protect his shirt-front, Forie had to spread his napkin over it. He turned his head away in the hope of avoiding the tide of caresses, like a man who has grown impatient at the hairdresser's. Camped on his knees, swaddled in a rose-pink dress, Kranile was the ideal barber: she was certainly giving him a close shave! But it was me that she was really intent on shaving; I noticed that her eyes never left me. The tramp was watching me; both eyes, darting beneath their lids, lay in wait for every quiver of my face, every tightening of my fingers.

'If you will not refrain for my sake, think of the waiter,' I told them, in the end. 'I feel like a voyeur. It must be humiliating for you.'

'I can't imagine what came over her,' Forie told me, as we left. 'It's the first time anything like this has happened. She can't possibly feel that way about me! She's drunk!'

'No, just green,' I replied, in their frightful argot.

Next day, I sent her two pink pearls and a bouquet of black irises. I have not seen her since.

Izé Kranile has told all and sundry that I am impotent.

If she only knew! If they only knew!

Oh, the nights in Naples and Amalfi, excursions by boat in the gulf of Salerno – and the long and insatiable kisses I shared with two Hungarian sisters at the hotel in Sorrento! The evenings in a gondola on the dead lagoon in Venice; brief intervals in the abandoned canals of Judea . . . and the unexpected encounters, the passionate adventures of Florence . . . adventures without tomorrows which seemed eternal. And the exhausting hallucinations of Sidi-Ocba and Thimgad; vampire kisses in the midst of the mirage of the sands, and the salty breeze of the desert!

If she only knew! If they only knew!

ENCHANTMENT

July 97

The obsession of the eyes has returned to possess me.

Ever since the low comedy of that girl – since the dinner at Paillard's with that Kranile and Forie – the liquid green eyes that I once saw shining beneath the plaster eyelids of the *Antinous*, the plantive emerald lying in wait like a gleam in the orbits of the eyes of the statues of Herculaneum, the alluring gaze of the portraits in the museum, the challenge of centuries captured in the painted eyes of certain faces of infants and courtesans . . . all the deception and the mystery, all the legend and the eeriness . . . has returned to persecute me, hallucinate me, solicit me and oppress me, filling me with hatred, shame and sexual excitement.

Another man has take up residence within me . . . and what a man! What frightful atavism, what sinister ancestor has it stirred up in the depths of my being? That gaze . . .

And the abominations whispered by my desire in the appalling solitude of my nights . . . appalling! For my nights are haunted, now . . . oh for the nights of my childhood, long ago and far away, in the old family residence, when I never lost a wink of sleep!

Same month, same year.

It is a veritable demon that obsesses me.

I am convinced of this now, for yesterday evening I was unexpectedly confronted with the apparition of the gaze in circumstances which were thoroughly banal. I saw the unanticipated gleam of the emerald in the course of an excursion in a boat. On some suburban stretch of the river, so near and yet so far away, the eye of Astarté suddenly illuminated the eyes of a crewman. It smacks of the supernatural and the beyond. There is more than mortal sickness in my suffering; there is active evil: an occult influence; an enemy will; witchcraft; *enchantment*.

The boat was going slowly downstream, cutting through the heavy water scaled with waterweed and bristling with rushes; here and there, floating on the surface, lay large clusters of somnolent water-lilies. The stream was steeped in shadow and bathed in light. It was the same waterway which enters Poissy and Vilennes and yet, behind the poplars and the willows of the island I knew there was a military camp, a barracks. The Auteuil viaduct was on the horizon, as was the Eiffel tower. The hour was quite exquisite after the oppressive warmth of the day. We were surrounded by the quivering of leaves and the freshness of grass, beneath the shady and delicately roseate silk of the suburban sky, full of the smoke of factories and the play of the sunlight . . .

The splash of the oars lulled me and filled me with a sense of well-being, when – quite by chance - I caught the eye of the oarsman seated in front of me. It was all I could do to prevent myself from crying out.

In a suntanned face, cooked and ripened like a smoked fish, two large blue eyes burned: the most intense, the most violent and the purest blue; two hallucinatory eyes of such transparency and such profundity!

Those eyes! They immediately recalled to me all those other eyes, living and dead: the eyes of Willie and those of the actress Dinah Salher in *Lorenzaccio* or in *Cleopatra* – in *Cleopatra* above all, for in that part the saffron with which the tragedienne coloured her skin had brought out all the exoticism of her eyes. The eyes of the boatman were also the eyes of children in certain portraits of Bastien-Lepage, and certain eyes I had encountered at Basle in the portraits of Holbein and Albrecht Dürer. With my hands clasped on top of my head, trying to contain the painful hammering, I was just about to ask the name of the man when the two liquid sapphires suddenly grew dim, and became green. They had changed into two emeralds, so transparently deep that I had the sensation of standing on the lip of the abyss. Seized by vertigo, not wishing to be engulfed, I stood up in the boat.

'Is Monsieur ill?' the rower asked me. 'Does Monsieur wish me to put into shore?'

The man's eyes had become blue again: the fresh and vivid blue of the eyes of Willie and Dinah. The boat had passed through a patch of shadow, and the reflection of the bright green foliage of the willows had briefly illuminated his gaze.

That, at least is the explanation which I have since given myself – but it is not a satisfactory explanation. This is by no means the first time I have gone boating on the Seine, and I have never before encoutered the plaintive emeralds which lurk in the eyes of the statues of Pompeii, the liquid eyes of the *Antinous*.

Astarté has come again, more powerful than before. She possesses me. She lies in wait for me.

December 97
My cruelty has also returned: the cruelty which frightens me. It lies dormant for months, for years, and then all at once awakens, bursts forth and – once the crisis is over – leaves me in mortal terror of myself.

Just now in the avenue of the Bois, I whipped my dog till he bled, and for nothing – for not coming immediately when I called! The poor animal was there before me, his spine arched, cowering close to the ground, with his great, almost human, eyes fixed on me ... and his lamentable howling! It was as though he were waiting for the butcher! But it was as if a kind of drunkenness had possessed me. The more I struck out the more I wanted to strike; every shudder of that quivering flesh filled me with some incomprehensible ardour. A circle of onlookers formed around me, and I only stopped myself for the sake of my self-respect.

Afterwards, I was ashamed.

I am always ashamed of myself nowadays.

The pulse of life has always filled me with a peculiar rage to destroy. When I think of two beings in love, I experience an agonising sensation; by virtue of some bizarre backlash, there is something which smothers and oppresses me, and I suffocate, to the point of anguish.

Whenever I wake up in the middle of the night to the muted hubbub of bumps and voices which suddenly become perceptible in the dormant city – all the cries of sexual excitement and sensuality which are the nocturnal respiration of cities – I feel weak. They rise up around me, submerging me in a sluggish flux of embraces and a tide of spasms. A crushing weight presses down on my chest; a cold sweat breaks out on my brow and my heart is heavy – so heavy that I have to get up, run bare-foot and breathless, to my window, and open both shutters, trying desperately to breathe. What an atrocious sensation it is! It is as if two arms of steel bear down upon my shoulders and a kind of hunger hollows out my stomach, tearing apart my whole being! A hunger to exterminate love.

Oh, those nights! The long hours I have spent at my window, bent over the immobile trees of the square and the paving-stones of the deserted street, on watch in the silence of the city, starting at the least noise! The nights I have passed, my heart hammering in anguish, wretchedly and impatiently waiting for my torment to consent to leave me, and for my desire to fold up the heavy wings which beat inside the walls of my being like the wings of some great fluttering bird!

Oh, my cruel and interminable nights of impotent rebellion against the rutting of Paris abed: those nights when I would have liked to embrace all the bodies, to suck in all the breaths and sup all the mouths . . . those nights which would find me, in the morning, prostrate on the carpet, scratching it still with inert and ineffectual fingers . . . fingers which never know anything but emptiness, whose nails are still taut with the passion of murder twenty-four hours after the crises . . . nails which I will one day end up plunging into the satined flesh of a neck, and . . .

It is quite clear, you see, that I am possessed by a demon . . . a demon which doctors would treat with some bromide or with all-healing *sal ammoniac*! As if medicines could ever be imagined to be effective against such evil!

61

Why does the memory of that stupid encounter pursue me so insistently? It has stirred up in me I know not what: something unnamable and unhealthy; something I never suspected ... and yet, on due reflection, what could have been more straightforward than my encounter with those two masqueraders?

The female student, peaked cap perched atop her ears, wearing a tunic with metal buttons; and with her that ignoble droll in a cassock, dragging priestly dignity in the gutter − certainly a sight to behold. There was nothing there to invite misinterpretation; it was the night of Mardi Gras. The waddling of the woman, her wide hips beneath the drape of her tunic, the shameless make-up of her face ... it all stank of the partying and debauchery of carnival night: all of it, including the smug attitude and the oblique smile of that street-hawker in clerical costume! But in that badly-lit street in Les Halles, at the door of that cheap hotel, the silhouettes of those two masqueraders became dangerous and disquieting. The hour was ominous too; it was close to midnight. What were they going to do together in that flophouse? The impression imposed upon me by the image of the androgynous student accompanied by the pseudo-priest was somehow abominable, ignominious and sacrilegious.

I have always loved masquerades; masks fascinate me. The enigma of the face that I cannot see attracts me strongly; it is the vertigo of the brink of the abyss. In the great throng of the Opera balls, as in the vulgar and noisy crowds of the music-halls, eyes glimpsed through the holes in black velvet *loups*, or beneath the lace of mantillas, have for me a particular charm, a sensual mystery which excites and intoxicates me with an occult fever. There, when I am seized by the hazard of the game and the fervour of the chase, it always seems to me that those liquid eyes of pastel green that I love − the distant gaze of the *Antinous* − shine and look out at me from behind the masks.

What a strange dream I had last night! I wandered in the warm streets of a port, in the low quarter of some Barcelona or Marseille. The streets were noisome, with their freshly-heaped piles of ordure outside the doors, in the blue shadows of their high roofs. They all led down towards the sea. The gold-spangled sea, seeming as if it had been polished by the sun, could be seen at the end of each thoroughfare, bristling with yard-arms and luminous masts. The implacable blue of the sky shone brilliantly overhead as I wandered through the long, cool and sombre corridors in the emptiness of a deserted district: a quarter which might almost have been dead, abruptly abandoned by seamen and foreigners. I was alone, subjected to the stares of prostitutes seated at their windows or in the doorways, whose eyes seemed to ransack my very soul.

They did not speak to me. Leaning on the sides of tall bay-windows or huddled in doorways, they were silent. Their breasts and arms were bare, bizarrely made up in pink, their eyebrows were darkened, they wore their hair in corkscrew-curls, decorated with paper flowers and metal birds. And they were all exactly alike!

They might have been huge marionettes, or tall mannequin dolls left behind in panic – for I divined that some plague, some frightful epidemic brought from the Orient by sailors, had swept through the town and emptied it of its inhabitants. I was alone with these simulacra of love, abandoned by the men on the doorsteps of the brothels.

I had already been wandering for hours without being able to find a way out of that miserable quarter, obsessed by the fixed and varnished eyes of all those automata, when I was seized by the sudden thought that all these girls were dead, plague-stricken and putrefied by cholera where they stood, in the solitude, beneath their carmine plaster masks . . . and my entrails were liquefied by cold. In spite of that harrowing chill, I was drawn closer to a motionless girl. I saw that she was indeed wearing a mask . . . and the girl in the next doorway was also masked . . . and all of them were horribly alike under their identical crude colour-ing . . .

I was alone with the masks, with the masked corpses, worse than the masks . . . when, all of a sudden, I perceived that beneath the false faces of plaster and cardboard, the eyes of these dead women were alive.

Their vitreous eyes were looking at me . . .

I woke up with a cry, for in that moment I had recognised all the women. They all had the eyes of Kranile and Willie, of Willie the mime and Kranile the dancer. Every one of the dead women had Kranile's left eye and Willie's right eye . . . so that every one of them appeared to be squinting.

Am I to be haunted by masks now?

THE TERROR OF THE MASQUERADE

April 98.

Masks! I see them everywhere. That dreadful vision of the other night – the deserted town with its masked corpses in every doorway; that nightmare product of morphine and ether – has taken up residence within me. I see masks in the street, I see them on stage in the theatre, I find yet more of them in the boxes. They are on the balcony and in the orchestra-pit. Everywhere I go I am surrounded by masks. The attendants to whom I give my overcoat are masked; masks crowd around me in the foyer as everyone leaves, and the coachman who drives me home has the same cardboard grimace fixed upon his face!

It is truly too much to bear: to feel that one is alone and at the mercy of all those enigmatic and deceptive faces, alone amid all the mocking laughs and the threats embodied in those masks. I have tried to persuade myself that I am dreaming, and that I am the victim of a hallucination, but all the powdered and painted faces of women, all the rouged lips and kohl-blackened eyelids . . . all of that has created around me an atmosphere of trance and mortal agony. Cosmetics: there is the root cause of my illness!

But I am happy, now, when there are *only* masks! Sometimes, I detect the cadavers beneath, and remember that beneath the masks there is a host of spectres.

The other evening, in that café-cabaret in the Rue de la Fontaine, where I had run aground with Tramsel and Jocard, who had taken me there to see that supposedly-fashionable singer . . . how could they fail to see that she was nothing but a corpse?

Yes, beneath the sumptuous and heavy ballgown, which swaddled her and held her upright like a sentry-box of pink velvet trimmed and embroidered with gold – a coffin befitting the queen of Spain – there was a corpse! But the others, amused by her wan voice and her emaciated frame, found her quaint – more than that, quite 'droll' . . .

Droll! that drab, soft and inconsistent epithet that everyone uses nowadays! The woman had, to be sure, a tiny carven head, and a kind of macabre prettiness within the furry heap of her opera-cloak. They studied her minutely, interested by the romance of her story: a petite bourgeoise thrown into the high life following the fad which had caught her up – and neither of them, nor anyone else besides in the whole of that room, had perceived what was immediately evident to my eyes. Placed flat on the white satin of her dress, the two hands of that singer were the two hands of a skeleton: two sets of knuckle-bones gloved in white suede. They might have been drawn by Albrecht Dürer: the ten fingers of an evil dead woman, fitted at the ends of the two overlong and excessively thin arms of a mannequin . . .

And while that room convulsed with laughter and thrilled with pleasure, greeting her buffoonery and her animal cries with a dolorous ovation, I became convinced that her hands no more belonged to her body than her body, with its excessively high shoulders, belonged to her head . . .

The conviction filled me with such fear and sickness that I did not hear the singing of a living woman, but of some automaton pieced together from disparate odds and ends – or perhaps even worse, some dead woman hastily reconstructed from hospital remains: the macabre fantasy of some medical student, dreamed up on the benches of the lecture-hall . . . and that evening began, like some tale of Hoffmann, to turn into a vision of the lunatic asylum.

Oh, how that Olympia of the concert-hall has hastened the progress of my malady!

May 1898

> *O brothers, sad lilies, I languish in beauty*

That I might be desired amid your nakedness,
And towards you, nymphs, nymphs of these fountains,
I come in the pure silence to offer my vain tears.
The hymns of the sun have faded. It is evening.
I hear the golden grass growing tall in the holy shadow
And the perfidious moon holds up its mirror,
So that the bright fountain is extinguished by the night.
Thus, thrown in the harmonious reeds,
I languish, O sapphire, in my sad beauty;
Antique sapphire and magical spring,
Where I forgot the laughter of the ancient hour,
How I lament your pure and fatal outflow!

Formerly, in my hour of need, I had only to open my caskets and to rest my temples upon a cold pool of gems in order to refresh them. The sombre azure of sapphires calmed me best of all; the sapphire is the the stone of the solitary and the celibate; the sapphire is the gaze of Narcissus. Franz Ebner, the jeweller of Munich, brought me back such beautiful sapphires from India: sapphires whose depths were so profound and clear that it seemed the transparent nights of Ceylon still dwelt therein; nocturnal sapphires in which I was able, not so very long ago, to drown my fever whenever I caressed them with my fingers and my eyes.

And the beautiful lines of Paul Valéry! What calmness their sublime nostalgic melancholy brought me! Those lines substituted for my horrible sickness the plight of Narcissus; and thereby cooled that suffering and phosphorous soul which the plaintive eyes of the *Antinous* has lighted in my being. But sapphires no longer appease me, now that I am haunted by the masks.

1st June 1898
Is it because I have taken so much pleasure in the cold depths of jewels that my eyes have been taken captive by this atrocious clairvoyance?

The simple fact is that I am suffering and dying of something which is not seen by others, but which I can see!

My 'hallucination' is only an extra sense: it is some unnamable facet of the human soul which is brought forth to bloom upon the skin, and which lends to every face the semblance of a mask.

I have always had some defect which makes me suffer from the ugliness of people encountered in the street, especially the little people: labourers going to work; clerks to their offices; housekeepers and servants. The ugliness of a saddened and miserable clown is further aggravated by the vulgarities of modern life, the degrading promiscuities of modern life . . .

Oh, the horror of a shower of rain in November, the interior of a bus station! All the ugliness of a Parisian street: the poverty of certain necks beneath the thin hair and weaselly faces of certain hurrying housewives; the exhausted and vicious chlorosis of the excessively-pallid lips and the oblique eyes, always sunken under bulging eyelids, of certain woman-chasers! The perfect hideousness of a Paris street! With the first frosts that hideousness becomes terrible! All this, at any rate, is easily explicable.

The poor downcast faces of aged artisans and shopkeepers display all the everyday cares of menial work: the burdens of petty preoccupations and the anxiety of the unpaid bills which made the end of every month fearful. The lassitude of the penniless at odds with life – a soured life without foresight – and all the unhappiness of simply existing, without a single elevated thought in their heads, has created those flat and mournful horrors.

How could one hope to find an expression in *those* eyes, fixed by stupefaction or hardened by hate: the glassy, criminal eyes of all those poor devils? Naturally, the thought occurs that perhaps there is one among them who is not entirely sordid and worthless; but one only sees the light of money and theft glimmering in their eyes. Lust, when they experience it, is venal and vandalistic. Each one, in his secret thoughts, dreams of nothing but the means to cheat and rob others.

Modern life – luxurious, pitiless and sceptical – has

formed the souls of these men, and their women likewise, into those of prison guards or bandits. It has given them the flattened heads of venomous snakes, the pointed and twisted muzzles of rodents, the jaws of sharks and the snouts of pigs. Envy, desperation, hatred, egoism and avarice have re-created humanity as a bestiary in which every low instinct is imprinted with animal traits . . .

But those ignoble masks! To think that I have believed for so long that they were the sole prerogative of the poorer classes. Mere racial prejudice has made me think so.

The poorer classes! What blasphemy! I have not looked closely enough at my own kind.

10 June 1898.
The one joy in my Hell, the one consolation to be found in the haunted shadows where I struggle, if there is any consolation at all, is that I am no longer alone in my struggle!

There is another man who has the same obsession as myself, another man who is haunted by the masks, another man who sees them and dreads them. That man is a great painter, an English artist known throughout Europe, one of the most famous men in London. It is Claudius Ethal, the renowned Ethal, who has removed himself from England and set up home in Paris in the wake of the notorious lawsuit involving Lord Kerneby.

Ethal also sees the masks; more than that, he immediately sees *through* the mask of every human face. The resemblance to an animal is the first characteristic that strikes him in every being he encounters . . . and he suffers so acutely from this dreadful clairvoyance that he has been obliged to renounce his calling. This great painter of portraits will henceforth paint nothing but landscapes – Claudius Ethal, creator of *The Young English Rose* and *The Woman in Green!*

By means of what secret presentiment has that visionary become aware of my own sickness? Was it instinct, or intelligence communicated to him by the indiscretions of my acquaintances, that brought him to me so quickly in the salon, the day before yesterday, with a familiarity that the mundane introduction before dinner hardly authorised? Why did he speak to me in that low and distant voice – a completely different voice from that which he had displayed at dinner – why did he say to me with that air of mystery and complicity: 'Do you not find, Monsieur le Duc, that the Marquise de Sarlèze is strangely reminiscent of a stork this evening?'

It was insane, but it was true.

That evening, with her long stippled neck, her narrow face, her round eyes with membranous lids, above all with her great nose tapering like a beak and the evident artifice in the wig imperfectly secured to her cranium, the Marquise de Sarlèze was a horrid stork out of some nightmare. The resemblance suddenly seemed to cry out to me, and I felt my reason darkened by the unknown, for in the vaporous luminosity of the chandeliers, along the high windows draped with pale green satin and in the doorways, the rooms of the Sarlèze apartments were suddenly populated with masqueraders.

It was the Englishman who evoked and imposed them on my vision. The half-naked woman at the piano, who was singing as if weighed down by the burden of her throat, had the profile of a bleating sheep; her blonde hair had the dull and woolly aspect of a fleece. The muzzle of a fox emerged from Tramsel's face, the mouth of a hyena from the novelist Mireau. In the group of seated women – all the flowers of the faubourg in a single basket – there were heavy bovine faces: the aqueous eyes of ruminant cows, ranged alongside the receding brows of carnivores and the round eyes of birds of prey.

That terrible Englishman identified all the resemblances for me. Standing next to Pleyel, the woman with a sheep's face, the Comtesse de Barville, continued to bleat a song by Chaminade; her pianist – a professional with the protruding eyes of a batrachian in a crushed and stupid little face – provided desultory and jerky accompaniment.

Claudius Ethal, leaning close to my ear, continued to put names to these monsters. The entire suite of the Sarlèze apartments – with their long parallelograms of ancient panellings, slightly touched up with gilt – was populated with ghosts by that diabolical Englishman. As if by means of some magical rite, the whole atmosphere swarmed with larvae, like a drop of water viewed through a microscope. The dreadful faces were allowed to become transparent to the instincts and ignoble thoughts of the souls within. All around us was a great whirlpool of grimacing mouths of shadow.

The nightmare immediately lost its grip when the Englishman fell silent.

THE HEALER

June 98

What kind of man is this Ethal? Is he genuine? Is he a great artist or a mountebank? I left his studio confused, intrigued, but nevertheless under his spell. For a moment I believed myself cured . . .

Well, given that I am just as disturbed as I was before, I evidently am not – but this is a different disturbance. I am less anxious about my problem but so disquieted by the man!

What a marvellous improviser he is; what an awakener of new ideas – strange ideas which nevertheless seem true!

This Claudius Ethal has bewitched me. I saw nothing in his studio: not a drawing, not a sketch, not a trace of oil-paints . . . and what a singular workplace for a sensual and sumptuous artist like him! Four bare walls lit by the cold daylight of a huge window with a view of rooftops – and what roofs! The Pantheon and the steeples of Saint-Sulpice. The Englishman has seen fit to settle on the other side of the river, at the end of the world, behind the Luxemburg . . .

In that vast hall, its ceiling so high that it seems to recede into shadow, there is not a single ornament, not a single bright patch of antique fabric, not a single gilt frame. It is a painter's studio denuded of all the customary décor. There is a certain luxury, though, in the austerity: the silky smoothness of a waxed and polished floor in which one can see one's face, the parquet gleaming like a field of ice – and, in one corner, a tall Imperial cheval-glass, mounted in a mahogany frame decorated with masks.

There were Debureau masks: the pale faces of Pierrots with pinched nostrils and tight smiles. There were Japanese masks, some in bronze and others in lacquered wood. There were masks from the Italian *commedia*, made of silk and painted wax, and a few of black gauze stretched over brass wire. There were enigmatic and cleverly horrid **Venetian** masks, like those of the characters of de Longhi.

An entire garland of grimaces had been posed around the sleeping pool of the mirror.

I had come to see a painter and his paintings, but I had fallen upon a collection of masks. I experienced a moment of near-dread.

'I have brought them out for you,' said Claudius Ethal, with the graceful gesture of a dancing-master. 'I have a fairly full collection here. Debureau masks are becoming rather scarce; I have had enquires about those from Venice, they simply cannot be found today. I don't have to tell you about the Japanese; all Edo has come to London and the avenue of the Opera.'

I remained on my guard, and he continued. 'Don't stand in awe of them: the only chance you have of being cured of your obsession with masks is to familiarise yourself with them, and to see their ordinariness. Study them at your leisure; handle them; penetrate their inspiring and horrifying ugliness – for there are those among them which are the works of great artists. Their ugliness born of dreams has extended for you the distressing qualities of human ugliness. The best cure for such delusions is homoeopathic. I am quite familiar with your problem; it is my own. It is the only reason for my voluntary exile from London. The fuliginous atmosphere and the fogs which rise out of the Thames fashion spectres and mannequins out of all mankind, in a manner too dreadful by far to be endured. I can breathe so much more easily since I began to live with masks! So I have brought them all out for you.'

Moving aside, with the peculiar grace of a dancer, Ethal displayed to me a mahogany sleeping-couch decorated in the same fashion as his cheval-glass: a whole heap of masks encumbered the cushions.

There were charming ones as well as terrible ones, that I must admit. The painter was particularly entranced by Japanese masks: warriors', actors' and courtesans' masks. Some of them were frightfully contorted, the bronze cheeks creased by a thousand wrinkles, with vermilion weeping from the corners of the eyes and long trails of green at the corners of the mouths like splenetic beards.

'These are the masks of demons,' said the Englishman, caressing the long black swept-back tresses of one of them. 'The Samurai wore them in battle, to terrify the enemy. The one which is covered in green scales, with two opal pendants between the nostrils, is the mask of a sea-demon. This one, with the tufts of white fur for eyebrows and the two horsehair brushes beside the lips, is the mask of an old man. These others, of white porcelain – a material as smooth and fine as the cheeks of a Japanese maiden, and so gentle to the touch – are the masks of courtesans. See how alike they all are, with their delicate nostrils, their round faces and their heavy slanted eyelids; they are all effigies of the same goddess. The black of their wigs is rather beautiful, isn't it? Those which bubble over with laughter even in their immobility are the masks of comic actors.'

That devil of a man pronounced the names of demons, gods and goddesses; his erudition cast a spell. Then: 'Bah! I have been down there too long!'

Now he took up the light edifices of gauze and painted silk which were Venetian masks. 'Here is a Cockadrill, a Captain Fracasse, a Pantaloon and a Braggadocio. Only the noses are different – and the cut of their moustaches, if you look at them closely. Doesn't the white silk mask with enormous spectacles evoke a rather comical dread? It is Doctor Curucucu, an actual marionette featured in the Tales of Hoffmann. And what about that one, with all the black horsehair and the long spatulate nose like a stork's beak tipped with a spoon? Can you imagine anything more appalling? It's a duenna's mask; amorous young women were well-guarded when they had to go about flanked by old dragons dressed up in something like that. The whole carnival of Venice is put on parade before us beneath the cape and the domino, lying in ambush behind these masks ... Would you like a gondola? Where shall we go, San Marco or the Lido?'

He laughed.

His vivacity stunned me. I laughed with him, charmed by his fluency, dazzled by the scintillation of so many memories – and I no longer saw, in the eye-holes of all those masks, the frightful gleam of suffering which had previously shone therein for me.

'That's enough for today,' he declared, after an hour and a half of rambling. 'You must come again, as often as possible. Your case is so interesting! When you have become fully inured to the masks, we will thumb through the albums of the great caricaturists together: Rowlandson, Hogarth, and above all Goya. Ah! the genius of his *Capriccios*, the soothing horror of his witches and beggars! You have not yet made sufficient progress to face the terrible Spaniard, but his work is a philtre which will facilitate your cure. There is also Rops, but the lewd aspects of that artist would reawaken fevers in you which we must let lie for the time being. Perhaps Ensor and his modern nightmares, when you are better. This is an authentic cure that I have set in train.

'If we were in Madrid, I would tell you to go to the Prado every morning, so that you might enjoy the suggestive influence of Velasquez' madmen, the mad Hapsburgs; they provide a perfect diversion. As we are not, you must go instead to the Louvre. Antonio Moro's portrait of the Duc D'Albe's famous dwarf will teach you an important lesson. To begin with, he will familiarise you with my face: it is said that he resembles me. And on that note, *adieu*, or rather *à bientôt*.

'You shall certainly be healed.'

July 98

Why did Claudius Ethal tell me that he resembled the Antonio Moro in the Louvre? Was it to disturb me or to make a mockery of me?

This Claudius is, it appears, a terrible practical joker. In London, he has practised the art of 'fun' with such malice and refinement of purpose that he was forced to expatriate himself to France; his situation there had become untenable. His legal dispute with Lord Kerneby, regarding his portrait of the duchess, was nothing but a convenient pretext; the truth is that he has fled an explosion of the righteous wrath of rancorous old men: wrath and rancour stirred up with all the artistry of an ironist, who elevated the poser above the painter of portraits when he went into their homes. The scandal of his condemnation, the ruination visited upon him by the lawsuit, were only reprisals; the court did not lash out at the acrimonious, crabby and speechless artist but at the incorrigible and triumphant jester.

For ten years Ethal was painter by appointment to the aristocracy, and revelled in the impunity guaranteed by the status of his clientèle. Fortified by his talent and his great name, arrogance and hypocrisy led him to jeer and scoff at that same aristocracy which had taken him most painfully to its heart. Dreadful stories are told about him.

To begin with, there is the story of the Marchioness of Clayvenore, a princess and lady-in-waiting to the queen, who was invited by him to lunch in his studio at Windsor. Once there she was brusquely placed before a terrifying portrait of two grotesque clowns: the two brothers Dario – Reginald the giant and Edward the midget – who, for three years, had caused a considerable stir in the music-halls of New York and London. Lady Clayvenore had seen the two grotesques at the Aquarium two days before, and now experienced all over again the vision of their grimaces and their contorsions.

Lady Clayvenore had expected to find Ethal's studio replete with portraits of women and children, but she came by twilight upon a painted nightmare: the tortured faces of the two phenomena. Then the studio became dark. It was the end of December, and night falls quickly in winter. Lady Clayvenore perceived that she was alone in the deserted studio; Claudius Ethal had disappeared – and while, all a-tremble, she went to look for an exit-door behind the curtains, which were no longer drawn back, the hallucinatory portrait came to life.

Welcome to Crossroads!
DAVID checked out the following items:

1. Surviving : the uncollected writings of Henry Green
   Barcode: 58320326
   Call #: 823.912
   Due: Aug 08, 2013

2. Loving ; Living ; Party going
   Barcode: 2015113414
   Call #: Fic GREEN
   Due: Aug 08, 2013

3. Nothing
   Barcode: 12432522
   Call #: FIC GREEN
   Due: Aug 08, 2013

4. ILL TITLE - MONSIEUR DE PHOCAS
   Barcode: 2097040527
   Call #: IL105720992
   Due: Aug 01, 2013

First the midget leapt like a toad from the frame, then the huge and skinny giant sallied forth with vulturine wingbeats. Around the woman overwhelmed by consternation, a strange Sabbat commenced. With atrocious convolutions of the arms and the torso they repeated the act which she had seen at the Aquarium two days before, but in the solitude of the deserted studio it was a ghostly phantasmagoria; the dance of two larvae, made far more horrible by shadow and silence.

The two grotesques, hired and primed by Claudius Ethal, performed their exercises faithfully – but following that private séance Lady Clayvenore kept to her bed for eight hours, and since she was on the point of divorcing Lord Clayvenore, a full account of Ethal's nasty joke had to be given to the court.

'The divine Marchioness,' the painter said, by way of excuse, 'always declared that of all sensations she appreciated only the unforeseen, the violent and the profound. I believed that I was giving her exactly what she wanted.' Then, clicking his tongue like a connoisseur of fine things, he added: 'Poor milady! Never have I seen on a human face such a superbly intense expression of terror. I watched in ecstasy: there was such voluptuousness and charm in that distress and horror . . . I shall treasure it as the memory of a marvellous Lady Macbeth, a sleepwalking Lady Macbeth.'

And that is merely one of the lesser tricks attributed to that devil of a man.

In the escapade which took him to Whitechapel in the company of Lady Feredith – an American millionairess, married to a Yankee, who was temperamental, ill-bred and addicted to ether, and who had had an unhealthy curiosity about that district of thieves and prostitutes – things went even further. Two mercenaries hired and posted by the painter treated the old lady in search of sinister sensations as if she were one of the miserable girls who prowled the streets by night. The nocturnal mock-attack culminated in violence and in certain actions of which the American did not complain; stripped of her jewels, her modesty overwhelmed, this particular thirster for the unknown would have regretted nothing. Indeed, she inspired the artist to create one of his most beautiful studies, exhibited under the title *Messalina*. Claudius Ethal evidently found it an occasion for merriment.

Finally, to conclude the series of his acknowledged fancies, there is the story of the portrait of the Baroness Desrodes, a converted jewess, whose annulment awarded by the Court of Rome, fabulous dresses and furniture in asparagus-green laquer had kept the newspaper columnists busy for a year. In an acute crisis of snobbery, Elsie – as she was known to her intimates – had taken it into her head to have a portrait by Ethal. Helleu and La Gandara, her usual painters, were no longer good enough for her. In order to obtain the portrait she crossed the channel, installed herself in London, and set all her acquaintances to work. Whistler and Hercomer, who had already been commissioned to produce portraits of her, arranged for her to be introduced to Claudius. There was a series of dinners and receptions in a house in Charing Cross, to which Elsie had transported her entire Paris establishment in order to dazzle all the good citizens of England: her green-lacquered furniture encrusted with diamonds; her glass cases of unique Dresden and unobtainable white Sèvres; and her entire collection of frogs. She had frogs by Massier, by Carriès, by Lachanal, by Bigot, and frogs all the way from Japan, for she was a veritable fetishist, like all those of her snobbish and superstitious kind. Baroness Desrodes is the woman of the frogs, just as the Comte de Montesquiou is the man of the world . . . what poverty, what paltriness, what vanity!

To cut a long story short, the baroness obtained the desired sittings with the painter. Ethal consented without being begged too much; he agreed likewise to portray the baroness at Charing Cross, in her own setting, amid her green lacquer furniture, her frogs and her familiar paraphernalia. The baroness was exultant: she had tamed the wild and savage beast which was the great Ethal! She had become part of his circle of intimates! Ethal had agreed to paint her at home, which he had never done for anyone else! But there was, however, one condition: that she should not see the portrait until it was finished. He would take the canvas away after each sitting and bring it back with him for the next. It was a hard condition, but it was nevetheless accepted. The painter set about his work, and when the portrait was finished the whole shooting-match of friends and acquaintances was assembled in the studio of the painter in order to admire the portrait of Elsie.

Horror and stupefaction! Seated in the midst of her bronze and ceramic frogs, Elsie too had a green head, enormous briny and gold-circled eyes set in a squashed face, and a goitred throat. Her bare arms, their flesh stringy and flaccid, were crossed so that little palmate hands were raised in front of the goitre. The Baroness Desrodes was a frog: a human frog strayed from the land of Faerie. And here she was, enthroned in the midst of all her admirers!

The baroness rejected the portrait and referred the matter to her solicitors.

'What did she expect?' Ethal said. 'It is her own physique which is the root of the problem. She defies portraiture and demands caricature.'

And Claudius Ethal is rumoured to indulge less mentionable whims.

This is the man who proposes to cure me; I am in his hands. What does he want from me? I confess that a dire anxiety has taken hold of me. This Englishman frightens me.

UNDER THE SPELL

June 1898

Ethal was telling the truth; he does indeed resemble the Duc D'Albe's dwarf. I have returned three times to the Louvre to absorb myself in contemplation before the Antonio Moro, and the odious resemblance became more evident with every visit. Ethal is the frightful double of the Flemish master's hooded gnome.

The dwarf has an enormous head, a thick neck and an overlong trunk which does not seem to fit the excessively short and twisted legs. His gnarled and shaggy hands, and his crooked fingers circled by heavy rings, are the hands and fingers of Ethal. Ethal has his receding forehead, his bushy eyebrows and his bulbous sniffling nose; that sarcastic mouth is his too, as are the thick and heavy eyelids whose intermittent shelter conceals a gleam of malice.

The sensual and maleficent physiognomy of this kobold dressed up as a jester is the physiognomy of my painter; the resemblance is striking. One senses in him a cunning and attentive soul, all lust and irony: the soul of a satyr, which English arrogance and cant do not suit at all, although there is so much affected ambiguity in his being that flashy finery and a fool's cap and bells seem more becoming than a dinner-jacket.

One particular detail stands out: that hairy chest, cynically displayed beneath the immoderate expanse of his neck, like the chest of a carter or the body of some frightful spider, covered with bristly black hair . . .

I had not noticed all these hideous and repugnant things during our previous encounters: the spirit of that devil of a man exerted such imperious power over me! They only became clear to me in the course of time, and after Ethal had taken care to call my attention to the resemblance. I would not have discovered them at all had they not been pointed out to me, and yet it was he who sent me to the

Louvre, he who caused me to observe the horrible analogy which can be drawn between that horrible dwarf and himself!

Why? Strangely enough, that ugliness, instead of repelling me, attracts me. The mysterious Englishman has me under his spell; I am no longer able to pass him by.

Since I have come to know him, the presence of others has become even more intolerable to me, their conversation most of all. Oh, how it all annoys and exasperates me: their attitudes, their manners, their whole way of being! The people of my world, all my unhappy peers, have come to irritate, oppress and sadden me with their noisy and empty chatter, their monstrous and boundless vanity, their even more monstrous egotism, their club gossip . . . the endless repetition of opinions already formed and judgments already made; the automatic vomiting forth of articles read in those morning papers which are the recognised outlet of the hopeless wilderness of their ideas; the eternal daily meal of overfamiliar clichés concerning racing stables and the stalls of fillies of the human variety . . . the hutches of the '*petites femmes*' – another worn out phrase in the dirty usury of shapeless expression!

Oh my contemporaries, my dear contemporaries . . .

Their idiotic self-satisfaction; their fat and full-blown self-sufficiency; the stupid display of their good fortune; the clink of fifty- and a hundred-franc coins forever sounding out their financial prowess, according their own reckoning; their hen-like clucking and their pig-like grunting, as they pronounce the names of certain women; the obesity of their minds, the obscenity of their eyes, and the tonelessness of their laughter! They are, in truth, handsome puppets of *amour*, with all the exhausted despondency of their gestures and the slackness of their *chic* . . .

Chic! A hideous word, which fits their manner like a new glove: as dejected as undertakers' mutes, as full-blown as Falstaff . . .

Oh my contemporaries: the *ceusses* of my circle, to put it in their own ignoble argot. They have all welcomed the moneylenders into their homes, and have been recruited as their clients, and they have likewise played host to the fat journalists who milk their conversations for the society columns. How I hate them; how I execrate them; how I would love to devour them liver and lights – and how well I understand the Anarchists and their bombs!

Why has Ethal stirred up such an outburst of hatred in me? To be sure, this horror of mankind – especially the abomination of the worldly – has always been in me, but it was dormant, latent, smouldering beneath the ashes ... Since I have met Ethal, though, it has rapidly fermented, turning sour and seething. A furor has mounted within me like a new wine, a wine of execration and hatred. All the blood is boiling in my veins; all my flesh is sickening; my nerves are jangling and my fists are clenched; murderous desires run through my mind ...

To kill, to kill someone, oh how that would soothe me! That would extinguish my fever. I feel that I have the hands of an assassin.

So *this* is the cure I was promised!

And yet the presence and the conversation of Claudius brings about a sense of well-being. His presence reassures me and the sound of his voice calms me. Since I have known him, the shadowy figures which grimace all around me are less distinct. I am no longer obsessed with penetrating their masks ... and the vertigo of the green eyes – the glaucous irises of the *Antinous* – has been banished!

The eyes, the eyes, I no longer suffer the madness of the eyes. This man has bewitched my sickness. His conversation is so charming, he provokes so many ideas, the least of his phrases awaken such echoes in me! His words evoke and bring into being thoughts which are my own, although not yet fully formulated: thoughts still distant from my consciousness; ideas of which I had as yet no suspicion. This mysterious provocateur is telling me about myself, putting flesh on my dreams. *He speaks to me so distinctly that something like him is awakening in me.* It is as if another self more precise and more subtle, born of his conversations, has taken root within me. His gestures define my powers of sight; he has become light and life to me.

He has brushed aside and dissipated the shadows which gathered around me. Spectres no longer menace me.

And yet this atrocious hatred and murderous fury still increase!

Perhaps it is one of the phases of my healing – for I *shall* be healed. Claudius has promised me that.

July 1898

Like me, Claudius has a fascination for music-halls and dance-halls. The human body, whose ugliness normally saddens and irritates him, becomes a source of inexpressible joy when it chances to move with beauty. Purity of form – the suppleness and vigour of the human body – also soothes and brightens his spirits. Claudius has an eye of singular acuity for the discovery of this beauty, however it might be diguised by the most piteous and dreary rags and tatters. His artistic flair enables him to track down and dig up this beauty – which is especially to be found in the haunts of streetwalkers, destitutes and street-arabs – with uncanny skill. And yet this is a painter patronised by great ladies!

Claudius is drawn by his predilection to the flesh of beggar-women as hogs are drawn to truffles. For sores and tattered garments he has a perspicacious love 'as dependable as that of an evil Christ' – as he said of himself, in jest.

The other evening, on the way home from Versailles, we went into a dance-hall in the Rue de la Gaîté. In the heavy, saturated atmosphere of that overheated room we were surrounded by labourers dressed in their Sunday best, apprentices of every kind of trade and every mode of prostitution. His bright and crafty sensualist's eye was suddenly attracted to one particular couple.

The woman, still young, was slimly curvaceous; her straight hair was parted in the middle and bound in a headband. She was young, but already faded: the morbid, sensuous and depraved fading of the suburban Parisian. She was probably a burnisher. But her wicked smile was so feverishly pink, and beneath her great voracious eyes were deathly-dark rings – and what a black look she had as those eyes followed the gushing and gambolling of her dancing partner!

This dancer, undoubtedly her lover, had released her and was prancing like an escaped colt through the dance-hall, triumphantly snapping up the women in his path and making them pirouette like so many spinning tops. He was dressed in a threadbare velvet jacket, parted just a little in an untidy and aggressive manner. His chest was thrust out and his knees were tensed. One after the other, he carried the women off and lifted them up, then deposited them again on their toes.

Forsaken, the woman with the black headband, the narrow face and the hard eyes watched him closely, lying in wait for him in muted anguish and mounting anger. The other women made a circle around him, and he, overexcited, now played the part of a lone cavalier, risking ever-greater leaps in response to the tapping of feet, flinging his arms about. He rolled up the sleeves of his jacket, swayed his hips, and bowed low to the wan and silent girl – and, with his rump in the air, like someone playing leap-frog, made laughing faces at her between his legs, before resuming his twirling.

In the electrified room, laughter and applause burst forth. The girl had become green. She dug in her pocket under the table, but before she could achieve her purpose he seized her by the waist, snatched her up in a greedy embrace and crushed a kiss upon her mouth. Staring into one another's eyes with moist lips, supporting one another with their legs entwined, their whole bodies were touching. She was suddenly faint and forgiving, laughing as if she had been tickled; he was still vain, cocksure and proud – and off they went, waltzing and pirouetting, with all the defiant arrogance of overt mutual desire and peace finally made.

'The knave is handsome,' Claudius whispered in my ear. 'The little one will not be bored tonight.'

I started involuntarily, his voice having awakened me from a dream. His bright and glittering stare cut through me like a blade. I felt a sharp coldness enter into me. He looked deep into my soul, understood the as-yet-unacknowledged desire which that scene and that boy had disturbed in my flesh ... and I felt suddenly full to overflowing with hatred: hatred for Claudius and hatred for the mistress of that prancing lout!

So *this* is the promised cure!

I am afraid of this Englishman. His voice gives birth to abominable suggestions within me; his presence corrupts me; his gestures conjure up unspeakable visions.

20 July

Ethal has gone away. He went on Monday, summoned to Brussels by a letter; a sale of pictures and engravings has caused him abruptly to quit Paris. He ought to have returned two days later, Thursday at the latest, but he has now been there for eight days, sending telegrams all the while to announce his return. The dispatches mount up on my table, but my Claudius does not return.

What a vital role he has assumed in my life! How I miss him! His presence has become so necessary to me that since he has been gone it is as if a kind of hunger tears me and hollows me out. It *is* a sensation of hunger, absolutely – but at the same time it chokes and suffocates me.

And yet, I still feel that I fear and hate that misfortunate Englishman!

15 July.

The Three Brides by Toorop. Claudius has sent it to me, a very rare engraving which he bought at a sale in Ouudenaarde and which he posted with a letter anouncing his return on Monday. In three days! He will have been away for fifteen days.

Toorop. Jan Theodoor Toorop. I know the name; it is famous in Holland.

The Three Brides.

It is a sort of quasi-monastic diabolical vision. In a landscape populated with larvae – flowing and undulating larvae called forth like a cascade of leeches by tolling bells – three female figures rise up phantasmally, enshrouded with gauze like Spanish madonnas. They are the 'three brides': the bride of Heaven, the bride of the Earth and the bride of Hell . . .

The bride of Hell, with her two serpents writhing about her temples to hold her veil in place, has the most attractive mask: the most profound eyes, the most vertiginous smile that one could ever see.

If she existed. how I would love that woman! I feel that if that smile and those eyes were in my life they would be all the cure I need!

I could never tire of the study and contemplation of that hallucinatory visage.

The Three Brides is very peculiar in its detail and composition. It is the whimsy of a dream rendered with astonishing fastidiousness: the delusion of an opium-smoker composed in the style of Holbein.

'It is the product of an Asiatic Catholicism,' Claudius told me in his letter. 'A dreadful, terrifying and self-explanatory Catholicism – for the Dutchman Toorop is Javanese by birth. I know that you will love this Toorop, because there are only three painters in the world who can tease out the expression for which you are searching: Burne-Jones, the great Fernand Knopff and him.

'I know which of these *Three Brides* will excite your desire. It is the Infernal one, is it not, whose eyes haunt you?'

A SERIES OF ETCHINGS

'It is an Asiatic Catholicism, a Catholicism of ecstasy and perversity, a dreadful, terrifying and self-explanatory Catholicism – for the Dutchman Toorop is Javanese by birth.

'I know that you will love this Toorop.

'There are only three painters in the world who can tease out the expression for which you are searching: Burne-Jones, the great Fernand Knopff and him.

'I know which of the three brides will excite your desire. It is the Infernal one, is it not, whose eyes haunt you?'

And that is the one which haunts me now; my obsession with intense eyes has returned. By touching the scar, Ethal has reopened the wound. The scar? The wound had hardly closed . . .

Why has Claudius sent this etching, which disturbs me, and this letter, which causes me yet more anguish! Oh, the haunting of those emerald eyes!

So *this* is the cure that I was promised!

There is a practical joker in him. Is he playing some kind of cruel game, aggravating my sickness with fresh poison?

3 August 98
He should have returned. He said he would return yesterday.

A telegram arrived.

Antwerp. Departure delayed. Going to Ostend to see Ensor. Very curious artist. Will send you his masks if I can make a deal; difficult. Unearthed here yesterday, in second-hand dealer's, proof set of Goya prints: the series of Capriccios. A treasure. Am detaching one to send to you, for your patience. Study it. Letter follows. Best wishes.

The promised etching was delivered to me. The inking is

marvellous. It depicts a grimacing head with a snub nose and visionary eyes, feverish with a frightful ardour, lit up like beacons in their cavernous orbits. It is a socratic head, into whose gaze all life seems to be concentrated: the head of an alchemist or some ossified and desiccated cenobite; a batlike head with thin lips, well used to prayers; the lips of an old woman, whose creased mouth has turned into a mere hole. Under the mouth, the narrow chin abruptly recedes, giving the profile the aspect of a muzzle, while atop that ancient, shrivelled and decrepit thing, an inordinate forehead spreads out and overhangs, its enormous temples bulging: the dreadful disproportion of a gigantic brain.

The total baldness of the forehead gives the whole head the aspect of a fantastic glabrous skull: a skull whose sad muzzle is crumpled. The polished ivory of that prodigious skull fumes, ripples and breaks into waves; the skull seethes and fumes like the lid of a saucepan. And its pale and errant fumes become, in the darkness of the etching, snouts and beaks: so many grimacing beasts; so many larvae and venomous nudes. The abnormal brain peoples the night with mad and menacing grins.

In the margin, underscoring the abominable nightmare, this aphorism of Goya's appears in French and in Spanish:

Genius deprived of reason gives birth to monsters.

Why has Claudius sent me this? What is he trying to tell me? What is his objective? What is the meaning of this hideous etching, and of his sending it to me so that I might fall ill in looking at it? This rare proof attracts me, repels me, attaches itself to me. There is a kind of poison in those piercing and fixed eyes!

And the horror of those leeches with human faces, these rippling and and fluent tadpoles, to which the melting skull gives birth: the head is making me ill.

Afer the Toorop, the Goya! I have tried hard, but can find no explanation. And the return continually deferred, from day to day . . .

What sinister game is this mysterious Englishman playing with me?

5 August
All through the night, atrocious images of insects and infusoria swarmed within the curtains of my bed: strange reptiles with the beaks of storks; toads winged like bats; enormous beetles with gaping abdomens crawling with worms, moving towards newborn children fringed with leeches.

I sweated with anguish and struggled in the spasms of a shadowy nightmare. The Goya etching has given birth to these monsters. I shall have to double my usual dose of bromide this evening.

8 August 98.
A letter from Claudius, postmarked Ostend: a letter and a scroll of parchment. What has he sent now?

The letter first:

My dear Duc, please excuse me one more time. I have broken my word to you for the third time – and this year you have given up your summer expedition to take the waters and visit the Tyrol, in order to stay in Paris with me . . . I would be the most wretched man alive had I not the most serious motive to lay before you. The most marvellous curio – an extremely rare sixteenth century piece, of a kind of which I am excessively fond, a museum-piece such as one no longer encounters in the market-place – was brought to my attention by Ensor. It is very near here, in Holland; in Leyden, to be precise.

The piece is in the home of an old collector whose showcases are to be put under the auctioneer's hammer by order of the court. The poor man has gone mad and his family must liquidate his estate. The summer sales are the only ones available to them † disastrous for the seller, of course; the buyer always has the best of it.

I depart in an hour for Leyden, I will come back with the item in question if it is the last thing I do, for if Ensor has described it to me accurately it is a unique piece which will be my pride and glory. If I can secure it I will take up my brushes again and rediscover my talent. If I cannot paint this thing I shall never again set paint to canvas.

You shall see it, and you shall love it as much as I do — perhaps even more. Then we would be rivals!

I would not go for any other reason than to find some such thing as Ensor has told me about! Ensor sees with his imagination, but his vision is perfectly accurate, of an almost geometric precision. He is one of the very few who can really see. Like you, he has an obsession with masks; he is a seer as you and I are. The common herd, of course thinks that he is mad.

I have told him the story of your case, and he is naturally very interested in it. Although he does not know you he has been seized by a strong compassion for you; between sick persons there is always a bond of understanding. As a token of his sympathy, he has chosen one of the most beautiful etchings from his folio, and has asked me to offer it to you; I have dispatched it to you, bearing his signature. If not the most beautiful, it is at least the most intense of his series of Masques.

You shall see what sort of man Ensor is, and what a marvellous insight he has into the invisible realm where our vices are created . . . those vices for which our faces make masks.

Await now a telegram from Leyden, which will announce to you my success and — this time — my return.

ETHAL.

P.S. I could not strike a bargain with Ensor on my own behalf.

So yet again his return is deferred, his absence prolonged. When can I expect him now? It is as if he is firmly determined to exhaust and exasperate my patience.

And this unique curio, this collector's item that he has gone to Holland to acquire, and of which he wishes to paint a masterpiece — what could it possibly be? Yet more mystification.

I am seized by curiosity — and, at the same time, by doubt, suspicion and increasing terror.

I sense that all these dispatches of hideous and hallucinatory engravings are starting something. They are deranging and depraving my brain, populating my imagination with the produce of stupor and trance ... and the nervous trepidation of this perpetual waiting ...

I have entered into a mystery, and the mystery has entered into me. It is as if a vast net envelops me and closes around me. I feel that a mesh of shadows is contracting all around me, hour by hour.

And this etching by Ensor, this new dispatch? What horrible thing is winging its way to me now? No, I shall not even unwrap the parcel. I cannot bring myself to open it. This time I will not touch the parchment. No, I will not look at this engraving.

9 August 98
Lust.

My curiosity proved too strong, and I have broken the seal of the scroll. *Lust* – that is the title of Ensor's etching.

It seems, at first sight, to be set in a furnished room in some tawdry brothel. There is an armchair upholstered in velvet, a mahogany chest of drawers: the décor of banal and bourgeois depravity. Sprawled in the armchair, hands spread out on his stomach, is a hideous bespectacled gentleman, bald, smug, taut-necked and lantern-jawed: some old notary, pharmacist or churchwarden, a Flaubertian Monsieur Homais running to fat. His snout and his big myopic eyes are avidly savouring the spectacle before him: in an alcove there is a bed, set a little too high, its curtains gracefully swept back; and on the bed, languishing in semi-darkness, spreading out her two stout bare legs, there sprawls the pale puffy body of a fat prostitute, a whore with coarse features and a belly like some huge and hideous balloon, which gives the impression of being distended by the semen of an entire barracks.

Settled beside the sated girl, in complete contrast to her full and lazy flesh, is a thin and miserable figure in a long cassock. Waspishly hunched over her, he embraces the woman, gluttonously biting and sucking her neck! Oh, the hardness of that face contorted by desire, the whites of the eyes upturned by lust!

Lust! Wearing a Greek cap, sunk into his armchair, the fat man in the spectacles contemplates, rejoices and burns. It would be a thoroughly base spectacle were the phantasmagoria of the surounding walls not sharply heightened by a wild grandeur – for the brothel-chamber is haunted! Under the artist's etching-needle, the design of the wallpaper in the room has become a sinister and swarming tapestry. The room is infested with tadpoles and gnomes with sinuous flowing bodies. Ugly grimaces and taut smiles, blind dead eyes and slobbering mouths, float about the walls and in the bed-curtains.

The lust of the three masks displayed – an enfeebled and sterile' lust – has populated the room with amorphous and embryonic beings: a swarm of stillborn monsters has gushed forth from the enraptured eyes of the churchwarden, and from the greedy kiss of the seminarian.

At the bottom of the luxurious print, with a knowing but brutal and intransigent gesture, Ensor has signed his own name and added a line from Baudelaire:

Hypocrite reader, my fellow, my brother!

Lust. Quivering with disgust, I felt some ancient fire simmering in the marrow of my bones.

So the old madness was progressing still!

On closer examination of the figures in that vengeful etching, it seems to me that the seminarian resembles me. He has my thinness, my fixed and sad eyes. The resemblance is odious. Is it intentional, or mere chance? I have examined the print very carefully, and it seems to me that after the print was struck someone has used a pen and ink to retouch the figure of the man who is devouring the neck of the sleeping whore.

Yes, it has definitely been touched up. Who has done it? Ethal or Ensor? Ethal surely – Ensor does not know me.

Why have they sent it to me? Oh, it is evil to trouble me thus. I feel myself shadowed by the unknown; my mind is sinking; all the marrow in my bones is aflame; my heart, as if disconnected from my body, capsizes and floats free.

And this Ethal has promised me a cure!

THE DOLL COLLECTOR

13 August 1898

Pierre de Tairamond has just left me.

Tairamond is a distant cousin of mine – one of those vague and distant kinsmen by which every great family extends into the suburbs. It is one of the prerogatives of the nobility to trail such strings of relatives behind them, forever extending new shoots into every insignificant provincial town, however distant. It is a privilege and an affliction to possess such an army of collaterals, descendants of the same bloodline and pretenders to the same coat of arms!

Tairamond is one of the very few kinsmen of mine that I have ever been able to tolerate. He is also the only one with whom I maintain any kind of communication. He was at school with me, when we used to play together; now, in Paris, he touches me for loans to supply his needs and sustain his social life – and as he is poor and unpresumptuous I have consented to adopt the role of banker, occasionally providing him with sums of money which he has always neglected to repay. I like his careless cynicism. I think he has a certain affection for me, although he is incapable of gratitude. The loans he solicits from me are the principal reason for his maintaining the connection with me, although his ego – he is a clubman ten times over – revels in the ambiguity of my reputation.

Sharp as a needle, Pierre has always maintained a perfect discretion with regard to me. With an affected dandyism, he has always had the courtesy to appear to be ignorant of the abominations that are laid to my account. He has never interrogated me as to how I spend my days, or as to the mystery of my nights. He is a spoilt child, but tactful – a species which is becoming rare. I like him as much for his faults as his good points. Given the man that he is, the fact that he has taken the step of coming to me, and all that he has said to me regarding Ethal, should not be allowed to disturb me - for it was to talk about Claudius that Tairamond came.

For two hours he talked to me about Claudius. His conversation moved in fits and starts, listless and reticent, but I understood well enough that my liaison with the Englishman has caused him some alarm, that he was not the only one in my circle of acquaintances who was anxious about it, and that he had been virtually instructed to undertake his errand by the family and my old friends.

Half of Paris is preoccupied with my intimacy with that Englishman and, detested though I am, there is some concern over the fact that I am courting danger.

Tairamond had no precisely formulated accusation to level against Ethal, and the thousand and one rumours about his life in London and the Indies have nothing to teach me – nothing at all. I already know about all his practical jokes against Lady Clayvenore and other noble ladies. Pierre has added a few more nasty stories, aggravated by the intervention of the police, which would have precipitated the departure of Claudius even more effectively than his lost lawsuit – but grave as they are, these stories do not surprise me in the least. Ethal would not be the artist that he is if he were not an erotomaniac! But what *has* rather taken my breath away, and given me cause me to reflect, is the question which Tairamond has raised of Ethal's collection of poisons, and his opium cigarettes.

He has, apparently, brought back from his voyage to the Indies an entire arsenal of mysterious poisons whose very names are unknown in Europe: stupefiants, narcotics and aphrodisiacs – the most powerful and terrible aphrodisiacs – obtained from maharajahs and fakirs by means of prices paid in gold or by fabulous barter; a dangerous treasure-trove of powders and sinister liquors, whose preparation and dosages he has fully mastered. It is further said that he has employed this debilitating alchemy in the worst enterprises; there has been talk of broken wills and atrophied resistance, energetic men and women rendered powerless by means of certain cigarettes proffered or perfumes sent by Ethal. It is said that one of his acquaintances – an old school-friend and a painter as highly-valued and as fashionable as himself – became an idiot in less than two years as a result of frequenting Claudius' studio.

Certain cigarettes prepared by Ethal are said to provoke the worst debauchery; and it is said that the young Duchess of Searley was dead in six months, by virtue of having breathed the scent of certain strange and heady flowers in his home, whose peculiar property is to make the skin lustrous and the eyes delectably hollow.

According to Tairamond, dangerous elixirs of beauty are offered by Claudius to those who pose for him. The Marchioness of Beacoscome might have died too, if she had not been ordered by her doctors to suspend her sittings. These marvellous flowers which generate pallors and shadowed eyes contain within their perfume, it seems, the germ of consumption. For love of beauty, in his fervour for delicate flesh-tints and expressions swamped with languor, Claudius Ethal would poison his models!

Tairamond also asked me if I had seen Ethal wearing a certain emerald mounted in a ring, whose green depths contain a poison so powerful that a single drop on the lips of a man would suffice to strike him down. Ethal has allegedly tested that frightful glaucous death two or three times, before witnesses, on dogs.

Cantharidian cigarettes, opium pipes, venomous flowers, Far-Eastern poisons and murderous rings . . . I knew nothing about any of this. Ethal has never breathed a word of it to me. The tales which Tairamond told gave me entry into a fearful and dismal legend. The corrupter and perverter of ideas that I already knew him to be was overtaken by a new image: he was, definitively, a *poisoner*: an impish master of every kind of venom.

I received this account with outward indifference. With the characteristic lightness of the clubman, Tairamond – without putting any more faith in the rumours than was merited – had taken the trouble to warn me; he had come from Trouville and was due to depart the following day for Ostend. While passing through Paris he had come to see me, solely to exchange a few friendly words and to put me on my guard. He took his leave without borrowing the few hundred francs which was the customary tax exacted by his visits – and that omission caused me more disquiet than all his revelations. If his mission was not a pretext to ask for a loan then the matter was surely serious! A sportsman would not go to all that trouble for nothing.

20 August 1898.
I have just left Claudius.

Early this morning an express letter brought me news of his return: *The Leyden marvel is mine and I have it here. Come to see it. We both arrived last night.*

The Leyden marvel! Ethal had realised his desire. The incomparable curio – the museum-piece which had kept him fifteen days in Holland – was finally in his possession and I had been invited to come and admire the object . . .

I have seen the marvel, and the marvel has left me cold. And yet, what preparations and what ingenious staging Claudius employed in doing me the honour of displaying it!

One by one, Ethal threw back the draperies with which the showcase was veiled. It was as if he took pleasure in testing my patience – but at last, imprisoned within four fine panels of plate-glass, secured in place by copper rods, the Doll was revealed to me.

For it is a Doll, or rather a mannequin: a full-sized mannequin of wax, representing a little girl about thirteen years old, dressed in heavy clothes decorated with embroidery, silk arabesques and rosettes of pearls. She is eminently comparable to the Valois Doll that was exhibited for three months in the Georges Petit gallery in the Rue de Sèze.

Standing in her glass case, the Valois Doll had the air of a little princess of the Amboise court, captive in a block of ice. It is likewise an Infanta that Ethal has brought from Leyden: an Infanta with tresses of pale silk, almost silver, rather stiffly corsetted in crimson velvet glittering with aglets; an Infanta who might have stepped out of the frame of a Velasquez, with that suggestion of the embalmed dead which all wax figures have.

Ethal's eye, singularly lit up, caressed and brooded over the livid translucencies and tarnished pinks of that artificial flesh. To me, though, its yellow pallor, its drawn and hardened lips, and the purplish rings around the vitrified eyes were tormenting and terrifying. The fluid spareness of the little hands, almost as if they were molten, struck me with horror; to me the Doll smacked of the morbidity and dampness of crypts. The only thing which I liked about it was the sumptuousness of its clothing, which had taken on the colour of leather and tinder, discoloured and at the same time gilded by the passage of centuries. The silken embroideries lived again in the wildness of the velvet. These embroideries and their pearls held my gaze, but not by virtue of the richness that persisted in them so much as a determination to avoid the mannequin's dreadful immobile eyes.

Ethal and I looked on in silence. I felt that he was watching me, and that he regarded my apparent indifference as a deception. He had expected ecstasy − a flood of admiring and enthusiastic words − and my coldness was disturbing and distressing him.

'You are not yet ready for this kind of art,' he concluded, replacing the pieces of green serge around the showcase. 'I thought that you would appreciate the delicacy of the model, and the infinite nuances of the decomposition of that body. Think of that Doll as a portrait − better than that, as a statue: a painted statue, a precise and delectable effigy which, more profoundly than a canvas or a marble, has been imbued by the modeller's fingers with the exquisite and tragic soul of centuries . . .

'For my own part, I am mad about these wax figures. I worship them. I find them much superior to portraits. I wonder if you might like these a little better?'

He opened a little door, and brusquely pushed me into

an obscure annexe adjoining his studio. It was very high and very narrow, giving me the impression of a mine-shaft – more of a large cupboard than a room. It was lined with shelves like a library, but more spacious ones than would have been needed to house books; and in the shadows of the spaces between the shelves I saw the vitreous eyes and faded lips of more than twenty death-masks: twenty waxen images with historic and historiated hairstyles modelled in in colourless silk. Among these heads – all of which were women or adolescent males – I recognised renowned and classical images from the museums: one from the museum of Lille, resignedly gentle; the *unknown woman* and the mystery of her thin smile; and the historic profiles of Marguerite de Valois, Agnes Sorel, Mary Stuart and Elisabeth de Vaudemont. There was, in fact, a whole harem of dead womem in that lugubrious display of simulacra.

Claudius reached for one of the busts and offered it to me, turning it slightly towards the light, so that I might admire it.

It was the head of an adolescent with a blunt nose, the chin creased by a dimple, with a knowing expression of energy in the bulge of the forehead and the pre-eminence of eyebrows arched over sunken eyes. It was the dolorous, suffering face of a tragic child: a stubborn and defiant head, handsome by virtue of the silence of thin and pouting lips. The greenish pallor of the worn and emaciated but nevertheless angular face further accentuated the bitterness of the mouth. Underneath, on a coat of arms, were pearly tears: the three pilules of the Medicis.

THE EYE OF EBOLI

'Almost a Lorenzo de Medici, isn't it? But intense in a different fashion, wouldn't you say, with the sunkenness of the staring eyes and the stubborn defiance of that mouth? What energy and what rancour there are in the sweep of the jawline and the abrupt chin! One gets the definite impression that such a child, in the midst of Florentine riots and intrigues, ought to have furthered the course of tragic events. In truth, he has the expression of hatred and amazement of one who might have been seen violating his own mother.'

Ethal offered these judgments while complacently handling the bust. 'And yet,' he added, 'this wax figure is entirely my own work. I didn't find it in some little town of Umbria or some Tuscan village. That violent expression and that forehead furrowed by mulish and morbid thought are products of my own imagination. It was a little Italian boy who posed for me – a miserable little model afflicted with consumption. I encountered him one day loafing about on in the Boulevard de Clichy when I had a studio in the Place Pigalle.

'He was fifteen years old then. A little Neapolitan from the Place Maubert come to die, far from the sun, beneath the cold and gloomy Parisian sky. He had a heart-rending cough, poor thing! All a-shiver beneath the torn rags of his Roman costume, he was still prowling around the painters' studios, not daring to go home for fear of being beaten. He had already been wandering in the November fog for two days, timid and terrified, caught between embarrassment and fear at the prospect of offering himself at yet another studio. No one wanted him any longer; he was considered too thin. Scarcely had he lifted his shirt than he was politely shown the door by the daubers. When I picked him up he hadn't eaten for two days. There are many such starvelings in Paris.

'His thinness interested me immediately, and the peculiar cast of his features – that expression of ardent languor which idealises every consumptive face, furnishing them with such artistry. To cut a long story short, I approached Angelotto, confessed my interest and led him away to my lair . . .

'Poor mite! I ought to have used him more sparingly rather than requiring him to repay my hospitality so quickly, but I sensed that he was living on borrowed time and might easily slip through my fingers. The very next day I made him pose . . . What could I do? It isn't every day that one has the opportunity to make a masterpiece. It was terrible, I know, but I was besotted with the wild look in his huge suffering eyes. Angelotto posed, resignedly, for hours on end. That hateful stupor – in which I sometimes thought I read a hint of reproach – never left his eyes, and his mouth was sealed by such mute defiance!

'I worked unceasingly on the wax effigy, with a barbarous joy and a plenitude of sensuality that I have never found again, for I felt that I was moulding a soul which had passed utterly beyond the reach of misery and suffering. Every blow of the chisel contributed to the synthesis of that indignant and obstinate soul, whose rebellious surges animated my fingers with their electricity. His coughing grew worse and worse in spite of infusions, fumigations of tar and a warm bed placed next to the stove. I had to summon a doctor in the end, but I knew it was a lost cause.

'I took care of him as best I could between sittings. He never thanked me, but did exactly as he was told without saying a word. He died in my arms after twenty days. He passed away one morning in December – I remember that it was Christmas Day – with some little Neapolitan models of the Holy Family on his bed, which I had found by chance in a second-hand dealer's in the Rue des Abbesses and bought for him. Poor Angelotto! He had posed, the night before, from midnight to four o'clock; I would never have believed that he could slip away so quickly.

'It all became then a terrible nuisance: informing the parents, for whom I had to search and make provision; the official registration of the death; but these Italians . . .

'The whole affair cost me three thousand, without including the plot in the cemetery at Montmartre. Whenever I am in Paris for All Saint's Day I take flowers to the grave . . . but you must admit that I have a masterpiece here!'

Ethal's monologue was singularly animated, as though he were intoxicated by his own words, but for several minutes I had been listening without taking it in. Utterly captivated, I watched the enormous hand with hairy knuckles which he clenched like a claw about the heavy tresses of the bust. It was a truly vice-like grip, like the talon of some bird of prey. Its ferocious and animal qualities were further enhanced by three exotic rings, one on the thumb, one on the middle finger and the last on the ring-finger; these three huge pearls, irregular and misshapen, were like nacreous pustules on the dry and granular hand of the painter, exaggerating the impression which his fingers gave of a claw seen from the side.

By means of some bizarre retrospective hallucination, I saw that vulturine claw wringing the last gasp out of the little Italian model. Ethal's fingers, will and cruel sensuality had, beyond the shadow of a doubt, hastened the death of that child.

That Ethal! He smiled as though in ecstasy. I felt myself grow wrathful with the hatred of all the evil which that horrible hand had already done, and would do in time to come. Tairamond's tales came back into my mind. What sinister compound might be contained in those hideous and ghastly pearls raised like malignant blisters upon his fingers?

A sudden insolence moved my lips. I pointed to his rings, and said: 'Are those things poisoned?'

Ethal had replaced the wax figure on the shelf, and he promptly turned his attention to the strange jewels. 'Ah! Someone has told you!' He punctuated his remark with a light smile, and added: 'No, not these. But if such things interest you ... or if the idea worries you ... I can show you an extremely curious ring. Come on, then – let's leave the wax for now, shall we?'

Pausing only to seat me on the sleeping-couch in his vast studio, Ethal disappeared through a little door whose presence in the wall I had not previously suspected. He reappeared in due course and came to stand beside me, with a rather bizarre ring delicately held between his thumb and index-finger.

'Look at this!'

It was a square-cut emerald cabochon of a rather pale green – the milky green of chrysoprase – within which some herbal juice seemed to glisten and tremble. Two steel claws inlaid with gold, of rather crude workmanship, embraced it: two hawkish talons clenched upon the glaucous water-drop of the gem.

I felt the pressure of Ethal's gaze upon my own.

'You have never seen anything like it, even though you have visited Spain? Have you not seen such a ring in the Escorial, in the private apartments of Philip II, among the treasures falsely attributed to Charles the Fifth? A great green tear, said to be poisonous, gathered in the claws of an invisible bird of prey? There is a rather beautiful legend attached to it which, if it is not actually true, is a fine invention: the legend of the *Eye of Eboli*; the tragic story of a lovely princess.

'Philip II, it seems, was not an easy master to serve. He was a fervent burner of heretics, as jealous as a tiger, with manners more than a little like those of a wild beast. Poor Sarah Perez was his only favourite and royal mistress – what a scandal, that such a devout Catholic should fall in love with a Jewess! It was Israel's revenge: a jewess in the bed of the King of Spain, the inamorata of a Hapsburg! Do you really not know the story? It is surely apocryphal, but it is framed so well by the mournful splendour of the Escorial and it reflects so perfectly the black heart of the father of Don Carlos!

'For what it may be worth, for your education and

edification, this is what is whispered in those parts. This Sarah Perez had the most beautiful eyes in the world, those green eyes spangled with gold that you love so much: the eyes of Antinous. In Rome, such eyes would have made her a concubine of Adrian; in Madrid they helped her become the princess of Eboli ensconced in the bed of the king. But Philip II was extremely jealous of those wonderful emerald eyes and their delicate transparency, and the princess – who was bored with the funereal palace and the even more funereal society of the king – had the fancy and the misfortune to cast her admirable gaze upon the Marquis de Posa while she was leaving church one day. It was on the threshold of the chapel, and the princess believed herself to be alone with her *camarera mayor*, but the vigilance of the clergy was equal to the challenge. She was betrayed, and that very evening, in the intimacy of their bedroom, in the course of some violent argument or tempestuous tussle, Philip threw his mistress to the floor. Blind with rage he leapt upon her, tore out her eye and devoured it in a single gulp.

'Thus was the princess covered in blood – a good title for a *conte cruel*, that, which Villiers de l'Isle Adam has somehow omitted to write! The princess was henceforth one-eyed: the royal pet had a gaping hole in her face. Philip II, who had the Jewess in his blood, could not cleave so closely to a princess who had only one eye. He made amends to her with some new titles and estates in the provinces and – regretful of the beautiful green eye that he had spoiled – he caused to be inserted into the empty and bloody orbit a superb emerald enshrined in silver, upon which surgeons then inscribed the semblance of a gaze. Oculists have made progress since then; the Princess of Eboli, already hurt by the ruination of her eye, died some little time afterwards, of the effects of the operation. The ways of love and surgery were equally barbarous in the time of Philip II!

'Philip, the inconsolable lover, gave the order to remove the emerald from the face of the dead princess before she was laid in the tomb, and had it mounted in a ring. He wore it about his finger, and would never take it off, even when he went to sleep – and when he died in his turn, he had the ring bearing the green tear clasped in his right hand.

'The ring which you are holding, my friend, is identical to that one. I had it cut according to the model of the king's ring, and damascened in Spain. The original is still in the Escorial; it would have been pleasant to steal it, for I easily acquire the instincts of a thief when I am in a museum, and I always find objects which have a history – especially a tragic history – uniquely attractive. I am not an Englishman for nothing – but that which is easily enough accomplished in France is not at all practical in Spain: the museums there are very secure.

'I had, therefore, to resign myself to commissioning a duplicate from a jeweller in Madrid. They did the work very nicely. The claws are curiously shaped, but the true marvel is the stone; it is so very limpid and weighs many carats, but notice also how it is hollowed out! You see that drop of green oil which takes the place of the internal tear? It is a drop of poison, an Indian toxin which strikes so rapidly and so corrosively that it only requires to come into momentary contact with one of a man's mucous membranes to rob him of his senses and induce rigour mortis.

'It is instant death, certain but painless suicide, that I carry in this emerald. One bite' – and Ethal made as of to raise the ring to his lips – 'and with a single bound one has quit the mundane world of base instincts and crude works, to enter eternity.

'Look upon the truest of friends: a *deus ex machina* which defies public opinion and cheats the police of their prey . . .'

He laughed briefly. 'After all, we live in difficult times, and today's magistrates are so very meticulous. Salute as I do, my dear friend, the poison which saves and delivers. It is at your service, if ever the day should come when you are weary of life!'

THE THOUGHT-READER

Look upon the truest of friends: a deus ex machina which defies public opinion and cheats the police of their prey . . . After all, we live in difficult times, and today's magistrates are so very meticulous. Salute as I do, my dear friend, the poison which saves and delivers.

September 1898

'It is at your service, if ever the day should come when you are weary of life.' How strangely Ethal spoke those words to me! One might almost have thought that . . .

For a moment I saw red. I think I might have leapt at his throat.

What does he take me for? Is it by chance that he has gathered me into that company of sadists and child-molesters which comprises nearly all of his compatriots? Those English puritans with faces flushed by port and gin, gorged on red meat spiced with pickles, who seek by night to soothe their overheated senses in the employment bureaux where Irish servant-girls can be acquired . . . that tribute of poor pre-puberal girls with large flowery eyes, which wretched Dublin despatches every month to the Minotaur of London!

Oh, the stiff and cruel sensuality of the English: the brutality of the race, its taste for blood, its instinct for oppression and its dastardliness in the face of weakness. All of that had flared up in Ethal's eyes while he lingered, with feline delight, over the tale of the agonising death visited upon his little model!

Angelotto, the little Italian consumptive of the Place Maubert!

I felt a mute hatred rising within me. With what cynicism he had laid out before me the pus of his moral wound – and yet it had oozed out of him with such horrible charm! The more I studied that dolorous head, the more I admired its tragic stupor and its air of defiance, the more I regretted not having known the wretched child. Myself, I would have snatched him away from the murderous grasp of the painter. My aversion for Ethal festered alongside a strange rancour. I wanted not so much to have killed the monster as to have understood him.

It was like jealousy! Jealousy! What miry depths is this Englishman stirring up within me?

15 September.
I do not want to see that man again. Ought I to depart for Venice, for the soothing calm of its lagoons, the charm of the grandiose and dead past of its palatial waterways? Oh, the slick flight of gondolas over the heavy oily depths of the canals, the *e poppe!* thrown into the silence, in the deserted corners of the streets and, in the morning – in the first rosy tint of dawn – my long hours of dreaming and rapt contemplation before the city's awakening, at the windows of the palace Dario: alone before the solitude of the grand canal, when the domes of Santa Maria della Salute seem to be made of satin, in a Venice of pearl!

Yes, Venice would cure me. There I would be able to escape the tyranny of my obsession with Ethal; there I could repair my soul, restoring the soul of yesteryear – a sumptuous and beautiful soul – before the Tiepolos of the Palazzo Labia and the Tintorettos of the Academy; there, perhaps, I could cultivate – nay, reanimate – a lost candour before the divine figures of Carpaccio. Exchanging one madness for another, would it not be more worthwhile to lose my heart to Schiavoni's St George or the Academy's St Ursula than to dream villainous dreams before some morbid wax effigy wrought by that dreadful Ethal?

Yes, I must go. Besides, has not Orbin recommended Venice to all neurasthenics? The climate is gently soothing, and there is a kind of narcotic balm in the silence of that watery city, Venice will save me from Ethal. There I will come to life a little more. Venice, what memories it holds!

Venice! I thought I might encounter once again the imploring expression which obsesses me, that troubled green gaze
which has made me an unbalanced wretch, an outcast and
a madman.

I remember now. It was at the *Ospedale*, in the venereal
section, in the tepid and insipid atmosphere of a huge
room with whitewashed walls and windows fired by the
sunlight of a most beautiful afternoon. She was stretched
out amid the dubious whiteness of the hospital sheets, and
her mahogany-red hair, spread out on her pillows, made
her jaundiced syphilic face seem even more sickly. She was
silent, immobile, surrounded by the whispers − scarcely
lowered in tone when we entered − of twenty other
women: twenty convalescents, or those less sick, huddled
together around a table encumbered by glass beads, num-
bers and cards. Everyone in the ward who was fit enough
was playing *loteria*, with all the animation of voice and
gesture typical of their race. Only the sick woman with the
pallor of wax did not speak, nor move. Between her half-
closed eyelashes, though, there was the gleam of a green
eye spangled with gold: an eye that was weary and sad, yet
incandescent with light, as if it were the bed of some
sheltered spring in the light of noon. Such a dolorous smile
played meanwhile upon the poor faded lips, and in the
corners of the bruised eyelids, that for an instant I believed
I saw the same glistening expression of infinite lassitude
and intoxicated ecstasy I had seen in the eyes of the Antinous!

Curiously, I leant over the bed, but the features had
already become slack, and the eyes had closed. 'A mere
spasm − as if she suddenly remembered something,' said
the doctor who accompanied us. 'She has cancer of the
ovaries; she is doomed.'

The plaintive emerald had flashed in her eyes for the
space of a single instant; for a moment, the eye of Astarté
had risen to the rim of her eyelids, and my soul had risen
likewise to the edge of my lips. It is clear to me now that

the moribund woman of the *Ospedale* displayed, throughout her bloodless face, the same greenish translucence as the bust of Angelotto, the haunting wax figure.

A strange coincidence: two expressions of the death-agony. Both she and he were already stricken and destined for death!

Those glaucous and desirous eyes – I have thought of another evening when I encountered them.

It was in Constantine in Algeria, in the Rue des chelles – the street of street-walkers and other prostitutes, which descends so steeply to the Oued Rhumel.

In the underworld of Moorish cafés, Spanish inns and Maltese bars one often stumbles across the haunts of smokers of *kif*, where shrill and monotonous music is barked out by fifes and derboukas. On this occasion, in the centre of a circle of squatting arabs there were two bloodless beings with dead and drawn eyes, swaying abominably and strangely gyrating their loins, with snake-like sinuousity.

Oh, the desperate, almost convulsive appeals which those thin arms made as they moved above the hard-set faces with painted eyes and painted jaws. The twisting dancers were incredibly slender, dressed in rags of gauze and gold lamé tulle like those worn by women. They were periodically shaken from top to toe by abrupt tremors, as if electric shocks were passing through their entire bodies. All of a sudden, one of the dancers became still, absolutely rigid, letting loose a piercing cry like that of a hyena; glittering in his suddenly-animated eyes I saw the elusive green gaze. I sprang towards him, and took him by the wrists. He collapsed, foaming at the mouth. The poor man was an epileptic and, to add to his troubles, quite blind. He was just some wretched Kabyle dancer, utterly exhausted by depravity and consumption, destined soon to die.

The Venetian woman in the *Ospedale* was similarly damned. Could I have fallen in love with the agony of death itself? This invincible attraction towards all who suffer and all who are dying is a frightful and baffling thing! Never have I seen so clearly into the depths of my own being. Had Ethal already divined this irreparable defect of my sick soul on the evening when he set before me, first that doll, and then that wax figure, in which I found – modelled with love – the same effigy of dolour ... of the particular species of dolour which pleases me?

The Kabyle dancer, the dying woman in Venice and the consumptive little model of Montmartre are elements of the same series. That Englishman has read my deplorable instincts like an open book. How I hate him!

28 September
I am no longer going away. I have seen Ethal again, and he has recaptured me. I was standing by the table, just about to buckle the straps of my trunk – I had already rolled up my canes and umbrellas in my travelling rug – when a hand fell upon my shoulder, and a sneering voice from the shadows recited:

> *I want to forget the one I love!*
> *Take me far away from here,*
> *To Flanders, Norway or Bohemia,*
> *So far that the road soothes my cares!*
> *But what will remain of myself,*
> *When I have succeeded in forgetting?*

It was him. How had he found out that I was leaving? It is easy to believe that the man possesses second sight.

'You will not find it,' he said, gesturing vaguely towards his little gleaming eyes. 'The gaze is in yourself, not in others. Go to Sicily, or to Venice, or even to Smyrna, but sick man that you are, you will carry your sickness with you. It is a Museum gaze that you seek, my friend; only the decadent civilization of a great city like Paris or rotten London has anything to offer you. Why are you stealing away in mid-cure? Have you found fault with me? You are no longer haunted by masks now, and even though the murderous lust still seethes within you, at least you no longer suffocate by night as unreal beings swarm around you. I have saved you from dreams and am bringing you back towards instinct – for the murderous instinct is good, solid and natural, every bit as sacred as the instinct to love.

'You are an unwitting victim of the pressure of *laws*; only wretchedness and the corruptions of prostitution can give you a glimpse of the gaze which tempts you.

'It is the eyes of the tortured that you seek: the fearful, imploring, divine ecstasy and terror-stricken sensuality of the eyes of St Agnes, St Catherine of Sienna and St Sebastian. I give you my word that we will find those eyes – but you must not defy me!

'Don't go; it's useless. I have promised that you will be healed. I swear by the grave of my little Angelotto that I will keep my promise!'

SOME MONSTERS

8 October 98.

Keep tomorrow evening free for me and come to enjoy for the first time some green tea which has been sent to me directly from China. I have a whole set of cosmopolitan eccentrics to show you, including two compatriots I met by an extraordinary stroke of luck yesterday, while taking tea in the Avenue Marbeuf. They are eager to meet you and I have promised to settle their curiosity; you will find it equally interesting to meet them.

The tragedienne Maud White — do you know her? — has a peculiar way of reading Baudelaire, without the slightest accent. You will probably like her brother better. They will both be there tomorrow, and others too.

After midnight, we will see if we can organise a little opium-smoking session. This is not actually part of your cure, but the occasion will serve as a medical consultation. I will heal you; that much is certain.

Until tomorrow, then; be here about ten o'clock.

Your accomplice,
CLAUDIUS ETHAL.

So Ethal greets me in this fashion now! What is this international consignment to which he has promised to exhibit me? On whom does he wish to play his jokes tomorrow — these English persons or me? I do not like this invitation at all, and I mistrust Ethal's Asian tea and drugs. Am I some exotic beast to be displayed to parties of tourists conveyed by Lubin or Thomas Cook, at a little feast of opium in the course of which the Duc de Fréneuse will undergo an operation?

I have seen some rather captivating photographs of this Maud White. The costumes of her Shakespearean roles have been reproduced several times in the *Studio*. I remember her particularly as an enigmatic Cordelia — but her talent is said to be second-rate. She has never been seen in the West End of London.

I shall not even reply to Ethal. His English guests will have to remain curious.

10 October

What a strange and singular soirée! These creatures with their automatic gestures and their too-brilliant eyes have left me with the impression of having spent the night in some kind of abnormal, hallucinatory half-dream state. All of them seemed much more like phantoms than real people, by virtue of their somnambulistic conversations and their ambitious affectations of elegance!

If I had not touched their hands and brushed against their clothing I could have believed that I had dreamt the whole thing . . . and yet, I do not regret having attended that tea-party.

The strange décor of Ethal's studio was utterly transformed for the evening by the unusual luxury of immense floating tapestries suspended from rings mounted on copper curtain-rods. All the busts from his wax museum, brought out for the occasion from the little room where they were kept and posed on small pedestals, kept solemn vigil. All these images of suffering or sensuality incarnate mingled, in bizarre fashion, with the woven characters of the overhanging tapestries: a throng of noble barons straitened by iron corselets, their ladies in heavy skirts, and their liegemen in doublet and hose. It was as if a huge crowd of olden times were forming a procession about the walls, with the faces of spectres emerging here and there from the shadows in the form of the precisely-modelled features of the wax heads: each one haggard, with empty eyes and a painted smile. In each corner, set in enormous chandeliers like those of a church, twelve long candles burned in groups of three. Their smoky light made Ethal's studio seem even larger, its alcoves and recesses stepping back into the unknown.

Strange décor, to be sure – but the company of Maud

White and her brother was even stranger. She was lissom, soft and pale, her milky flesh sprouting from a low-cut armless sheath of black velvet which shamelessly exposed her breasts. He wore a suit with watered silk lapels, so tight that he seemed corseted by it, and a black brocade waistcoat. They both had pale blonde, almost silvery, hair – the blond of Spanish Infantes in Velasquez portraits – styled in such a similar fashion that their resemblance to one another seemed to desexualise them both.

Then, there was the Duchess of Althorneyshare. Her shoulders were shiny with powder, her arms plastered with white lead, and her rouged cheeks seemed to have been lit by the fire of the profuse stream of diamonds which trickled from her ears to her throat. The Duchess of Althorneyshare was mauve from the roots of her tinted hair to the toes of her silk-slippered feet; she was mauve not only by virtue of her mauve dress, but also by virtue of the withering discolouration of her patched-up flesh, marinated for thirty years in balms, unguents and friar's balsam. The fabulous choker of pearls which she wore seemed to be supporting in a vase of nacre the frightful face of Queen Elizabeth. The Duchess of Althorneyshare had been a dancer long ago, when she married the Duke. Nowadays, widowed and permanently enriched by her inheritance, she tours the world from Florence to the Riviera and from Corfu to the Azores, parading the Lord Burdett's millions and her own vices. She was not even at the Opera – she was a star of the music-hall.

Then, there was Mein Herr Frederic Schappman, a tall thin German with an equine head and skipping gait, whose careful gestures were complemented by a rattling of opals, a long string of which he wore about his right wrist. Mein Herr Schappman was dressed in a long black frock-coat, his cravat an enormous knot of white silk. He gave the impression of an opossum encrusted with diamonds, so glittering with jewels was he.

Then came some London-tailored outfits, buttonholes flourishing with orchids, the accompanying faces painstak-

ingly shaven, with thick fluid tresses and impeccable part-
ings. Then a dark face turbanned in white: a great Hindu,
very formal in a dinner-jacket, with Sinhalese sapphires
and pearls on all his fingers. I gathered that the splendid
Hindu had been brought by either the duchess or the
German.

'You aren't afraid of the police, I hope? What a fine haul
they could net, this evening, if they descended upon us.
For a moment I was tempted to tip them off.'

Such were the words with which Ethal greeted me.
Introductions followed.

Maud White, rolled up in her velvet like a statue in its
drapery, deigned to put her arms around me with an
almost tender gaze in her large green eyes. She had the
most beautiful eyes, leaf-green in colour, unfortunately let
down by the somewhat slack oval of her face. Her brother,
Sir Reginald, favoured me with a bow and expressed his
pleasure at making the acquaintance of the celebrated collector.

'Her head is heavy,' Ethal said to me, in a low whisper,
'but her skin is divine. As for the body . . . but it can't be
helped. Maud is chaste, repelled by contact with men. Is
that a vocation or a vice? The truth is that she plays *Zohar*
. . . yes, certainly, the brother and sister together. That is
what is said, and it does not displease me at all to believe it.
In the interest of their fame it would be rather imprudent
to contradict it. She has built herself quite a reputation here
and in London with the aid of Swinburne, Baudelaire and
Incest. She loves to perform the work of poetic outsiders;
she will read to us this evening from Baudelaire.

Leading me to the far end of the studio, he said: 'I shall
not present you to the duchess. For one thing, you're not
her type; for another, she only has eyes tonight for the
Hindu and Monsieur Schappman: she will certainly gather
in one of the two. Why, then, invite the monster? Well,
she furnishes a room so horribly, and emphasizes the
beauty of other women. What a splendid idol she makes
beneath the spolia opima of her diamonds, and how she

115

blackens beneath her powder and paint! I can't look at her without thinking of the Biblical Esther, who was soaked for six months in myrrh and cinnamon before Mordecai presented her to Ahasuerus. Flesh discoloured by aromatic spices comes to have a special kind of complexion – but Esther was fresh meat, whereas this one has been well-hung by forty years of prostitution. What beautiful putrefaction one detects beneath the armour of that make-up, in the ravines of those wrinkles! I like the impression she gives of one diseased, like some Black Virgin dressed in satin, such as can sometimes be seen in Spanish churches. How well she would serve as a Madonna of the Terror, in a procession of penitents painted by Goya! She is Our Lady of the Seven Deadly Sins, as Forain called her one evening – and you must admit that the name becomes her.

'I shall not introduce you to Schappman, nor to Schappman's Hindu. Dear Freddie is only interesting when he explains the reasons for his voyages to Japan. He undertakes such excursions to the lands of Nippon every spring, after leaving Alexandria; he goes there, he says, to see the plum-trees in flower. Deep down, he has the soul of a milliner. He really ought to be named Charlotte, and to be employed buttering the bread of the descendants of Wilhelm Meister.

'I'll wager that he'll tell these fellows all about his enthusiasm for plum-trees, or the adventure of his last purchase – that string of opals which he wears coiled about his arm. He collects them – souvenirs of the Orient! They're the rosaries of Mecca, found throughout Algeria.

'As for my fellow-Englishmen, they're typical John Bulls. They're of no importance, although they don't like to stay any longer in London than your obedient servant. They're all collectors of some kind or another. One favours Queen Anne belt-buckles, another shoes worn by the king of Rome, or sabretaches of the handsome Prince Murat: they have to do *something* and because they have no other way to occupy themselves they retreat into little worlds of their own. Anyway, they don't understand a word of French and insist on speaking nothing but their own lingo

– as if it were becoming to foreigners to distinguish themselves by imperfection!

'I shall present you in due course to someone who, although he too is from the British Isles, is well worth the trouble and will interest you. We are also expecting some Russians . . . but if you will pardon me, I must ask Miss White to read us something.'

Maud White – who was in the midst of flirting with her brother with regal immodesty, eye to eye and nearly mouth to mouth – indolently rose to her feet as Ethal approached. She greeted his request with liquid eyes peering out from half-lowered lids and feline movements of the spine and hips. Her breasts were almost springing out of her bodice, as if offering up her entire being, to the extent that she ignited the sleeping gaze of the Hindu – and, in consquence, the bloodshot eye of the ancient Althorneyshare.

'No, not Baudelaire, I'm rather fed up with him,' simpered Miss White, a dab hand at fashionable slang. 'Isn't that right, Reggie?' Reginald chipped in, seconding his sister's nomination of Albert Samain's *Au jardin de l'Infante* – a book so fully charged with thunder and lust that its charm is altogether oppressive and unhealthy.

'*On feverish evenings as strong as venison,*' she quoted, '*My soul is burdened with the ennui of an ancient Herod* – that's true enough, isn't it? Personally, I find that every image smacks of treachery. It's the same for all of us, isn't it?' She lingered coquettishly over every word: 'I'd like to read you *Lust*, if I may – you know the wonderful litany:

> '*Lust, fruit of death upon the tree of life!*
> '*Lust, advent of the sense of splendour!*
> '*I salute you, O most secret and most profound*
> '*Lust, idol and terror of the world.*'

Roguishly extending her tongue between the white rows

of her teeth, she added: 'The ode to Lust is certainly well suited to the occasion, and to the frame which your studio provides, dear Claudius – isn't that so?'

THE LARVAE

'The black Goat fades away into unhealthy shadows,
'The evening is red and naked! The last vestiges of your
*   modesty*
'Dissolve in an enervating pool of odours;
'And midnight sounds in the hearts of obscene witches.

'The desert simoom has swept over the plain! . . .
'Plunged in your tresses replete with bitter vapour,
'My flesh covers yours and ponders drowsily
'The love which tomorrow might turn to hatred.

'Face to face, our Senses, as yet unsated,
'Devour one another with stigmatised eyes;
'And our desiccated hearts are like stones.

'The Ardent Beast has made litter of our bodies;
'And, as prescribed for those who watch over the dead,
'Our kneeling souls – up there – are at prayer.'

In a monotous voice, shading slightly into a sob at the end
of each stanza, Maud White proceeded to read a third
sonnet. It was like the chanting of liturgical prose; and set
as she was against the backcloth of the floating tapestry and
its vague congregation the tragedienne seemed indeed to
be in a church, her performance an incarnation of the
sacred rite of some long-forgotten religion resuscitated in
her gestures and in the solid curve of her breasts.

The black Goat fades away into unhealthy shadows,

'An appeal to ghouls, a summoning of larvae,' murmured
the sardonic voice of Ethal from behind me. And, indeed,
while Miss White assumed her priestly role – her two pale
arms reaching out, as though the long fingers were plucking

invisible flowers, her exposed armpits dotted by golden rust – the studio of the painter had increased its population. More visitors had entered silently, supplementing the crowd of hennaed women and helmeted cavaliers which ranged about the walls. It seemed as if they had been evoked by Maud's slow voice.

Thanks to Maud White, the atmosphere had acquired a dream-like quality; it was not until the Irishwoman stopped speaking, her deathly figure slightly brightened by the nacreous trace of a smile and an oblique glance, that I recognised the newcomers.

The fat shoulders and heavy jaws of the Marquise Naydorff sat atop a gleam of satin and pearls: the Marquise Naydorff who had once been Letitia Sabatini. In spite of the fact that she was over forty her profile, like the face on some Sicilian medal, was helmeted by glistening black tresses. Princess Olga Myrianinska was at her side, her eyelids lowered in her swarthy face. Age had made her stout and she was rendered more bestial still by the fatigue of her face; once a bacchante, she was now a ruminant. Although the two were of different races, they had come to resemble one another; they had the same faded complexion, and the same drawn-out daze in their eyes and in their smiles. They were both puffed up and weighed down by morphine, indelibly marked by its stigmata.

The Slav and the Sicilian had entered almost at the same time. The Princess of Seiryman-Frileuse had followed a few seconds after, accompanied by a man of means: the Comte de Muzarett. This svelte pair also resembled one another; it was as if they were two sharp silhouettes neatly cut from the same template, like a couple of tall and elegant greyhounds. On closer inspecton, however, the slimness of the woman was slightly more muscular, and the lines of her profile were more wilful. The obstinacy of the overlong chin and the forehead which exploded beneath the pale gold of her light tresses, and the hard and surly grey of the steely eyes complemented the stiffness of her attitude, sheathed as she was in an upright scabbard of pearly satin!

The man, with a little hawkish head bearing a thick and frizzy shock of hair, carried a wilful affectation and a knowing litheness in the elegance of his body. His skin was very fine and intricately creased; the thousand little wrinkles at the temples and the chiselling of his tight lips were reminiscent of a portrait by Porbus. His translucent and protruding ears were decorated with earrings; his taut and thin neck seemed freshly-milled, like one of the Valois. An astonishing family, the Comtes de Muzarett! So affected was his hauteur that with the three females gathered about him he had the air of a museum-piece illustrating the text of three naughty books. Four hundred years of nobility without a single dilution by mismarriage was spattered by the mud of their cosmopolitan company.

This group was quick to surround the tragedienne. The evocatrice accepted the compliment gracefully. The women had a hard gleam in their fixed eyes, their jaws contracted in spite of their evident effort to smile. All three had become singularly pale. Muzarett, on the other hand, with a lithe inclination of his slim and elegant being, affected the eagerness and enthusiasm of a dilettante passion conspicuously free of all desire.

'Look at those ogresses!' said Ethal, scathingly. 'What a lustre they lend to the youth of Maud White, and how they undress her with their eyes! Follow the sharp glances of the American; they plunge like daggers into the bare bosom of the Irishwoman! If those eyes had the cutting-edge of their steel it would be a long time before the lovely girl would bare her bosom again! How they stab their two rivals! Youthful flesh draws them like a magnet; they have only come for her sake.

'As for the dear Comte, he is all sublime indifference. He pays court to none but the reciter. The entire display of idolatry is designed to the sole end of placing in Maud's hands certain items of verse. Tomorrow he will send to her, with an appropriate inscription, his ten volumes – and the *Winged Rats* of Comte Aimery de Muzarett will have one more Muse to their account. His fame as an artist

121

requires very tender care. Look what a mask of diplomacy is painstakingly formed by the whole of that fine profile; he is as wily as a cardinal. He has scented in Miss White a useful agent of celebrity, and he has come solely to harness her to the cause of his glory. It is himself that he courts by means of the salaams he offers to her; he only ever flirts with himself. He is the Narcissus of the inkpot . . .

'Oh good – look who's coming to stir things up!'

This remark was occasioned by the smooth-stepping entrance of a handsome little man, slender and ethereal, with bright blue eyes and blond eyelashes set in a diaphanously pale face. His cheeks were slightly touched with pink – so gently that one might have thought it a dash of rouge – and his light, disorderly hair was the colour of oats. This young and delicate Saxon threaded his way towards the group of socialites ecstatically gathered around Maud; the Marquise Naydorff introduced him to her. The Comte de Muzarett, who had been shaken by a perceptible shiver when the newcomer appeared, stepped aside slightly to make room for him but continued to monopolise the tragedienne, airily ignoring the new admirer.

'An amusing encounter!' said Ethal, bursting into laughter. 'It was Muzarett who discovered him, two years ago, and now no longer condescends to notice him. He found that the musician had more talent than the poet, and the melodies of Delabarre were better appreciated than the verses they accompanied. The dear comte launched the composer in order to provide backing for his rhymes, but did not anticipate that the world might give a better welcome to the pizzicati than the pentameters. He dismissed him for ingratitude – 'ingratitude' is the name which avatars of Narcissus give to the success of others – but the little one has a good head for tact and intrigue. He is a pupil who does honour to his master: he has climbed over the back of the comte. He has the advantages of his youth and his physique; it would hardly be possible to find anyone more handsome.

'See, even the ogresses are looking at him! He's as merry

122

as a clown, and Maud herself has deigned to favour him with the distant regard of her green eyes. She is no longer listening to the dear comte; it's the little one who is making the pace. He has come to push his music just as the comte has come to push his poems; they're both counting on Maud to make them fashionable in London – and in Paris too. Will Miss White, this winter, recite the verses of the one or declaim the virtues of the other's music? A clash of interests! The entertainment will be that their interests will bring them together, and perhaps – who knows? – repair the the break. Perhaps they will leave together, reconciled by Maud White. If Muzarett sees that it is in his interest, he will stifle his rancour; he is a very strong man.'

With a strangled laugh, like the clucking of a hen, Ethal continued: 'Little Delabarre is driving each and every one of them crazy. Look at the Duchess of Althorneyshare, showering Maud with compliments and drawing ever closer to her – and look at Herr Schappman and the English clan! They're all coming to breathe the air around the young rose-bud. The larvae! The scent of young blood entices and draws them closer. There's no need to venture into antiquity to evoke the shades of the dead. Do you remember the doves whose throats Odysseus slit as an offering to the Stygian deities? Look! Even the Hindu mingles with them, in his turban embroidered with gold. Now, at last, the princesses have ceded their place. He is committed to the duchess – a one-time dancer, a woman who has slept with men for money. Shame on her! A Messalina, but not a Thaïs! And yet, Messalina is a good enough name; we apply it to priestesses of the Great Goddess, don't we? No man was ever initiated into the mysteries of Isis.'

Maud White and her brother were now receiving the adulation of the grovelling frock-coats decked with gardenias and the German with his string of opals. The spectral duchess, her face varnished like a doll's, had drawn the pianist to a divan. Wallowing there, a mass of flaccid flesh submerged in mauve silk, she loomed over him. The diamonds arrayed upon her bosom hung like brilliant stalactites over the handsome smiling man; he recoiled slightly, moving away. Behind the divan, the black eyes of the Hindu were inflamed. In the shadows, vaguely animated by the glow of the candles, the phantom procession of armoured knights and embroidered ladies made its patient way along the tapestry.

'But Thomas Welcome has not arrived!' grumbled Claudius, inspecting his window-display. 'It was his acquaintance that I particularly wanted you to make. It is important that you see him. The others ... ' – a careless gesture finished off the phrase. 'Princess Seiryman-Frileuse is the only exception; she is interesting. Very ostentatious. What a clever contrivance it was to marry – in name, at least – the old prince, settling eighty thousand francs on him in order that she should carry his name while parading before the world her depravity and her independence. She is honest and passionate, that one! There is so much snobbery and morphine in the perversion of the others. The marquise was badly married, brought to her present condition by the hostility of the world and the vileness of her husband. Myrianinska is almost broke; her daughters maintain her now that she can no longer earn her keep in the bedroom. Enervated, intoxicated, tired of themselves and everyone else, they are no longer disturbed, even rarely, by the sensations which would provide the only excuse for their aberrations; their level of intelligence does not go much beyond the brutality of the habituées of brothels and drinking-dens. Princess Seiryman is beautiful in her perverse fashion – look at the bitter wilfulness of her proud profile, and look how those hard and mournful grey eyes, the colour of melting ice, shelter the energy of thought and obstinacy!

'Look at her! How attentively she studies the Duchess of Althorneyshare, although everything about that woman ought to horrify her: her decrepitude and her past. But Aliette Montaud was delectably beautiful once; thirty years ago she was one of those who can move hearts and millions. Princess of Seiryman, knowing that, seeks regretfully among the ruins for the adorable but long-lost instrument which was once incarnated by sensuality and desire.

'Napoleon must have looked in like fashion at the field of battle when someone other than himself had won the victory. By the way, do you know the princess's surname?'

He whispered the joke.

'Lesbos?'

'Absolutely: *Lesbos, land of warm and languorous nights*. But Welcome has not come! In that case, perhaps I should ask Maud to recite another poem for us? All this coming and going has caused a cold draught, for which Baudelaire seems to me to be the obvious remedy. Come with me then, Fréneuse, and we will beg her to favour us with *Les femmes damnées*. We have a few of them here tonight. *Like pensive livestock lying on the sand* . . . Ah, but the other duchess is here now. This one is a veritable innocent, a seer who lost her way in life. We can't possibly risk Baudelaire before Her Royal Highness. You must excuse me.'

Another woman had indeed entered, escorted by two men.

TOWARDS THE SABBAT

Who could have failed to recognise the newcomer? Her photograph was displayed on hundreds of billboards in the boulevards and featured in reports of all the receptions of ministers of state. There was no mistaking the classic shoulders, uplifted bosom and pretty Austrian head of the Duchess of Meinichelgein.

This evening, like every other, Her Royal Highness was accompanied by Dario de la Psara, the painter commissioned by all the fashionable cosmopolites. His sallow complexion and large velvety black eyes – like those of a Portugese Christ – provided a perfect compliment to the blonde fragility and pearly splendour of the duchess. The other man was Chasteley Dosan, the tragedian of the Comédie-Française. It was claimed that Her Highness Sophie had a positive passion for the actor's work – that she assiduously followed all Dosan's performances at the Comédie, and even, it was said, passed part of her evenings in the tragedian's dressing-room. The overbearing snobbery of Germany considers the glories of the Parisian *monde* to be more than a little faded; but the fashions of Berlin even lag behind those of London. Apart from La Psara, whose authentic talent and exotic profile had seduced Her Highness, Duchess Sophie was an also admirer of the trite works of Benjamin Constant, Carolus Duran, des Falguière and other common-or-garden hacks.

Her honesty was, however, legendary. She was as straight and as trustworthy as an épée, universally respected in spite of the unexpectedness of her caprices: she was wont to depart abruptly to continue her wandering existence, which carried her throughout Europe during the six months of every year which she spent far from her own country and her conjugal palace.

Claudius rushed to meet her. A high-backed armchair was brought forward. Seated approximately in the middle of the hall, isolated from the other women, with a smile in her eyes and on her lips, Duchess Sophie greeted the queue of men which her host led to meet her: Muzarett, Delabarre, Monsieur White, Mein Herr Schappmann, and the well-scrubbed Englishmen. Not a single woman was presented to her.

Although the Duchess Sophie was new to Parisian society, she was sufficiently well-informed to know what kind of company she was in. Shunted to one side, the Marquise Naydorff and Princess Olga simulated an animated discussion; the Princess of Seiryman-Frileuse absorbed herself in the contemplation of a bust, her back turned to the Austrian; the old Duchess of Althorneyshare contrived to monopolise Maud White.

Standing behind the milky shoulders of Her Highness, La Psara and Chasteley Dosan formed a discreet and smiling guard of honour, assisting with the introductions.

'I shall have to ask her to recite some Heinrich Heine, or a song by Goethe,' Claudius said, derisively, while wending his way towards Maud White. 'We are now in German territory.'

He gripped my arms firmly. 'Hein! How they detest one another, a reunion of those who have come down in the world, like this evening's, provides a fine focus of hatred. There is an extensive spectrum of contempt, with the German at the top of the ladder and poor Aliette Montaud at the bottom. Even that one can be ferociously contemptuous of the innocent Mein Herr Schappman, who is the only one here contemptuous of no one, having the soul of a Gretchen.'

'But what could possibly bring the duchess here?'

'To my studio? Why, nothing – except the desire to be painted by me. La Psara launches, but Ethal consecrates. La Psara is a Parisian talent, but not a European one; he is of some account in New York, but he simply does not exist in Vienna. The Museum does not want him, while the Champ-de-Mars . . . but she is completely Delabarre's for now – they must be debating as to whether Wagner or

Glück is the greater musician. I will wait before making Maud declaim . . . Ah, the tea!'

'The famous green tea?'

'Yes – but we shall be drinking another soon, once the spoilsports have gone.'

Seeming almost naked beneath floating gauzes and shell-like breastplates, two Javanese servants, male or female – their sex was as amibiguous as their race – carried two big copper plates laden with little cups into the room. They were impeccably harmonious in their form and their light brown colouring. The ivory whites and carnal pinks of the scallop-shells seemed to be engraved in cameo upon their skin. Jade rings embraced their slim ankles and strange bronzed necklaces made entirely of minerals, glittering greenly like the bodies of cantharid beetles, ran around their necks.

Golden silences whipped by the wings of cantharids!

An aromatic beverage was steaming in the proffered porcelain cups. A profusion of jostling hands came to take up the cups, with much laughter, wheedling whispers and inquisitive questions addressed to the little idols. Javanese servants were at a premium in Paris, and the women immediately cornered them, holding the exotic figures prisoner in a circle of black costumes.

'The Marquise Naydorff and Princess Olga are withdrawing, now that the orgy is beginning,' I commented to Claudius.

'You think so! Spite is driving them away. They are no longer the game of the moment, with whom the men choose to mingle. Then again, the presence of the Duchess Sophie may have reawakened their modesty. They'll make some catty remark to me, I'll wager.'

Indeed, the Sicilian and the Slav were wending their way towards Ethal.

'Very successful, your soirée! Are you waiting for the Infanta?' asked the Marquise.

'She might still come. Have you been introduced?' Claudius riposted.

'If you supply a list to *Le Figaro*, please do not include our names,' the princess put in.

'As you wish.'

How the Marquise exaggerated her farewells! 'So you know the entire nation?' she persisted. 'All Gotha bears a path to your door.'

'And all Gomorrah too,' riposted the painter.

The two women left. The atmosphere became more relaxed after their departure.

An *Intermezzo* provided by the lovely Maud brought Her Highness and the tragedienne together. Duchess Sophie complimented the brother and the sister. 'What day will you come to dinner with me? You must both come tomorrow. What time would you prefer?'

The groups were fusing now. The ancient Althorneyshare took over the handsome Dario – after the musician, the painter. 'What a marvellous talent you have, monsieur,' simpered the ancestral doll. 'I have seen pictures by Velasquez in the Prado in Madrid which are not equal to yours; some of your portraits . . .'

'Oh, mere variations on the theme of women's faces,' protested La Psara, who did not believe such flattery.

Little Delabarre, having escaped the fleshless fingers of the ex-dancer, had fallen into the chaplet-entangled hands of Mein Herr Schappman. 'From Charybdis to Scylla,' Ethal breathed into my ear as he passed by; but the pretty little composer was thinking about a series of concerts in Berlin – perhaps even, the following winter, a season in Cairo – and so he tolerated the German opossum's little gestures, touches and infantile babble. In his turn, the musician made polite inquiries about the export trade.

Muzarett was interviewing the sombre Chasteley Dosan: the great and noble poet fawning over the member of the Comédie-Française. 'How could the committee have accepted that piece?' complained the clipped voice of the

Comte. 'I can only put it down to the influence of the author's dinner-parties.'

To which the actor, under pressure, replied: 'That's theatre.'

And when the count bewailed the inferiority of poetry, Dosan declared, with his lips drawn back to expose his strong white teeth, as if he were the voice of the oracle, 'Verse is perfectly okay' – which official declaration reassured the author of *Winged Rats* while annoying the poet.

'Vanity Fair!' observed Ethal mockingly, having returned at last to my side. Ethal seemed truly diabolical in the middle of his sabbat of covetous desires, hypocrisies, rivalries, rancours and base instincts, which he had set in motion and now left to its own momentum.

'Am I a good enough director of consciences?' he chortled, choking on a contented laugh. 'Do you like me in that role? How their lovely little souls rally in order to embellish their skin with petty blushes, eh? Except, of course, for the ancient Althorneyshare and the Princess of Seiryman. They make no concessions, those two. Look at the princess!'

The American, standing a little apart, was talking to the two little Javanese, who replied in a strange and twittering English. All the while, the princess was touching their shoulders, feeling the grain of their skin and testing the weight of their necklaces like a collector noting the details of some rare trinket. Then she abruptly turned her back on them and came straight towards us.

'They are very amusing, Ethal, your Far-Eastern idols. Would you like to lend them to me for a day or two – long enough for three sittings? I would like to make a sketch of those little heads.'

When Ethal silently bowed the Yankee continued: 'What day would you like to send them to my studio? I am there after two o'clock.'

'Whenever you please, Princess.'

'Very well – tomorrow. I may count on it, may I not? Where is Monsieur de Muzarett?'

Muzarett hurried over; the princess demanded her cloak.

This was the signal for a mass departure. Her Highness Sophie followed, with La Psara and Chasteley Dosan, who had brought her. Mein Herr Schappman removed his Hindu. Little Delabarre slipped away on his own.

The florid English clique remained stubbornly in place, intoxicated by a combination of raki and cigarettes – short, slim cigarettes which the Javanese were now bringing round. They also offered decanters of Greek liqueur, raki, mastic and *eau de jasmin*: a whole alcoholic perfumery, sickly sweet and yet wild, dangerous to European brains. The Duchess of Althorneyshare, stiff and still beneath her diamonds and her face-powder, seemed more and more like a Madonna of Depravity, stigmatised by her nickname of Our Lady of the Seven Deadly Sins. I wondered what could be keeping the old crone. What was she waiting for? Ethal did his utmost to retain – and, indeed, succeeded in hanging on to – Maud White and her brother, who were talking about leaving.

The candles were already burning low, half-consumed in the copper chandeliers liberally spattered with tears of wax. There was something funereal in the atmosphere, although it remained warm and tepid; it was as if the odour of the decaying flowers of a memorial wreath were suspended there. Something else was in preparation but had not yet begun. Ethal, visibly wearied by impatience, launched frequent glances in the direction of the door. Taking the hint, all other eyes followed his. We were waiting for someone whose arrival was imminently expected.

Finally, the door-curtain was lifted up and a tall young man in a tight black suit came through. He was perhaps a little too tall, and too loosely-built.

'Thomas! At last!' Ethal exclaimed, hurrying towards the new arrival. He seized his hands feverishly, bringing him to join us.

'My friend from Ireland – Sir Thomas Welcome!'

I had never seen Claudius so emotional.

Sir Thomas Welcome bowed, rather coldly. He was a very handsome gentleman with a gentle and mournful bearing, lightened by two great bright eyes of some indefinable colour: green and violet at the same time, like the water of a stagnant pool. Those eyes immediately attracted my curiosity. A long blond moustache divided his charming face, and yet the wavy hair of his head was black. He had very pale skin and huge hands: the huge hands of a well-groomed executioner. They were well-scrubbed and, like Ethal's hands, boasted rings on every finger. His robust body seemed subject to an infinite lassitude, as if labouring under some heavy and mysterious burden. His expression was melancholy.

Welcome made hardly any response to the effusions of his host, and seemed to regret having come.

'We may proceed now,' Claudius declared, giving instructions to the Javanese servants. Then, taking the newcomer to one side, he said: 'Why are you so late, Thomas? I was worried. I feared that you might not come at all.'

To which the Irishman replied, in a calm voice: 'You knew that I would come. I promised that I would.'

OPIUM

The Javanese servants had provided each of us with a small pipe crammed with greenish paste. A negro dressed entirely in white, who suddenly appeared between the tapestries, lighted each of them in turn with brightly-glowing charcoals from a small silver brazier. Seated in a semi-circle on cushions set upon the Asian carpet, with our hands resting on squares of embroidered silk or Persian velvet, we smoked in silence, concentrating our whole attention on the progressive effects of the opium.

The company gathered in the studio, which had earlier been so noisy, had now fallen into silent meditation. At Ethal's signal, the agile hands of the Javanese had unbuttoned our waistcoats and loosened the collars of our shirts in order to facilitate the effects of the drug. I was seated next to Welcome. Maud White – whose figure, freed from restraint, moved sinuously beneath her black velvet peplum – was stretched out beside her brother. The English formed a separate group, already subdued by the increasing oppression of the narcotic. Still seated in her armchair, rigidly encased in her armour of precious stones, the old Duchess of Althorneyshare was the only one present who was not smoking. Pipe in hand, Ethal was still caught up in the comings and goings, giving orders.

All the candles in the chandeliers had been extinguished. Only two had been replaced and relit, burning brightly in the middle of the room. Their flames lit up two opposite corners of a carpet laid out there, about which the negro had distributed flower-petals. He had strewn them around like a shower of rain, and had then retired.

Candles and flower-petals! One might have thought that we were at a solemn wake. The smoke from our pipes ascended in bluish spirals. A dreadful silence weighed upon the studio. Ethal came at last to stretch himself out between Welcome and myself, and the ceremonial dancing began.

In the mute and heavy atmosphere of that vast vapour-filled hall the two Javanese idols began to sway on the spot, the rhythmic movements of their feet extending through the length of their bodies into the contortions of their arms. Their extended hands seemed boneless and dead.

Standing in the midst of the flower-petals, in the spectral glow of the two candles, they feverishly crumpled the wool of the carpet beneath their hammering toes. Their legs glistened from their narrow ankles to their slim thighs in a flux of transparent gauzes. They were now wearing strange diadems on their heads, like conical tiaras, which made their faces seem triangular and intimidating.

While they silently shook themselves, with slow and cadenced undulations of their entire bodies, the scallop-shell breast-plates slipped gently from their torsos, and the jade rings slid along their bare arms. The two idols gradually divested themselves of their garments. Their finery accumulated at their feet with a light rustling sound, as of seashells falling on sand. The tunics of white silk followed the slow fall of the jewellery. Now, as they stood on tiptoe, very slender in their exaggerated nakedness, it was as if two long black serpents shot forth from the cones of the two diadems had begun a delicious and lugubrious dance within the bluish vapours.

The sound of snoring was already audible, but amid the plucked petals the naked idols continued to dance.

All of a sudden they took hold of one another at the waist, twirling while tightly interlaced, as though they had but a single body with two heads ... and then they suddenly evaporated. Yes, *evaporated*, like smoke – and at the same time the hall was filled with a new light.

A whole section of the tapestry was moved aside. Dressed as a stage, Claudius's model table appeared: cold and waxed like a parquet floor, lit from behind by the pearly and frosty glow of a wan nocturnal sky.

It was a sky padded with soft clouds, against which stood out the sharp and black silhouettes of roofs and chimney-stacks: an entire horizon of chimney-pots, acute angles and attics, formed in salt and iron filings. In the distance, the dome of Val-du-Grâce could be seen. It was a silent and fantastic Paris, as seen by a bird in flight – the same panorama that could be seen from Claudius' windows, framed like a stage-set by the skylight of his hall.

Above this improvised stage, as if sprung from a dream, a whiteness appeared: a flocculence of tulle or of snow, something silver and impalpable. This frail whirling thing, which leapt and fluttered delicately beneath the moon, in the *ennui* of that corner of a deserted studio, was the slender naked form of a dancer.

She spun around in the mute air like a winter snowflake, and nothing disturbed the fearful silence save for the soft pitter-pat of her footfalls. Were it not for the silky rustling of her tulles she would have seemed supernatural in her transparence and thinness. Her legs like slender stems, the rigid projection of her bosom, her pallor blue-tinted by the moonlight, and her astonishingly fragile waist combined to give her the appearance of a phantom flower: a phantom and perverse flower, funereally pretty. The scenery of Parisian roofs and chimneys completed the illusion. It was some little ghost strayed from Montparnasse or Belleville which danced there, in the cold of the night. Her flat yet delicate face had the ghastly charm of a death's-head; long black hair descended to either side of her head, and in her hollow eyes there burned an intense alcoholic flame, whose blue ardour made me shudder.

Where had I seen that girl before? She had the slenderness of Willie and the smile of Izé Kranile, that triangle of ironic pink flesh revealing the hardness of enamel . . . oh, the shadows playing about those shoulder-blades . . . it was as if the skeleton were showing through beneath the platitude of her breasts!

All around me, the rattle of heavy breathing emerged from somnolent chests, but they were no longer snoring. My head was heavy, and the moistness of icy sweat was all over me . . . and the snowflake danced on and on.

She flared up suddenly in a flash of violet, as if bathed in projected limelight . . . and instantly flew back up into the sky as the chimneys and the roofs invaded the studio. They were now in the friezes and in the bay-window dazzlingly lit by the same flash of light. It was as if the invisible houses beneath the roofs and chimneys had suddenly surged up from the ground – and I was lying, among my Asian cushions, on the pavement of a street in the middle of a deserted Paris.

No, not Paris, but at a road-junction in some lugubrious suburb: a place bordered with newly-built houses as yet uninhabited, their doors boarded up and their grounds concealed, stretching into the distance . . . it was a cold and frosty night. The sky was very clear, the pavement very hard. I had a harrowing impression of absolute solitude.

From one of the streets, all of whose buildings were white, two horrid louts were emerging. They wore velvet coats, linen jackets, red handkerchiefs tied around their necks, and had vile fishy profiles beneath their high-peaked caps. They hurtled forward like a whirlwind, dragging with them a struggling woman in a ballgown. A sumptuous fur-lined cloak slid from her bare shoulders. She was blonde and delectable, but her face could not be seen and I dreaded that I might recognise it. The violent scene was utterly noiseless.

I could see nothing of the silent and brutalised woman but her lustrous back and the soft blonde hair at the back of her head. The two thugs were gripping her tightly by the arms. She had fallen to her knees, paralysed by terror. I wanted to call out, to run to her aid, but I could not: two invisible hands, two talons, took me by the throat also. Suddenly, one of the bully-boys knocked the woman down, pressed her face to the ground, and knelt on top of her, sawing at her neck with a cutlass. Blood spurted out, splashing the green velvet pelisse, the white silk dress and the delicate golden hair with vivid red. I woke up, choking hoarsely on my stifled cries.

The other smokers were all around, sleeping heavily,

with their faces contorted. The tapestry had fallen back into place over the studio skylight. The night was dark. The two candles were still burning, but the greenish light they emitted was distorting the faces. What a sight they were, those stretched-out bodies! Ethal's studio was strewn with them. We were not like that to begin with; whence came all these cadavers? For those people were no longer sleeping; they were all dead, just so many corpses. A veritable human tide of cold green flesh had risen to the flood and broken like a wave ... but an immobile wave, cast at the feet of the Duchess of Althorneyshare – who still remained, rigid, with her great eyes wide open, seated in her armchair like some macabre idol!

She too was greenish beneath her make-up; it was as if the purulence of all the bodies heaped at her feet cast a humid glow upon her flaccid skin; her corruption was phosphorescent. Her diamonds had become so livid that she now seemed to be embellished with emeralds, like some bloated green goddess – and in her hieratic face, the colour of hemlock, only the gleaming eyes remained white.

I watched that abomination. The ancient idol – so stiff that she seemed to be on the point of breaking up – was leaning over the body of a young girl prostrate at her feet: a supple and white cadaver outstretched upon the floor, of whom nothing could be seen but the back of the head. The back of the head was blonde and broad, like that of Maud White. Althorneyshare, with a sinister mocking laugh, put her voracious mouth to the nape of the neck as though to bite it – or, rather, to suck at it like some vile cupping-glass, for in her haste the teeth had fallen from the rotten gums.

'Maud!' I cried, brought bolt upright by anguish – but it was not Maud after which the horrible hunger of the idol was lusting, for in that same instant I saw, shining in a violet halo, the smile and the oblique expression of the tragedienne. Her mysterious mask was all aflame in that aureole above the horrid Althorneyshare ... and everything faded away into the shadows, while a familiar voice murmured in my ear:

> *The chastity of Evil is in my limpid eyes.*

It was her voice – the voice of Maud White!

SMARA

At this point, the sequence of my memories is disrupted.

I sank into a chaos of brief, incoherent and bizarre hallucinations, in which the grotesque and the horrible kept close company. Prostrate, as if I were being garrotted by invisible cords, I floundered in anguish and dread, oppressively ridden by the most unbridled nightmares. A whole series of monsters and avatars swarmed in the shadows, coming to life amid draughts of sulphur and phosphorus like an animated fresco painted on the moving wall of sleep.

There followed a turbulent race through space. I soared, grasped by the hair by an invisible hand of will: an icy and powerful hand, in which I felt the hardness of precious stones, and which I sensed to be the hand of Ethal. Dizziness was piled upon dizziness in that flight to the abyss, under skies the colour of camphor and salt, skies whose nocturnal brilliance had a terrible limpidity. I was spun around and around, in bewildering confusion, above deserts and rivers. Great expanses of sand stretched into the distance, mottled here and there by monumental shadows. At times we would pass over cities: sleeping cities with obelisks and cupolas shining milk-white in the moonlight, between metallic palm-trees. In the extreme distance, amid bamboos and flowering mangroves, luminous millennial pagodas descended towards the water on stepped terraces.

Herds of elephants were on sentry duty, using the tips of their soft trunks to gather blue lotuses from the lakes for the gods. This was the India of Vedic legend, far beyond mysterious Egypt. At times, when we were passing overhead, strange idols stood guard upon the banks of rivers and pools. Some were angular, some cut by hatchet-blows out of solid granite; they were seated, with their hands on their knees, their petrified watchdog heads staring down into the water. Quadruple rows of teats covered the torsoes of others. Some had a glitter and radiance about them, as if they were all newly forged; others seemed covered in leprous sores, so old that they no longer had faces. One had a nest of interwoven serpents crawling under the armpit; another, so beautiful that it seemed musical, had a brow gemmed with stars.

Among these idols, at prayer by the light of the moon, were the kneeling faithful; among these worshippers there were beasts as well as men.

Three matrons with heavy hips and ripe breasts were washing their linen at the foot of a Sphinx. Their hands were wringing out and beating the mysterious laundry, and the water trickling out of it was stained with blood.

One of these laundrywomen resembled Princess Olga, another the Marquise Naydorff; I did not recognise the third. An opossum, at prayer in the shadow of a Buddha, appeared to be the ghost of Mein Herr Schappman: like Ethal's friend from Berlin, his careful paws were picking over a string of opal beads . . .

And a whole procession of storks, perched on a high wall beside a Turkish cemetery and silhouetted by the night, looked up as I passed overhead, and mocked me with their beaks.

Now we were flying over marshlands. All of a sudden, the hand which was carrying me released me.

Sticky walls . . . greasy ground . . . a choking and insipid darkness . . .

I was in a crypt whose vaults were oozing, lying in a strangely moving mire, which rose up in places and plunged into depths in others. It was like a warm tide, dreadfully thick and fluid, in which my rocking body was bogged down. There were silky murmurs, light rasping sounds . . . I know not what unnamable things brushed against me, an obscure crawling sensation extended from my legs to my back, vile warm breath scarified my flesh . . . and then, under my groping hands, I felt the horror of little fat and hairy bodies, all of them shifting, wriggling under and over me . . .

For a few moments, flaccid wings fluttered against my face; then frightful kisses from little pointed mouths, whose teeth were tangible, settled on my neck, on my hands, and on my face. I was a captive of hopeful caresses, my entire being tortured with cunning little bites until I lost my strength. From top to toe I was prey to innumerable blood-suckers: fetid beasts shared my body between them, insidiously violating the entirety of my naked form.

Suddenly, in the gloom which had become greenish, I saw the singularly bloated faces of the two Javanese servants, laughing mockingly. They floated in mid-air, disembodied, like two transparent varnished bladders, whitely diademmed. Percolating from their half-closed eyes, as if shining through two slots, was a dead and greasy gaze. The two bladders laughed, while four hands without arms came towards my face: four soft and cadaverous hands, menacing my eyes with their sharp fingernails, splayed like claws at the ends of long golden cigar-cases.

And by the light of the two ghostly faces, I saw what a frightful enemy it was that had conquered my flesh. A whole army of enormous bats – the heavy and fat bats of the Tropics, of some vampiric species – was kissing my body and sucking my blood. The caress persisted, sometimes so precisely that I was forced to quiver with atrocious pleasure. Enfeebled, close to some climactic spasm, I stiffened in order to shake off the pullulation of that collective kiss – and as I did so something hairy, flaccid and cold entered into my mouth. Instinctively, I bit down on it, and it filled my throat with a sudden spurt of blood: the taste of some dead animal was bitter on my tongue; a tepid gruel adhered to my teeth.

It caused me to wake up . . . at last!

An alkaline burn was pricking my nostrils; a hand clapped a refreshing wad of damp linen to my temples; there was hurried movement all around me, and the half-sleep from which I was slowly emerging was penetrated by the noise of comings and goings, of voices . . . and I opened my eyes.

Ethal was kneeling beside me. Into the disorder of the studio, invaded by the morning light, came a draught of cold air from an open bay-window. It revived me. One of my hands was between those of Sir Thomas Welcome, who was slapping my palm, The anxious eyes of Maud White watched me considerately over the shoulder of her brother.

'He ought never to have smoked,' opined Sir Thomas.

In the sullenness of the sad and dusty studio, the first light of dawn was the last gasp of the orgy. In the morning light the tapestry had faded to the colour of piss, the busts were cadaverous, the flower-petals were a stain upon the carpet, and all along the chandeliers wax had clotted into green stalactites.

Everyone was preparing to leave. The English, brought to their feet by the negro, retired stiffly, with closed and sinister faces; they almost had to be inserted by force into their overcoats. Maud, reassured, wrapped herself in a long pelisse of straw-coloured silk. Set upright on my cushions, I sipped the water tinted with arnica which Sir Thomas gave me. What pity there was in those huge bright eyes looking down at me!

'Let's go,' said the Irishman, offering me his hand. 'We can leave now.' Monsieur White also offered a supportive hand. While we were saying our goodbyes I saw that Maud had a ring on her finger set with two big black pearls surmounted by a ruby: an enormous trefoil of gems, which I had seen on Althorneyshare's finger before the smoking-session began . . . and Maud's eyes were as fresh as water, the pallor of youth restored to them!

The Duchess was leaving Ethal's rooms at that very moment. Trailing waves of cerise silk, rustling with gold lace, bundled up to her ears, and recently patched up. Powdered and freshly replastered, her old satyr's face was smiling in the midst of a cloud of white lace. 'Time to go,' she said – and left, leading away the brother and the sister.

'We must do the same,' insisted Thomas Welcome. 'The morning air will make you feel better. Do you want me to take you home?'

'The Duc de Fréneuse has his coupé,' Ethal put in, brusquely.

An open carriage would be better. I won't take you along the Bois – we'll take the quays, following the Seine.' As Claudius made a careless gesture, he added: 'Monsieur de Fréneuse lives in the Rue de Varenne and I am at the Hôtel du Palais.'

THE SPHINX

9 November 1898

Thomas Welcome has just left me. I am still under his spell and yet, at the same time, I feel fearful.

Thomas Welcome took a risk in coming to me. His visit was most unexpected and disconcerting, and yet most amicable. What driving force caused him to take such a step, given that he hardly knows me? I only met him for the first time three days ago, at that horrible opium party organised by Ethal. What can have moved him to take me into his confidence, and to make that sort of life-saving attempt on behalf of one who is a stranger to him, whose fate ought to be a matter of complete indifference?

I hunt for an explanation but cannot find one.

Was it some irrational and spontaneous feeling of sympathy? I cannot believe it. My appearance is a deterrent; at first sight I am disquieting and frightening. In addition, there are the things which are said about me. I am withdrawn; the word 'likeable' has never been applied to me – and if it ever were applied to me, I would make every effort to disassociate myself from its implications. A 'likeable' person is one of those who aproaches people around and about the Loggia; it is a word to apply to the interpreters in Florentine hotels and the rogues of the gallery Umberto in Naples. Such a notion would be unworthy of Sir Thomas Welcome and myself.

Could it be some resentment against Ethal, a suddenly-conceived hatred for the painter? The step he has taken might be reckoned a disservice to Claudius. But Ethal has told me that Welcome is his best friend – and then again, I have a definite feeling that there is some kind of complicity, some obscure and unbreakable bond between the two men.

From pity, then? Pity for me! I would not like to think so.

What if this is the latest stratagem of Ethal's, calculated to disturb me and increase my distress? Might it be designed to precipitate the kind of enveloping madness by which I feel myself to be gripped, suffocating me in its meshes like that frightful hand: the purposeful raptorial talon of that sinister Englishman, decorated with horrid rings? What if these two men are acting in concert to delude me and – by means of suspicion and terror – to push me ever closer to the brink of the abyss into which Claudius wants me to fall?

I no longer know what I am doing. I am no longer in control of myself. I am turned upside down and bumped about, and I feel that I am staggering into an ambush, into terror . . .

Since that last soirée in Ethal's studio, the nightmare figures and hallucinations of that appalling night . . .

I have not recovered my soul!

15 of the same month
I have thought long and hard about the visit of Sir Thomas Welcome. No, that man does not wish me any harm; the impulse which brought him to me was sincere. It is impossible to lie when one has eyes like those; they are bathed in such sadness! Pity abides there, and I felt the immense kindness of his expression embracing me. I recall the anguished tone which shaded his question: 'Have you known Ethal for a long time?'. And I recall the kind of solace that filled his face in response to my reply: 'For five months!' It was the expression of pleasure which illuminates a doctor's face as he realises that the illness of his patient is of recent provenance, and still curable. It was as if hope had been renewed in his eyes when he said to me: 'For five months!'

Without too much insistence in his words, without pressing too hard on the wound, he made me understand with a few well-chosen phrases that he knew and pitied my sickness, from which he himself had suffered. He told me how dangerous Ethal had formerly been to him, and in what peril I now stood.

'He is a great – a very great – artist. He has an inquiring mind and is a very firm friend. But his bizarrerie – and, worse than mere bizarrerie, his *love* of the bizarre, the abnormal and the exotic – might be fatal to a sensitive and imaginative being. One such would surely be led astray were he to fall under Ethal's influence. Not that I place any faith in the rumours regarding Claudius which circulate here and in London – rather less credited in London than in Paris; your fellow Frenchmen have a mania for hawking around rumours and anecdotes – but it is nevertheless true that my friend Claudius has strange interests. The horrible attracts him, sickness too. Moral perversity and physical affliction, mental and emotional distress, constitute for him a field of distracting and intoxicating experiences: a source of complex and guilty pleasures, which thrills him like no other. He has more than a dilettante interest in vice and aberration; his is an innate predilection – a kind of fervent and passionate vocation.

'Like certain great doctors and philosophers, he is fascinated by various rare and little-known maladies; he approaches such cases with a cerebral fascination. He watches out for them, researches them and selects them; he is a collector of the flowers of evil. You saw what a divine collection of orchids he carefully brought together the other evening. You may be certain that that great exhibition of cosmopolitan depravity, pent up all night in his studio, was one of the most delectable evenings of his life. He has the flair of an Indian tracker for the discovery of such beings; he is drawn to vice like a hog to truffles, and he snorts them up with avid pleasure. The scent of decadence intoxicates him; he understands his specimens fully, and he has a complicated and profound love for them. He is, as you say in France, a *voyeur* of unsavoury souls. *Voyeur* is undoubtedly the word!

'Ethal cultivates and develops these flowers of criminality, much as he is accused in London of cultivating pallor, anaemia, languor and consumption in his models because of his artistic affection for certain pearly flesh-tints and darkly-ringed eyes. Not that I lend any credence to those unfortunate rumours; certain expressions and smiles transform suffering into beauty by the particular tightening of the mouth and the delicate fading of eyelids and complexions, but we must not lend Ethal's fantasies a tragic grandeur that they do not have.

'It is still the case that our friend Claudius has the fully-developed mind of a poisoner, and one who poisons for pleasure. This is a psychological refinement, but not one of the few which are nowadays permitted by law. He has this in his favour, though: he confines his operations to people who are already sick and only finishes off those whose are condemned to die. Slaves were once put to death by poisoners in front of Roman emperors desirous of admiring their skills, but Ethal is Caesar and poisoner at the same time; it is for his own edification that he contrives marvellous spectacles. He will collaborate wholeheartedly with a man's vices, in order to see how far that man will carry the torch of depravity. One day, one of his subjects will go as far as murder – but it is not necessary that the Duc de Fréneuse should be the one.

Sir Thomas was ready for my reaction. 'I might have been the one myself,' he said, swiftly. 'Like you, I have been possessed by the dream; it has taken hold of me. Beset by hallucinations, conscienceless, with no other will but that of the extending dream itself . . . numbed, annihilated, for years on end, I have lived a wretched waking nightmare. In those days, I was compelled to spend every winter in Algiers, or Cairo, or Tunis, like a captive: captive of a gaze, an undiscoverable gaze. It was the gaze of the same Goddess who disturbs and haunts the sleep of your own nights . . .

'For ten years I travelled through the Orient in search of an obsessive and delirious vision which came to me one ecstatic and insomniac evening. But the Goddess – the Goddess who will likewise appear to you, one evening or one day, if you do not fight your dream – has always deceived me!

'A lover of phantoms, that is what I have been these last ten years – and that is what you are, Monsieur, and will become irredeemably, if you cannot restore yourself to good order. For the gaze is undiscoverable, and Astarté is a witch, whose very essence is deception. That which has lied before will lie always!

'That gaze! And yet, one winter, I really believed . . .

'Four years ago, one moonless night on the Nile, when the crew of the *dahabeah* were asleep at last, we were slowly . . . oh, so slowly! . . . sailing down the stagnant stream of the river. I can still see the profound blue of night descending upon the immense Egyptian landscape, extending to the distant horizon: infinitely flat; infinitely red; scarcely shaded . . .

'On that particular night, I fully believed that Astarté would appear to me – that the Goddess would reveal herself at last!

'We were drifting down the Nile . . .

'For an hour, I watched a strange black dot curiously rising up and growing larger, at a still-distant bend of the river. I thought it might be the entablature of some ancient temple or merely a half-submerged rock looming up from the water. The *dahabeah* slid through the water, slowly and heavily, without rocking, as if in a dream. In the silence of the starless night, the shadow which intrigued me approached by slow degrees. As it took form and became distinct, it revealed the rump of an enormous sphinx of roseate stone whose outline had been worn away by the centuries.

Everyone aboard was asleep: a truly disconcerting slumber had plunged the entire crew into a leaden torpor. The movement of the craft, approaching the immobile beast, filled me with an increasing terror – for the sphinx, now, appeared to me to be luminous. It was as if a vaporous glow emanated from its rump. In the hollow of its shoulder a human figure became visible, standing up but dormant, with its head tipped back.

It was a young and slender figure, dressed like a donkey-driver, in a thin blue robe, with rings of gold at the ankles. It was an adolescent male, but I could not tell whether he was a prince or a slave, for the attitude of the sleeper seemed both royal and servile, embodying royal confidence, servile complaisance and conscious abandon.

The robe was open at the neck, exposing a flat chest, as white as ivory – but there was a gaping bloody gash across the neck: a huge scar or an open wound! As regards the face, I found it quite delectable, with the sole exception of the narrowed oval of the chin – but it was all steeped in shadow, by virtue of the figure being supported from behind.

Terror-stricken, I called out loudly, but I was unable to awaken anyone; the native crew and the English servants were all overwhelmed by magical sleep. They did not wake until dawn, by which time the sphinx had disappeared into the distance.

When I recounted my adventure next day, the dragoman responded by saying that it must have been some donkey-boy whose throat had been cut by the arab bandits which abounded in these parts. He suggested that the cadaver of the murdered child had been placed as a warning to travellers – an ironic and salutary lesson!

But how was I to explain the luminous sphinx, the intense glow which had gently and harmoniously animated the roseate stone, and the superhuman beauty of the figure sleeping in its shadow? I felt that I had passed through an enchanted moment, that for a few seconds I had dwelt in a miraculous and divine realm which was nevertheless wholly deceptive.

Ethal also assured me that I had been dreaming – Ethal, inevitably, was aboard, exasperating my sensitivity, exercising the power of suggestion over my morbid dreams.

So you see, Monsieur, that you have nothing to envy me. There was a time when I was a miserable wretch, tortured exactly as you are now.'

SIR THOMAS WELCOME

'To depart towards the sun and the sea, to go to heal oneself – no, to *rediscover* oneself – in lands which are both new and very old, where faith still endures, and which have not been tamed by our bleak civilization; steeping oneself in the tradition, the virility and the health of uncorrupted peoples; to live in India and the Far East, bathed in the brightness of the sky and the sea; to disperse oneself in nature, the only thing which never deceives us; to liberate oneself from all those conventions, futile attachments, relations and prejudices that are so many burdens weighing us down, and so many dreadful prison walls erected between ourselves and the reality of the universe; to live at last the life of the soul and the instincts, far from the artificial, overheated and hysterical existence of Paris and London: far from the whole of Europe . . .

'And yet, there is in Italy and Spain, and certain Mediterranean islands: Sicily, Corsica . . . there are the light mornings of Ajaccio when the blue of the open sea is revealed between cypresses and pines . . . there are the almond-tress in flower on the slopes of Taormina, and the giant shadow of Etna over the antique dream of Greek theatre . . . there are the ancient isles of the Archipelago, certain tiny Adriatic ports, the unknown Venices of the coasts of Istria, more forgotten and even more ruinous in their sunbathed silence than the city of the Doges and the palaces . . . and there is the sleepy and profound charm of Turkish towns, the narcotic of the shadow of palm-trees . . . Yes, far from the realms of Baedeker and Thomas Cook, there are still corners where one may spend hours in the intimacy and complete sensuality of one's own company . . .

'What am I saying? The spirit which knows how to find solitude can claim its bounty in Tunis, or even in Malta, despite that it is nowadays infested wih Englishmen . . .

'Oh, the complex and wholesome intoxication of removal! To put the sea – league upon league of the shifting and changing sea – between oneself and one's ancient hurts, between one's own life and those of intruders! But to achieve this end, one must no longer know anybody. One cannot even love a dog, if one has to leave it behind; a departure is a little death. Invisible bonds hold on to us too well. Only the adventurous, multifarious and splendid world will heal all our wounds: those atrocious little wounds inflicted on the modern soul by education, comfort and civilization . . .

'There is a healing power in long sea-crossings, beneath constellations one has never seen before; in the cruel and nostalgic joy of brief encounters, those without tomorrows because the packet-boat which brought you both to Corfu will also take you away while she is bound for Alexandria; in the doubly-lived moments when the pulse is quickened by foreknowledge of departure and the sense of the irreparable; in the souls drunk in a kiss, the hearts given in a brusque embrace, the entire existence relinquished with a grip of the hand . . .

'That is the secret of life as it ought to be lived: impassioned, inviting, taken, given, then carried away into the unknown and the beyond, without taking heed of conventions, and prejudices of caste or race . . .

'The marvellous secret of life as it ought to be, in thought and action alike, is glowing in the great sad eyes of voyagers and the clear eyes of sailors, set against the scenery of some ancient Islamic port, in the shadow of some arabesque mountain, their lungs dilated by the brisk trade-wind of the Eastern seas, their hearts seized by all the delicious oppression of life . . . !

'The secret of life is to be a voyager! To be a voyager, one must love skies and countries; one must be able to fall in love with a city or a race, and to detach oneself entirely from individuals.

'The cure, the secret of good fortune is this: love the universe in all its changing aspects, in its marvellous antithesis and still-more-marvellous analogy. The external world will then become for us a source of unalterable joys, so much more perfect because our being is only their mirror. Shocks and injuries are only visited upon us by individuals. Avoid people; avoid Ethal; study races. You will find in one of them the gaze that you seek and you will find your soul therein: your crippled, dislocated and feverish soul. We all have within ourselves an atavism, which binds us to one of the ancestral races, and each of us can rediscover his true fatherland hundreds of leagues from his birthplace.

'Like you, I have been obsessed with death and the horrible. The hallucinatory masks which haunt you took the specific form in me of a severed head. Oh, how I suffered from that malady, that disequilibrating obsession! I saw it everywhere; on every side that rictus of decapitation was railing at me, taunting me. The hallucination haunted me most intensively in the suburbs, in that sinister wilderness of byways which extends beyond the old city walls. As my sickness caused me to fall in love with my own malady, I knew exactly where and how to give birth to the torturing and evil vision.

'Oh, the moonlit nights . . . the mad carriage-races from the toll-gate on the Boulevard Bineau to the banks of Billancourt . . . the slow evocative walks along roads ringed with palisades and a few widely-space villas with closed shutters. How easily the vision emerged and ascended in those poor and leprous regions, from the suggestion of crime, the flowering of evil, that Claudius loved in me! How well that stony province of prowlers played host to contemporary nightmares, and how complaisantly the deceptive Astarté – who so obstinately refuses to display herself in the enchanted towns of Islam – condescends to reveal herself in all her ghoulish finery at the borders of vacant sports-grounds and neglected pleasure gardens . . .

And always with Ethal, who appointed himself as my guide. I came to know, as you will, the byways of the Revolution, the race-courses of Montrouge and the kilns of the plain of Malakoff . . . all the sinister Parisian suburbs which constitute the empire of the mocking Astarté of the slums, extending from the Bièvre to the wilds of Gennevilliers.

'What misery! To be in Gennevilliers, Malakoff or Montrouge when there is the triangular forum of Pompeii, the receding hills of Sorrento and Castellamare, all the enchantment of ancient Campania, the Bay of Naples and the Concha d'Oro, the arabesque epic of Mount Pellegrino, at Palermo, the temples of Agrigento and the race-courses of Syracuse, the splendour of their sunken arenas, funereal and yet so white, where footfalls stir the dust of centuries and of tombs . . . Syracuse! Taormina, Agrigento, Catania: all the blue memories of the grandeur of Greece, still sleeping beneath the olive-trees and the green oaks of Sicily!

'There is your only cure. To allow the universe to enter into yourself, thus to take slow and voluptuous possession of the whole world; that is the breviary of the voyager. To be a wise and conscious wax which takes the impressions of nature and art; to find in the shade of a sky, the line of a mountain, the attractive eyes of a portrait, the profile of an ancient bust or the silhouette of a temple, the intellectual and yet sensual coitus by means of which the refreshing and fecund *idea* is born . . .

'The life and physiognomy of a city – have you never dreamed of that? To wed a city as one would wed a wife, taking possession of it and enjoying it at length, keeping one's troubles to oneself; to be the conscious awakener of one's own sensuality, and with each analysis to take a step towards the sublime synthesis, which is the joy which comes when one knows life.

'Cities, especially ancient and populous cities, with a past rich in adventures and stories, are as tasty as ripe fruit, luscious with the mystery of such existences as were once lived there, luscious with all the striving for profit and for love that still goes on within them. Coastal towns, especially: Marseilles, Genoa, Barcelona . . . all the happy ports of the Mediterranean, with the hustle and bustle of their harbours, the sun-drenched reverie of their old docks and that tantalising fanfare of 'elsewhere', of unknown lands and distant shores, that sounds in the rigging, the sails, the halyards and the masts of so many outward bound ships.

'That is where you must go, to ripen your spleen in the sun and to breathe in the taste of conquest and action which the sea wind carries.

'Ports! Seamen are a childish and cynical race. The gaiety of their manly instincts pours forth when they are on the spree, and their innocent eyes are always dreaming: those eyes of water and of sky which one is always surprised to find in the rude tanned faces of buccaneers.

'Ports! Their industrious, enigmatic and cosmopolitan population displays in the sordid setting of their streets the quaint rags of galley-slaves and corsairs. Base prostitution – which is all mire and squalor, hunger and misery in our cold lands of the north – there borrows some mysterious beauty from the sun; the girls crudely offering themselves have something luminous, gaudy and Oriental in their accoutrement. Their cheeks are spattered with powder, their eyes are blackened, and their tinselled mops of hair make them exact replicas of one another, as if they were so many eternal dolls stamped from a template, destined to overflow with lust and dedicated to the comfort of men. In such places there is something animal about sex, which excites and relaxes at the same time the brains of intellectuals . . .

'Oh, the continual hazard of adventure which prowls and shines in the eyes of passers-by, the visions of attacks by armed hands, of rapes and knife-blows which haunt the corners of certain shady steets: the streets of Tunis, for example, and those of old Genoa and Toulon, and those of Villefranche, close to Nice, and of old Nice itself. And in the stink of their markets, in the midst of the detritus of fruits and vegetables, and there alone, Astarté will appear to you in some beautiful human flower, robust and oozing health, too rosy and russet, with mysterious animal eyes . . . like the butcher's wife with the profile of Herodias who was glimpsed by the Goncourts in the market of the

Récollets in Bordeaux. You would agree with me that the originals of certain portraits in museums – the very same ones which disturb you – flourish only in the masses. At Venice, the dogeresses of the Academy and the 'St Ursula' of Carpaccio are easily encountered in the Merceria and the little canals of Murano. La Cavalieri has sold oranges in Naples, and Caroline Otero in Cadiz; and those are probably the two most beautiful girls to be found in Paris.

'You, who are tortured by the malady of beauty and oppressed by the unanimous ugliness of modern cities, whose palaces are banks and whose churches are factories, must flee from anaemia and chlorosis and from that depravity which is the pitiful invention of souls in distress, in connivance with hunger. Flee from all the refined filth of alcoholic London and wretched Paris; leave them, go to live your life elsewhere. Tomorrow I depart once again for the Indies. Would you like to go with me? I shall take you! I no longer have obsessions or nightmares since I have begun to live my own life. To live your own life, that is the final aim; but what a wealth of self-knowledge must be acquired before arriving there! No one lights our way; friends cheat us of our own instincts, and experience alone can help us discover it. Ranged against us we have our education, our family and our entire milieu – and that is not to mention all the prejudices of the world and the legislation of our fellow-men. On top of all that, we encounter everywhere an Ethal. When that happens, it is too late to live the authentic existence, the only one for which we are born – and yet, in the same hour, the way is shown to us.

'Too late, too late . . . such is the vulgar cawing of fate in response to the sad lesson of experience. *Nevermore! Nevermore!*

'I saw you, the day before yesterday, during that opium-smoking session, the floundering prey of horrible visions. It was not opium, by the way, but hashish: opium does not vaporise in that fashion, and I easily recognised Ethal's hand in that deception. I saw you becoming pale, sweating

155

profusely, rattling and choking with gestures and incoherent words: an entire pantomime of agony in which I rediscovered some frightful memories of my own – and a great pity took hold of me, the pity of a sick man cured for another man overtaken by the same sickness. A deeply personal sympathy impelled me towards you. Having divined that we share the same tastes, affinities and sufferings, I have come spontaneously to see you. As I am your elder, if not in years, at least in experience, I have come to lend you my torch and cry out a warning as you teeter on the brink of the precipice.

'You can still avoid the fall.'

I drank in his words as though I were taking medicine.

ANOTHER TRACK

16 November 1898

I am still here! The rain is falling; the trees in the avenues stand up lamentably against the flour-paste sky; amid the puddles of black water, one must suffer the horror of cab-stands and the ceaseless scrimmaging of umbrellas. This is the Paris of November, the Paris of spleen and mud – and Sir Thomas Welcome is making haste towards the sun. Some mail-carrying packet-boat is bearing him off to the distant and odorous Indies: the Indies of bamboo forests, sacred pools and temples . . .

One word from Ethal, a single hour of conversation with the Englishman, a single evening spent with him in a restaurant, was sufficient to hold me back.

It is as if he sees clearly into the depths of my soul! Nothing can be hidden from that man! I can still see him, in the lounge of that restaurant, between the high mirrors bright with electric light, amid the dazzle of lustrous crystal, with the 'public' all around us: men in black suits and their female companions. The dining-tables were tiny. The girls were all alike in their low-cut dresses glittering with ersatz jewellery and their pastel make-up; all svelte, amenable, with overlarge and overmobile eyes set in oval faces, and all of them with their carefully-styled hair doing their utmost to evoke the image of Willie Stephenson: that vaporous and sharp stereotype of the end of the eighteenth century first made fashionable by dealers in cheapjack trinkets and small-time stock-market gamblers, which ended up imposing itself on the world of high society. In the aisles between the tables there was a continual coming and going as customers arrived and took their leave: a riot of sumptuous evening-cloaks, shimmering silks and gauzes, 'hellos' and 'good evenings' cried from one table to another with affected voices, and the little winks of satisfaction of calculatedly cool and bored men, playing all their gestures

for the gallery . . . all the costumed comedy of that menagerie of lust which is a late-night restaurant.

Why did Claudius, who knows my hatred of politeness
and the world, steer me to that restaurant? Exasperated by
all those affectations, all those powdered leers and all those
brothel smiles, how could I help but recapitulate, by way
of contrast, my conversation of the previous evening: the
idea of the great escape into the free and wholesome life, of
the intoxication of the instincts, of cultures still uncorrupted, of the blue of the sky and the sea, of all the health
and vigour of life in the tropics? I poured out before him
the entire philtre of energy that had been gifted to me the
day before by the enthusiasm of Welcome.

'Yes, I know the old song,' Claudius interrupted, with a
sneer. 'Bilbao, Marseilles and Barcelona . . . the bright eyes
of seamen . . . the secret of life . . . the love of action
apprehended in the wide eyes of voyagers . . . and doubtless
in the argot of hauliers on the docks. I know dear Thomas
all too well.

'But he has not told you everything.

'Be forewarned that alongside the beings of instict and
passion to which the dockyards and harbours of a great
coastal town give birth, there are creatures of lust and
perversity too: frightful products of cosmopolitan lust and
the *ennui* of civilization, much like the bejewelled ghouls
whose presence here you find so oppressive.

'Sir Thomas has not spoken to you about those. More
than that, he is neglectful of your needs in sketching this
portrait, for he has become part of a company: the company of the surfeited, the seekers of the impossible. One
finds them everywhere, in Bahia as in Marseilles, in Tangier
as in Cadiz, in Toulon as in Brest, in Le Havre as in Cairo,
rolling the dregs of their closed and filthy minds around
the opium dens just as their counterparts do in the music-
halls and the 'American Stars'.

'Would you like me to describe them to you? Women
with androgynous silhouettes, dressed in the blue cloth of
seamen; English millionaires with cooked complexions the

colour of port wine, their necks tanned and fierce, their expressions sharp and pale; all the proprietors of big yachts and all their passengers; a perverse and drunken army of Wandering Jews, which you must know as well as I do, given that you have been to Algiers and to Cairo . . . all of those who, being idle or crippled, or having come down in the world, go forth to parade upon the restless seas the fever of their worn out feelings or the embarrassing renown of their defectiveness.

'Oh, Sir Thomas Welcome pretends to be cured – he told you that, didn't he? Well, he's a liar. He has deceived you, like the possessed wretch that he is. Neither in the climbing streets of the casbah, nor those surrounding the mosques of Cairo, nor in the bright-dark of the souks of Tunis, nor in the mud and reed huts of the villages of the Nile, has he ever encountered those liquid green eyes whose distant and captivating promise has made him abandon everything. He has told me so himself. To me, he does not lie; he cannot lie to me. From the deadening backstreets of Constantinople to the Moorish cafes of Biskra, that intoxicating phantom of the Orient, the Syrian goddess Astarté has always disappointed him, always cheated and deceived him – just as he deceives himself, so enamoured is he of the deception which he pursues.

'I have travelled with him for years, but we have chased them long enough: these women of the Tropical lands, parcelled up in silks and veils; arab and moorish women taking themselves off to the mosque or the baths, tottering as they descend the steps of back-streets steeped in shadow. Their long, languid and ecstatic eyes, uniformly smeared with kohl, are as imploring as those of gazelles, but when one looks more closely at them, they are as hard and as brilliant as the flashing eyes of birds: cold and empty eyes of jet. All eyes are black beneath those lapis lazuli skies, and none of the creatures encountered in such regions – whether they be Ouled-Naïl or donkey-boys, found in the shadow of the great pyramid of Cheops or in the stony wilderness of Petra – will keep the promise of Astarté.

'Not a single one out of all these Oriental animals has ever been known to offer us the terrible and gentle expression of sea-green that Sir Thomas seeks – and which he still pursues, in spite of the fact that he pretends to be fully cured.

'At bottom, he is even sicker than you are! Yes, more even than you, my poor friend.

'Welcome is the worst of the possessed. I have seen to it that you made his acquaintance for the specific purpose of enabling you to get a better feel of your own sickness, and to prove to you to that the cure is *not* to be found down there, but *here*, where the very least of these women – or the very best, if you prefer – can yield to you the undiscoverable gaze, under the imposition of a particular sentiment which you have yet to determine . . . oh, it is neither desire nor love, you are too rich to inspire those.'

'What is it, then?'

'I will tell you, if you promise me not to leave. If you give me your word that you will not try to join Sir Thomas Welcome – from whom, I suspect, you will receive a telegram tomorrow, dispatched from Nice or Marseilles. But this salmi of woodcock is going cold! You know, dear chap, that woodcock cannot be kept waiting.'

19 November 1898

The Lahore *departs on Monday; you have time to pack your bags. Pack your trunk and come to join me at the Hotel de Noailles. The* Lahore *is the fastest ship the company has. We will be in Singapore on 5 January.*

WELCOME.

Claudius guessed correctly. I found this telegram on returning home. Should I show it to Ethal?

20 November 1898

'I knew it,' Claudius said, negligently placing the dispatch between our two place-settings. We dined together this morning, and after the oysters I could not resist the temptation to show him the telegram. He did not greet it with the sardonic smile I anticipated; his triumph was a mere matter of course. He asked the headwaiter for cumin – he seasons eveything he eats with a profusion of exotic and bizarre condiments. He demanded celery and saffron in order to make some fierce-tasting hors-d'oeuvre for himself in a radish-dish; then he mixed in a delicate tongue, and suddenly resumed the conversation.

'So you are not going? Well, so much the better! I would have been sorry to know that you were travelling with Sir Thomas Welcome – some rather disturbing stories have been told about him in London.'

'What stories? You would have let me go without telling me?'

'Of course. I would have influenced your decision if I had communicated the rumours before the decision was taken. We Englishmen have an absolute respect for the liberty of others; you were free to leave if you wished, and it was my duty not to interfere with that freedom in any way.

'I was able to warn you about the uselessness of such a voyage, and to convince you, using Thomas as an example, of the vanity of your hopes, because Thomas had lied to you in boasting of his cure. I had the right to demolish his deception, given that he based his argument on it, but I did not have the right to reveal details of Welcome's life or past which, if not actually preventing your departure, would at least have given you something to think about.'

'Is there any such detail?'

'Now that your decision is taken,' Claudius said, 'I am able to relate to you that which is called in London 'the unhappy adventure of Sir Thomas Welcome' – and the dangerous risk you have run.'

'Danger? And you would not have stopped me? With a light heart, you would have let me run into it?'

'Of course. No man can avoid his destiny. In any case, would you not have deserved it fully, by virtue of your lack of confidence in me?'

'But it would have been a betrayal!'

'No worse than yours, given that I have promised you a cure and you would have been changing doctors.'

'And what is this story about Thomas – this 'unhappy adventure' as you say it is called in London?'

'Such impatience! Control yourself. I shall not be so naïve as to recount it to you. You would be able to suspect me of having invented it, for the sake of the cause: *testis unus, testis nullus*. I will make sure that you hear every detail in due course, from one of my compatriots: Sir Harry Moore, the great racehorse trainer of Maisons-Lafitte. We will certainly be able to find him this evening – in Tattersalls, at about five, or at a bar in the Rue Auber around midnight. It is useless to insist; I shall tell you nothing. You would have every right to suspect my narration. But let me congratulate you on having been wise enough to resist the melancholy eloquence of Thomas's great eyes – they have the reputation of being very persuasive.'

'What is it that you want to tell me?'

'Nothing. Harry Moore will explain it to you. In the meantime, shall we pay a call on Jane de Morrelles?'

'Jane de Morrelles?'

'Yes, at 62 Rue Washington. I received a circular this morning. A new consignment has come in from the provinces, absolutely fresh. One of them is a little girl from Bayonne. Basques have a purity of form and a certain elegance which is rare in the Parisian marketplace. The most beautiful Celtic eyes are sometimes to be found among the populations of the Pyrenees: eyes which reflect the water of mountain-streams, the cold green of torrents. In an amber face those sorts of eyes are singularly bright. Then again, little provincial girls new to the trade and not yet broken in sometimes make such pretty startled gestures: the semblances of modesty, the cowering of beaten bitches. They are true keyboards of sensation. When one knows how to dose them with surprise and fear, one can obtain such pretty expressions . . . terror is such a powerful agent of excitation: the most potent pepper of sensuality!'

THE SPECTRE OF IZ

25 November.

What a vile and horrible day it has been! First, the time we spent in Jane de Morrelles' brothel; then that gruesome and disgusting session at the Moulin-Rouge; and finally that frightful couple of hours in the English bar, with that apoplectic giant Harry Moore, and his nasty revelations regarding Sir Thomas Welcome . . .

Sir Thomas Welcome! one of the few beings ever to have shown me a little sympathy; the only soul, in truth, towards whom I have ever felt drawn.

One would think that Ethal derives pleasure from suppressing all the energy that is in me, and destroying all my illusions . . . he leaves me with nothing, after such physical and moral wretchedness!

That Claudius! When I am with that Englishman, I have the sensation of plunging into dirt and darkness: the tepid, flowing and suffocating mire of my opium nightmare. When I listen to him the air becomes thin, and his atrocious confidences stir up my basest instincts and dirtiest desires.

He carries the atmosphere of the slums with him wherever he goes. There is something unspeakable in his insinuations and whisperings. And this is the man who should be healing me! He has found the means to increase my moral distress. The moral distress of the Duc de Fréneuse – what a sorry sight! I am as deeply enmired there as I ever was: stuck in a whirlpool of warm and perfumed silt, in the soft but tenacious grip of that man with the stare of a vulture!

Oh, the disturbing glint of his differently-coloured eyes beneath their membranous lids! One would think that his irises were sneering. And the odiously carressing but nevertheless insistent embrace of his fingers circled by enormous jewelled rings! And the hideousness of his hairy chest: that huge street-porter's chest which he bared in Jane de Morrelles' whorehouse, in the cleft of his unbuttoned shirt, as he put himself at ease in order to receive the little girls . . .

I am still asking myself how I refrained from strangling him, so pained was my heart by his off-handedness and his foul mannerisms. Today he has infected my few remaining presumptions and my last treasured memories with the pestilence of the swamp. Everything within me has faded and withered beneath that malarial breath. How I hate him for wreaking such total havoc within me! How I detest him for soiling my regard for Sir Thomas Welcome! I shall never forgive him for that.

Oh, what a day! The whole day was designed and contrived by him in order to pillage the last vestiges of hope from my soul. I will never forget it, for it has killed the last trace of innocence which survived within me!

I have now begun to descend into the great abyss of fear and nausea. From this day forward, I shall slide into the blackness of the unstable and the unknown. I shall have the utmost disgust for everything, including myself.

2 December 1898

Yes, the more I reflect upon it, the more certain I am that the day of 20 November was designed, contrived and orchestrated by Ethal. That encounter with Izé Kranile in the rooms of the brothel-keeper was deliberately set up. He knows that I was attracted to that girl three years ago, when she was in her heyday, and that – notwithstanding the fact that she mowed down my desire with all the clumsiness of an unbroken filly – her image has remained captivating in my memory.

He made certain that I would find her again, in that bawdy-house: Izé, her price fallen to two hundred francs and less; the dish of the day at Jane de Morrelles; the everyday convenience of husbands who only have an hour to spare when the Bourse closes; fresh meat for fat foreign visitors to the Rue de Washington! Oh, the claws which pinched my heart – I feel them still! – and the strange sensation of cold which ran up and down my spine when, in the boudoir with closed shutters where the impubescent girls with their grinning made-up faces were miming their insipid caresses, the slightly heavy ripple of Izé's laughter burst out from the room next door. How brutally I pushed away that fourteen-year-old gamine – advertised, of course, as eighteen – who was lazily straddling my knees, making pressing appeals to my wallet! Oh, the clumsiness of those false innocents, their musky hair curled with little tongs! Madame de Morrelles' little lambs! And Izé Kranile was there!

I pressed the electric button; Madame de Morrelles answered it herself, all smiles beneath the complicated scaffolding of her coiffure.

'The lady next door!' My voice was so hoarse that its timbre was affected.

'The lady next door? She is free. The monsieur is about to depart; nothing else has been arranged. That Izé is so fantastic! . . . ' Madame de Morrelles stopped abruptly, as if she had said too much. 'Do you know her?'

'Yes – an old acquaintance . . . I'd like to see her, to talk to her.'

'No jealous scenes, mind!'

I shrugged my shoulders.

'I'll have to ask her,' said the bawd.

'Come on! Let him see her!' Ethal put in, shaking off two of the little ones, who were hanging around him like two goats after a vine left as an offering to the god Terminus.

'But it's five hundred francs,' Madame objected nervously, 'Izé Kranile . . . '

Five hundred francs! I gave them to the bawd. Claudius filled the champagne-glasses of the little ones, and we followed Madame's train of pearl-grey silk.

Izé Kranile was sitting on a sofa with her legs crossed, leaning back on the cushions smoking Oriental tobacco. She was wearing a corset and an under-petticoat; the shoulder-straps of her chemise had slid down her arms exposing the lustre of her shoulders. Her shoulders, moist and fat, glistened in the half-light of hermetically sealed and curtained windows. The room was oppressively heavy and warm; I stopped short at the threshold, taken in the throat by the wild shrillness I had breathed once before, in Izé's dressing-room.

'Izé, there are two gentlemen here to see you,' announced Madame de Morrelles, the words gushing from her painted lips.

'Why, it's you!' exclaimed Izé, without getting up. 'What a coincidence! Small world, isn't it? Sit down. So you're out on the town, in search of a little naughtiness. At this hour, too! You're keen, aren't you? Not that I should complain. I suppose Morrelles invited you to inspect her little ones – the new kids from down South. They're only good for walk-on parts at the Gaîté-Rochechouart – the Folies-Bergère wouldn't take them. You don't usually come up here, do you? You only come for something special – like the first-timers. Isn't it always the way? It's the same with me. See that lot! They want me costumed as *Princess Angora*, diamonds and all ... and then it's 'Is all that stuff fake?' when I've shown them my kicks.'

Izé slapped herself on the thigh as the filth continued to run from her lips. How crapulous she had become! In what hole had she come by that coarse voice and that common manner!

I had passed up a star of the stage and now I found a street-walker. I was crushed; my radiant vision of that magical evening – Salomé fuming with the powder and sweat of the Folies-Plastiques – had fallen into the gutter.

'Do you still have your beautiful rings?' she asked, as she took me by the hand.

'Do you still have *your* assets?' countered Ethal, mockingly. 'Let's see!' And he took hold of her chin, tilting back her head in order to look at her teeth. Jane de Morrelles got up and lit the candles.

Izé Kranile still had her assets. She still had her face, broad at the temples and narrow at the chin, like the mask of a satyress. She had her large and splendid eyes with whites like enamel and irises like agates, which radiated gleams of grey and green: those famous eyes which had 'looked long upon the sea'. But an expression of infinite lassitude had worn down and drawn out her features; her little triangular mouth was slack now, in spite of her effort to turn up the lips into a smile. Izé Kranile was a wreck, broken by the horrible and riotous life into which she had descended. The coarseness of her voice seemed to have spread throughout her being. She was common property now! What anguish that realisation caused me!

'What are these bruises?' I said, appalled. 'Have you been beaten up?'

'No, just loved a little too well. I've been with a Greek.'

'And a bully!' Ethal remarked, bursting out laughing. 'You're black and blue. You must be charging him at a high rate, to let him do that to you!'

She laughed in her turn, huskily. 'What about that?' she said, proudly showing off three little red blemishes on her left breast. 'How's that for a mug's game?'

'That?' Ethal riposted, leaning curiously over Izé's skin. 'That's nothing much, my girl – but you ought to have it seen to.' The monstrous Ethal spoke quite carelessly.

'Bastard!' said the dancer, 'It's five hundred francs a go, that's what it is, to those who have the fancy. Together with the one I have round the back they come to a mere trifle of two thousand, and from a real gent too. It's a cigarette burn.'

'Is it?' said Claudius. 'You mean that there are men who amuse themselves by burning women for their pleasure? Despoiling a creature like you! What swines you must have to do business with!'

'One must live,' answered Izé, cynically. 'And everyone has his little passions – haven't they, dear?' And she winked impudently, while looking at me. Her hand slyly slid around my shoulders, trailing caressing and prying fingers over the back of my neck.

I pulled back, nauseated: 'Five hundred francs a burn! Is that what you charge for every nasty act?'

'It's the going rate.'

The frightful Claudius made as if to light a cigarette. 'Five hundred francs! I'm tempted to try it – if you'll permit?'

I grabbed him and dragged him away forcibly. 'No, Claudius – not that. I won't have it. Let's go; I've had enough.' I threw a hundred francs towards Izé.

'Still cracked!' concluded the girl, sweeping up the bank-notes. 'Hey – Madame Morrelles! A soda, with a little ether.'

Outside, it was still raining. The muddy puddles twinkled in the hazy light of overworked gaslights. Ill-tempered pedestrians hurried along the glistening footpaths or lay in wait for girls at the street-corners. It was the hour when Paris lit up. All the dissolving mud of the city ran in the gutters – and I had all that mud in my heart.

We dined at a restaurant. Later that evening, we undertook a disgusting tour of the musical-boxes of Montmartre: a bitter pill of idiocies a hundred times rehearsed, harking back to the funereal gaities of the Butte; all the listlessness of a trawl through the usual night-spots. We finished up at the Moulin-Rouge.

We watched the poor girls eaten away by anaemia and miserable, impecunious vice – wretchedness in silk rags – and we watched the strollers excited by dirty desires prowling uncertainly around the professionals: all the disgrace of a proletariat stirring up its lusts at regular hours, in order to counter the *ennui* of shopkeepers and little shopgirls. And this is where Ethal proposes to guide me to an encounter with the gaze! Wherever we went, the spectre of Izé preyed on my mind; all the girls we encountered seemed to be weighed down by the same exhausted and dejected lassitude, hawking the same filth in order to ignite the swinishness of passing men, with the same depravity of voice and gesture.

'Calves, mere calves,' as the painter Forie was wont to say when we had trailed around all evening, only to find ourselves at ten o'clock in some nest of whores or cut-throats!

When we came out again it was still raining. The deluge flooded the city and flooded my heart. The frightful odour of beastly wetness was everywhere. Outside in the boulevards the wretched whores in mud-spattered petticoats walked their beats, while their pimps idly played cards behind the windows of the wine-merchants' shops.

Such is the Paris of lust and pleasure, whose praises the poets of Montmartre are pleased to sing!

At last, at half past midnight, to add the crown of thorns to that march to Calvary, there was the promised and long-anticipated meeting with Harry Moore, the trainer from Maisons-Lafitte. We found him in the bar in the Rue Auber, idling at the counter, drinking tart and poisonously spicy cocktails. The dirty stories which the bookmaker merrily dribbled out between gin-induced hiccups and bellows of laughter, on the subject of Sir Thomas Welcome, assassinated my fond memory of the melancholic and handsome figure of Thomas just as the odious Ethal had earlier destroyed my vision of Izé Kranile.

Izé had become a game-bird in a whorehouse; Thomas became a condemned criminal, fit for Devil's Island . . .

It was, in truth, a day of spectres.

CLOACA MAXIMA

[From this point on the manuscript is interrupted by baffling lacunae and becomes subject to errors of date – perhaps accidental, perhaps deliberate. There are alterations in the handwriting, and there is a disconcerting general incoherence. Its author was evidently struck down by illness.]

January 1899

That first-night audience! What an awesome parade of infamy was manifest at the lips of the boxes. All those diamonds: the spolia opima of fortunes acquired by crime and prostitution. All the sergeants of the great army of vice were there, half-naked in their dress-uniforms beneath the skilful make-up and the proudly-set smiles, like so many triumphal idols: all of them aflame with gaudy necklaces and the false gold of dyed hair; all of them flanked by junior ministers or apprentice academicians, basking in the notoriety of politics or letters; all the radiant ex-virgins *à la mode* – for they are espoused now – set amongst their husbands and their lovers.

And in the orchestra stalls, dressed up to the nines, all the frail and tormented grace of actresses from little theatres and today's bits on the side: a host of Izé Kraniles and Willie Stephensons; little women with diminutive and fervent heads, weighed down by their copious hair, posing like insolent and precious page-boys with their delicate and fragile profiles, emanating a haunting and perverse charm . . .

Further up, the listlessness of men out on the town, their boiled-fish complexions aggravated by the porcelain whiteness of their shirt-fronts: the rictuses of their soft mouths; the broken lassitude of their bearing; and the ugliness of their cooked eyes.

Then, the rancorous faces of the critics: the oblique

glances of augurs tacitly judging the piece; all the ignominy of their 'my dear chaps!' and the confidential handshakes of their old boys' network.

I had, of course, seen the spectacle a hundred times before – but never had I perceived with such acuity the ugliness of the masks! Never before had my nostrils so sharply extracted from all the routine deception of perfumes and powders the atrocious odour of putrefaction. I knew the vices and the defects, the scandals and the miseries, of every woman and every man in the boxes of that theatre – just as they knew all the frightful rumours whispered in connection with my name, and the distress of my life. Do we not go to such occasions – each and every one of us, quite cynically – primarily in order to display our fashionable Parisian personalities: all the glory of the boulevardiers, complete with the disgraces of yesterday and the disasters of tomorrow?

From the movement of a lorgnette aimed at me, and the contrived smile of an eavesdropping woman, I can always deduce that my name has been pronounced and the subject taken up . . .

In one of the stage-boxes sat Naiderberg: the stout Naiderberg enriched by ten bankruptcies, executions by the Bourse settled by the purchase of villas in Cannes and grand hotels in Switzerland; the bloated Naiderberg, swollen up with greasy unwholesomeness, with his leprously white face and his overblown bearing. Then, continuing along the tier of boxes, there were the three Helmann brothers, like avian skeletons with their high shoulders, their meagre, jutting torsos and their eager muzzles; their lips were thin, their noses thinner and their eyes thinner still – but gleaming metallic yellow beneath their blinking eyelids. All three are bankers, maintaining in limited partnership the beautiful Conchita Merren, blooming like a white camellia between their three black suits. Then Maicherode, another banker, Viennese this time – a Viennese expelled from Vienna – who makes an ostentatious display of poor Nelly Ferneil, his draught-screen, but whose motto

171

– whispered behind closed doors and well-known to the Prefecture – is 'Suffer the little children to come unto me.' All of them naturalised Frenchmen and true cosmopolites: the masters of Paris.

Extrapolating the line formed by the men of politics – both those *in* government and those who set the prices of abstentions and amendments – seated in the boxes, the eye arrives at the great journalists, paid so much per article, who – for a hundred francs or so – will either praise the piece, or not speak of it at all, or spitefully denigrate it as required. (If the director does not care to reach for his cheque-book, an invitation to supper with the star of the troop, or the favourable consideration of a manuscript, might well suffice.)

I recognised several members of the herd: Evrard, the beau of the Bois, who exploits the girls and will fight for them if need be, svelte and curved in his silk-lined dress-coat; de Marsonnet, the painter who has married his mistress Nina Marbeuf, without caring that her fortune was entailed and would pass, upon her death, to the three children she bore Baron Harneim; Destelier, the editor who only edits Dreyfusards, and Dormimo, his colleague who only publishes nationalists – but who both have covert operations, one of them issuing the books of Gyp because Gyp is profitable and the other the pamphlets of Ajalbert, because pamphlets are his bread-and-butter. All hypocrites and all cheats: a whole set of respectable fronts sheltering lizards beneath, from the espousers of adulterated dowries provided by natural fathers who roost in scrupulous and belated austerity to the likes of Saint-Fenasse, who pulls the horses which he rides in races for his brother, and Marforade, the anarchist poet in the hire of Fraynach, who reproaches Moreuse for liking the army of the *École militaire* and lives with a masseur.

Then – come to see the star of the show, the delicious and fragile Eva Linière, with the huge eyes of a Gozzoli angel, frightening and frightened, wild and promising, so ill-fitted to her ragamuffin face – there was the Lesbos of the premières: all the accursed women who bring to our spectacles the perverse charm of professionals in travesty. There was Maud White, blanched with the soft blonde beauty of the Irish, in the box of Althorneyshare, the old Duchess of Ethal's soirée. The duchess was even more plastered with unguents, and her ancient flesh seemed more greenishly ghostly than ever beneath the nacreous pustules of an armature of pearls. Maud's brother was there too. In a ground-floor box, the heavy throat of the Marquise Naydorff was side by side with the thick figure of Olga Myrianinska: the Slav and the Sicilian, corrupted by the same tastes, were also there for the girlish shoulders and the thin face of Eva Linière, to be diplayed in ephebic guise in the costume of some refugee from the *Oresteia*.

That Eva! It was for her sake, too, that Muzarett, the tightly-corsetted and refined gentleman poet was in his armchair, leaning over to display the top of his narrow, wrinkled and unquiet head. Delabarre, the musician everyone is crazy about, accompanied him: the two enemies had made peace, reconciled at last as fellow devotees in the arcane and sensuous cult of the actress.

All the starched and scrubbed Englishmen of Claudius's soirée were there too, dispersed throughout the auditorium, but recognisable by their heavy and elongated faces, as if weighed down by their heavy jaws; they too were all communicants of the new religion. It was as if the entire auditorium had been given over to the celebration of a rite, in which the thin legs of the actress held everyone in suspense, in the hope and the anticipation that some accident might befall her costume.

Superimposed on all those staring men with their pig's snouts and all those staring women with their ghoulishly convulsed faces, I saw the remembered image of an etching by Rops: a frightful but honest etching in which Lust, the empress of the world, is depicted as a skeleton crowned with flowers – but a skeleton that might be reckoned a siren, in that beneath the vertebrae of the torso there flourishes a fleshy rump, and two spreading legs, the rounded legs of a statue or a dancer, upon which the kidneys nestle like luscious fruit.

As this vision became more distinct and obsessive, it seemed to me that the actress on stage became fleshless, a death's-head apparent beneath the flesh of her face. The legs and the loins alone remained carnal and harmonious in their proportions, and I felt a shadow of terror pass over me as I watched that spectre, upon whose mad and empty eyes the whole vast hall of masks was concentrating.

Then, suddenly, a woman entered the left-hand stage-box. Every gaze, every pair of opera-glasses, turned towards her. I was caught up in spite of myself by the magnetic effluvium which steered my eyes towards the newcomer. It was a tall and slim young woman, very pale, dressed in an exquisite pale blue costume which made her seem paler still!

She had the disquieting pallor of a eucharistic host, her oval face thinned down by a suffering and spiritual expression which made her eyes seem very large. Their colour was ultramarine, shading to black in the dark rings which surrounded them like lustrous bruises. This strange and fragile creature semed to personify the ideal beauty of the twentieth century: that delicate nose, with its mobile and vibrant nostrils; the gentle rise and fall of that flat bosom; that excessively thin waist under the light plumes of her fan; that incisive and charming pearl-white smile; that laugh displaying the tips of the teeth between the red of her lips. Where had I seen all that before?

All eyes were devouring that pallor; the lust of the entire auditorium drank down the philtre of that feverish and morbid beauty. In the flushed eyes and smiles, there was exactly the same excitement which had greeted the entrance of the actress upon stage – and which, only a minute ago, had followed the comic steps and daring gestures of her performance.

The creature in the pale blue dress was accompanied by a man and a woman. The man I recognised as her husband: a man of letters, no less talented than many others of that vocation but no more either. The woman was the Princess of Seiryman-Frileuse, the yankee multimillionaire whose dowry had elevated her from the Faubourg, whose passionate and energetic face was familiar to me from Ethal's studio.

'The pretty Madame Stalis with the Princess of Seiryman . . . Then, she too must be . . . ?'

All the androgynes in the hall aimed their opera-glasses at the stage-box, studying the American and her new friend, some admiring and others denigrating but all cut to the quick by the same implication and the same lewd conviction. The men, staring and smiling, likewise took the hint.

On the stage, Eva Linière continued to mimic the anatomy of a young page-boy, in her mauve tights spangled with dull silver: an operatic Orestes, a hellene from Montmartre and a thoroughbred Greek from Asia.

'All marching in step, men and women alike,' Ethal whispered in my ear, sarcastically. I had quite forgotten that he was there, anaesthetised as I was by the stupor of the surrounding spectacle and the suggestive vision. 'All in step, as if they were stuck together.'

Paris on the March was the title of the piece: an idiotic revue, with spectacular scenery and an abundance of feminine nudity.

'Observe, if you will,' Ethal went on, 'that Eva Linière and little Madame Stalis belong to the same genre. They have the same gracile and consumptive beauty, the same chlorotic charm and sickly seasoning: Venus of Père-Lachaise, fleshed out in Venetian glass. It is the attraction of that fragility which sets alight the squeezed and sensual brutality of shady financiers, stockbrokers and parvenus . . .

'These arrivals of yesterday are understandably drawn to the fragile elegance of the finest of the species; their sensations are multiplied tenfold by the thought that they are bruising and smashing the refinements of duchesses or virgins; they grind down flesh as they grind out their gold; they are the movers of the world and the pluckers of lilies . . .

'We are refined, we sense the cadaverous odour which lingers about them – but it will not be necessary to run away. I am acquainted with the delectable apparition of the stage-box. Madame Stalis is in good health, and so is Eva Linière. That pallor, that languorous attitude, that febrile state of the eyes and lips is a deliberate mask which they have cultivated. It is by means of the douche and a healthy household routine – early morning walks followed by long hours of repose on the chaise-longue – that the Seraphita of the premières and the ephebe of the concert-hall have arrived at that charming and chimerical appearance.

'The precious beauty of Madame Stalis is the inspiration and *raison d'être* of her husband, who leads this specimen of a rare flower through all the salons. The cultivated consumption of little Eva excites the clients and fills the house. The public pays good money, and each one gives good value for it. Look how the whole auditorium drools over the two emaciates! What can the anarchists be thinking of when they put their bombs in cafes, or the entrances of railway-stations?

'Isn't a crowd like this the bitter end? Isn't each and every soul out there ripe for the final boiling? And yet, you cling to your petty modesty, your sense of shame, and your timidity! Frankly, my dear chap, you're behind the times.

'Behold – we are in Rome!'

SIR THOMAS'S MILLIONS

The evening before last, in the course of an intimate tête-à-tête in Ethal's silent studio, I forced myself to recapitulate in some detail the mysterious death of Monsieur de Burdhes, which compromised Sir Thomas Welcome in such a bizarre fashion – to the extent that from that day forward Welcome found the doors of every club in London closed to him, and now employed de Burdhes' millions in travelling through Asia, under the cloud of a permanently blemished reputation.

On that fateful night a couple of months ago, when Claudius dragged me to that bar to hear Harry Moore tell the story, we were unable to extract anything from the stout trainer but the mumbled utterances of a drunken man: obscene idiocies interrupted by heavy hiccups and Saxon curses. That apoplectic drunkard had belched and vomited his slanders regarding Thomas, soiling my imagination and saddening my memory of him – but had not, however, succeeded in obliterating the impression which the noble and melancholy Irishman had made upon me. The insanities of the surfeited bookmaker only served to repel me, sowing just enough disquiet to make me regret not having followed Thomas in his exodus to India. At the end of the day, the disgusting Harry Moore had not been able to spell out any specific charge.

Ethal filled in the gaps.

Monsieur de Burdhes had been found murdered in a small house on the outskirts of London to which Welcome was a frequent visitor. There the two of them, in collaboration with others, had set themselves the task of 'rediscovering' – as they put it – the celebration of the rites of a secret cult which Monsieur de Burdhes had imported from the Far East. This eccentric had the ambition to impose upon the world a new religion. The young Sir Thomas – then in the full flower of his twenty-three years – was not merely one of the affiliates of the sect; he was its leading adept, and the favourite disciple of its original instigator – de Burdhes' heir apparent.

Thus, on the morning when Monsieur de Burdhes was found strangled in the Woolwich sanctuary, Sir Thomas Welcome inherited ten million pounds. The young Irishman had passed that night with friends, and had a cast-iron alibi, but the fact remained that the tragic death of Monsieur de Burdhes had put into his hands – at twenty-four – one of the largest fortunes in the kingdom. Invoking the famous criminal theory of *cui prodest*, the whole of society immediately closed ranks against the young millionaire. He found himself excluded from clubs and salons alike.

The mystery of Monsieur de Burdhes' murder was never solved. I write 'Monsieur' because, although he was a Dutchman by birth and had lived in London for many years, de Burdhes had made the unusual choice of becoming a naturalised Frenchman – an option of nationality which invited the universal scorn of London. But the feasts which he held in Charing Cross, three times at year, and the eccentricity of his being the founder of a religion recommended him, in spite of everything, to a world of arrogance and elegance enamoured of ostentation and determined individuality. The English have the greatest respect for the liberty of others: any manifestation of energy and personality is certain to please them, for it satisfies a taste for independence which is inherent in their race. To begin to be English it is necessary to be scornful of the ideas and the customs of other countries; to complete the operation one must distinguish and particularise oneself with a full spectrum of idiosyncrasies and an insolent insistence on maintaining one's own habits. In spite of being a naturalised Frenchman, therefore, Monsieur de Burdhes met all the conditions required to interest and win the favour of London. But to permit himself to be killed by an assassin, and by that same act to make a millionaire of a penniless Irishman with the compromising good looks of a Greek shepherd . . . that was too much!

London society made Thomas Welcome pay dearly for the double scandal of the unexpected fortune and the mysterious death. English cant, which had tolerated the disciple of Monsieur de Burdhes, could not accept his heir. . .

Thomas Welcome was forced to leave. His travels were a form of voluntary exile. Nowadays, he travels incessantly.

Without being too precise in his insinuations, but with a feline artistry of implication and hazardous hypothesis – a total mastery of the disturbing science of probability – Ethal sowed his doubts. His slow and monotonous oratory appeared to be detached, but nevertheless contrived to fill me with horror and cut through my last illusions.

The painter went on to the particulars of Monsieur de Burdhes' character and the crime committed in the little house; he seemed to obtain a strange pleasure from it.

'The great Dutchman was always in a kind of waking sleep, stupefied by opium. His vitreous eyes and his bloodless complexion seemed to have preserved all the oppressive lethargy of Oriental poisons . . .'

In the last few months of his life, de Burdhes had tried to combat his terrible lack of sleep by foolish measures. He undertook veritable forced marches, late at night, along the bank of the Thames, all the way from the deserted streets of the West End to the Docks, and even into Whitechapel and other districts into which it was very dangerous to go alone. When Claudius – who knew of what he spoke – advised the madman as to the peril in which these nocturnal expeditions placed him he replied, with a shrug of his shoulders: 'I have seen worse places in the East. Nothing ever happened to me. Anyhow, I like the cut-throat aspect of it: the sinister modernity of the river after midnight, the emptiness of its quays and avenues.' There was a glint in his eye as he spoke, launching into an almost amorous description of the corner of some suspect street, where he had caught a fateful glimpse of a car parked on the bank, reflected in the water of the river – then he stopped suddenly, as if he felt that he had said too much. Nothing was more sadly eloquent than his silence.

This de Burdhes had a passionate love for silence and the night.

Was it as a result of one of these perilous sorties that de Burdhes fell victim to nocturnal aggression? Or was it, on the other hand, the complicity of one of the initiates of the new faith which had contrived to open the door of the house in Woolwich to anonymous assassins? The mystery which surrounded de Burdhes' life became even denser around his death.

It was a tragic and obscure end, in which elements of the criminal and the fantastic were combined. The murder must have been committed by someone familiar with the practises and habits of the victim, because Monsieur de Burdhes was struck down in the middle of his devotions, on a night when he had gone to the house employed by the cult. There he had stayed up late in order to conduct some rite – but what rite? Was he alone, or was someone else with him?

'Hurriedly prepared by Thomas Welcome,' Ethal went on, 'I was taken by him into the temple. The police were already on the scene. They had not moved the corpse. I had never been into the famous lodge before. There was nothing out of place in the hallway or the first two rooms we went through next. The only decoration was a pair of enormous ceramic peacocks posed against walls painted golden yellow. Only the third room merited attention. Thomas, quite overwhelmed, stood rooted to the threshold.

'That room! I can still see it, as if it were only yesterday. A Louis XIV tapestry ran all around it. It depicted a garden with terraces and colonnades, full of gods in the costume of Roman warriors and goddesses in the ankle-length tunics of the time – but a strange discolouration had blackened the faces and the bodies while singularly lightening the material, to such an extent that against the russet sky and amid the blue-grey of fountains the figures no longer seemed like gods and nymphs, but demons with negroid faces whose white eyes transfixed onlookers.

'A very low and very large bed – was it customary for the devotees to lie down on it, I wonder? – was spread out almost at floor level, curtained in mauve silk patterned with golden flowers. At its foot, a monstrous Buddha was on watch; its image reflected in an Empire cheval-glass. The bed had not been disturbed. The air was thick with incense and gum benzoin. A Turkish night-light was still burning.

'Two policemen were in the room. One of them lifted up a door-curtain.

'There, in an alcove line with dull pink silk, on a tumbled heap of cushions, de Burdhes lay dead. He was in evening dress; an enormous white iris was in his buttonhole. He had fallen backwards, so that his knees were higher than his head. That bloodless head, the nostrils already pinched, had rolled to one side. The jawline and the Adam's apple jutted out. The fall must have been violent, and yet his clothes were not crumpled; the front of his shirt had scarcely come apart. One of his hands was clenched about the silver chain of a marvellous censer. There was not a drop of blood, but on the neck, at the place where the flesh is softest and palest, there was a mark like a bruise slowly turning to yellowish brown, as if the flesh had been bitten or slowly sucked for a long time.

'The perfume of the adjoining room still held sway near the corpse, very strongly and tenaciously but it was complicated by the odours of pepper and sandalwood. A little bluish smoke was still rising from the censer.

'In the middle of what practises, I wonder – what secret rite of the mysterious religion – had death surprised de Burdhes? An enormous bunch of black irises and red anthuriums stood up in a silver vase, in a strangely hostile fashion. On a little Hindu altar, surrounded by tulips of glass and caskets of gold and bronze, stood a strange statue moulded in pure black onyx. It was a kind of androgynous goddess with frail arms, a full torso and slim hips, completely nude.

She was demonic and charming at the same time. Two glittering emeralds were inset beneath her eyelids – but between her slender thighs, at the swollen base of the belly, where the sexual organs should have been, there was instead a mocking, menacing little death's-head.'

THE ABYSS

As Ethal's slow and monotonous voice evoked the vision of the little onyx Astarté, the impassive accessory to the murder of Monsieur de Burdhes, the shadows in the studio seemed to become denser and more sinister. It was as if they were woven out of mystery by Ethal's narration.

So Thomas Welcome had supposedly committed a murder. Perhaps the enigmatic quality of his charm was the legacy of his crime. The man who has killed is always surrounded by an atmosphere of terror and beauty. Hallucinatory gleams dart from the eyes of the great murderers of history, forming an aura about their heads, and even the finest of heroes have corpses for their pedestals.

> *Death and Beauty are two profound things*
> *So full of mystery and the azure of legend:*
> *Two equally terrible and fecund sisters*
> *Sharing the same enigma and the same secret.*
> (VICTOR HUGO.)

Ethal did not articulate all these bloody thoughts, nor did he recite that quatrain, but he suggested them to me. Now that he fell silent, I realised that my unreasoning sympathy for Thomas had been, primarily at least, sympathy for the assassin. The melancholy of that handsome face, all its gentleness and energy, was the product of the regret of having killed, and perhaps also – who can say? – of the desire to kill again. The taste of blood is the noblest kind of intoxication, seeing that all beings have the instinct to murder. The struggle for love, the struggle for existence itself, requires the suppression of other creatures. Has not Jehovah himself said: 'By the deaths laid at my door, you shall know that I am the Lord'?

All these counsels of death were insinuated into my ear by a mouth of shadow: a mouth of shadow which might perhaps have been that of the symbolic skull of the little Phoenician idol.

Yes, Thomas Welcome was an instinctive person, and there was the root of all the puissance of his charm. Instincts! Had he not boasted of their wholesome energy in the course of that enthusiastic conversation where, sure of his own eloquence, he had laid out before me his theory that the joy of life was to be found only in adventure, and in the intoxication of sensations released by researches in the unknown?

That life of action had been granted to him by the homicide which made him the master of millions; it was by courtesy of a corpse that he had been able to live his life. But was he free from remorse?

What was that obsession of glaucous eyes which tormented him as it tormented me? What were those severed heads by which he was haunted? Whence came the nightmare of the assassinated native on the banks of the Nile? Whence came that furious compulsion to walk alone in the nocturnal suburbs? Had he inherited that too from Monsieur de Burdhes? Might it not rather be the mania of a criminal who is subconsciously drawn back towards the scene of his crime?

Ethal was silent, but I felt his gaze pressing upon mine. It seemed to bore into my congested brain like a cold sharp-pointed gimlet. His horrible ideas were populating my mind with bloody imagery: the red larvae of murder following the green larvae of opium! That man was a veritable poisoner, in having denounced Thomas to me! That man, who ought to have been healing me, was aggravating my sickness . . .

The impulse to strangle him that I had experienced before made my hands feverish and caused my fingers to clench involuntarily.

Ethal broke the silence himself. 'You really ought to go and look at Gustav Moreau's museum, you know – the one which he left to the State. You will find a valuable lesson in the eyes of some of his heroes and the daring of his symbolism.'

He got up to show me out.

He had lit a torch. Close to the door, he lifted it up, and called my attention to the glass reliquary enshrouded in green serge where his wax doll lay – 'the marvel of Leyden', as he called it. He had formerly reproached me for my failure to appreciate the indefinable and corrupt attraction of that morbid and ostentatious curio modelled in painted wax and dressed in old brocade. Now, he gently separated a flap of material and displayed the doll to me, upright in all its finery, the colour of amadou, with its hair of yellow silk floss flowing from its bonnet of pearls.

'My own goddess,' he said, laughing derisively, slyly caressing it. 'She may be dressed in the cast-offs of the centuries, but no death's-head grins beneath her robe. She is Death herself: Death with all her make-up and the translucency of her decompositions. Our Lady of the Seven Carcases! You are already acquainted with Our Lady of the Seven Lusts – and one cannot always worship Our Lady of the Seven Dolours.'

February 1899
'All marching in step, men and women alike!'

That ignoble refrain, which Ethal chanted in my ear the other evening – along with his anecdotes and his jeers regarding the mass of humanity assembled for that first night, with a leitmotif of infamy introduced into the biography of each and every one – continues to deform and deprave everything around me. The calumny has made its way from the dunghill of vices complaisantly retailed by Claudius to the cadaver of Monsieur de Burdhes, bringing forth a hideous flourishing growth of lubricious images and shameful thoughts. That Ethal! He has blighted eveything, soiled everything within me, like some virus poisoning my blood – and now it is mud which runs in my veins. 'All marching in step!'

I am haunted by obscenity. All objects, even works of art, have become obscene in my eyes. *Everything* has taken on an equivocal and ignoble taint, imposing base ideas upon me and degrading my senses and my intellect.

It is as if I were possessed, and walking abroad in the forest of Tiffauges described by Huysmans: that sexual nightmare of old forked trees with gaping crevices in their bark has taken odious form in the midst of modern life. I am accursed, wretched and mad. I have been bewitched by ancient black magic.

Six years ago I bought from a dealer on the quays a Debucourt which represents, in the softened and delicately shaded tones typical of the painter, two young women holding one another tightly and playing with a dove. Why does this Debucourt now inspire me with only unhealthy ideas? The engraving is fairly well-known; it's title is 'The Revived Bird'. The two figures, enveloped by the gauzes and floating buckrams of the epoch, have healthy powdered complexions and an aristocratic beauty. Why should such innocent and graceful creatures now be associated in my mind with the memory of the Princess of Lamballe and Marie Antoinette?

'All marching in step, men and women alike!' It is the most ignominious calumny of the time, the most odious pamphlets of Father Duchêne, all the filth of the Jacobite clubs, that this engraving now brings to life as I look at it. All of that is embodied in the gesture which one of the women is making, separating the folds of her buckram shawl and placing between her breasts a cowering dove. My memory is beset by all the scandalous ordure heaped upon the liaison of Marie-Antoinette and the unfortunate princess. It is as though I am seized by a fever: a frenzy of sexual excitement, and of cruelty too. I find myself suddenly transported into the remoteness of a bygone century, to the precincts of a prison on a warm and stormy day, seething with rumours of a popular uprising. A sweaty and clamorous crowd of men in red bonnets – street-porters with brutal faces, unbuttoned shirts on their hairy chests – jostles me and stifles me; I am surrounded by eyes full of hate. The heavy air reeks of alcohol, filthy rags and squalor. Bare arms are waving pikes aloft. A great cry goes up as I see raised towards the leaden sky a severed head: a head drained of blood, with fixed and extinguished eyes; the image of decapitation which haunted Thomas Welcome's nights.

The remorse of the handsome Irishman has become my obsession too.

It is the head of a woman. Drunken men are passing it from hand to hand, kissing it on the lips and slapping its face. Their low and receding brows are the foreheads of convicts. One of them has a mass of knotted viscera rolled around his bare arm like bloody thongs; he is joking with his comrades. His lips are ornamented with an equivocal blond moustache which looks as if it consists of pubic hairs. Under this false moustache he is smiling broadly, despicably, outrageously. The head swings above the crowd, brandished at the tip of a pike, cheered, barracked, insulted and mocked. It is the head of the Princess of Lamballe, which the revolutionaries powdered and revived with make-up, setting the hair in curls, before they carried it to Penthièvre, and from there to the Temple, parading it under the queen's windows . . .

I regain my self-possession, broken, revolted and charmed by horror. There is something corrupt in my being. The dreams which delight me are frightful.

March 1899
Slums!

Ethal has given me a taste for the slums; he has awakened in me a dangerous curiosity regarding streetwalkers and guttersnipes. The bulging eyes of cut-throats, the soliciting eyes of suburban strumpets, all the acute and brutal depravity of beings reduced by wretchedness to the elementary gestures of instinct, attracts and fascinates me.

I arrive in the outlying boulevards in the evening, to prowl about interestedly, surveying the scene, on the look-out for whores. Low prostitution excites and entices me with its reek of musk, alcohol and white grease-paint.

Worse: after the crapulous intoxication of cheap dance-halls, I am overtaken by a hysterical desire to follow the couples to the peep-holed doors and grimy staircases of cheap lodging-houses. There, with some chance companion on my arm, I have listened to the sounds which are audible through the partition walls: the delirious fevers of sexual excitement, like the love-making of wild beasts; the noise of surprise attacks! Sometimes encounters begun with kisses finish in blows, and one hears, from the room above, the scrape of muffled struggles, atrocious hand-to-hand conflicts, and the voices of strangled women crying out for help. The creaking of mattresses moved by vibration provides me with less pleasure than certain frightful silences which follow rattles and sobs. Then, a piercing anguish clutches as if at my heart, at the thought that a crime might have been committed, and the descent of the police imminent.

To think that I, the Duc de Fréneuse, have passed hours and hours waiting and dreading a raid: a terrible raid, which would send the pimps and the girls hurtling from their beds and hidey-holes, fill the corridors with frightened galloping, and end with my being escorted to the Prefecture.

Oh, the poignant fear of ambushes and brawls, the sweating vigils in the furnished thieves' kitchens of the Boulevard Ornano and the Quatre-Chemins – and the anticipation of the final stab which might perhaps put an end to everything!

Yes, I am on the very brink of the abyss.

Ethal can lead me no further.

A GLIMMER OF HOPE

One evening when I slept beside a frightful jewess . . .
                                      BAUDELAIRE

> *Adieu: I sense that in this life*
> *I shall never see you again!*
> *God passes, he leads me to you and forgets me.*
> *In losing you, I feel that I love you.*
>
> *No tears, no vain complaint!*
> *I know enough to respect the future.*
> *When the sail comes to bear you away,*
> *I will smile as I watch you go.*
>
> *You go away full of hope,*
> *Proudly you will return;*
> *But those who will endure your absence,*
> *You will not recognise.*
>
> . . . .
> . . . .
>
> *One day you will perhaps realise*
> *The value of a heart which understands you.*
> *The good which is found in knowing it*
> *And what is suffered in losing it.*

24 March 1899

I read these verses by de Musset quite by chance, while mechanically turning the pages of a book. Why do they fill my eyes with tears, today? I have not wept once in the last twenty years, and even in my childhood I was not as easily moved as other children. Why, today, am I dolorously and deliciously moved by reading that *adieu*? Why have I opened this particular book? Like others of my generation, I am deeply scornful of de Musset – but look how the quatrains of the author of *Rolla* have capsized my heart in a sea of tears.

> *Adieu: I sense that in this life*
> *I shall never see you again!*

It is because I have never felt that kind of poignant distress, or the pride of a lover resigned to the departure of a mistress who is abandoning him. I have never loved.

The joy to which even the least of artisans and the most humble of bureaucrats lay claim – that minute of superhuman existence which every man and woman is supposed to enjoy at least once, thanks to love – has always been a closed book to me. I am a freak and a fool.

I have never been prey to ignoble instincts, and yet all the base ordures to which existence is party, magnified by the imagination, have made my life a sequence of nightmares. I have never had the gift of sensibility; I have never known the gift of tears.

I have always sought to fill up the illimitable void which is within me by recourse to the atrocious and the monstrous. Lust has been my damnation. It has deformed my sight and depraved my dreams, multiplying tenfold all the horrors of ugliness and transforming all the beauty of nature, so cleverly that only the repugnant side of persons and things is apparent to me. Thus I subsist in the punishment of my sterile depravity.

Evil survives the annihilation of everything else.

I have never breathed the perfume of the little blue flower of sentiment, which even little working-girls – apprentice milliners and plasterer's labourers – have in their hearts at sixteen years of age. More than that: rancour has always led me to scoff at it, to jeer at that adolescent perfume when it found a home in the hearts of others. I have never had a true friend and I have never had a true mistress. I have only known birds of passage: one-night stands or month-long caprices; all the girls that ever had the honour of my breath and my lips were girls that I paid – generously – in the morning; they must always have known that I did not love them.

Women have never been anything to me but flesh to be experienced – not even a pleasure! Avid for sensations and analytical by temperament, I have studied myself in association with them as if they were so many anatomical models. Not one ever provided me with the anticipated thrill – and rightly so, because I watched out for that thrill as if I were hidden in a bush, lying nervously in wait for it. It is not to be discovered by knowing sensuality, but rather in unconscious and wholesome joy. I have spoiled all the pleasure in my life by making an instrument of it, instead of living it. The quest for refinement and the careful research of the unusual are fatal; they lead to decomposition and to annihilation.

That moment of abandon which the meanest of streetwalkers, once her day's work is complete, gives to her pimp, I have never obtained for myself. God only knows if I have squandered all the money I have paid out to such women! Everyone, man and woman alike, senses that I am a being somehow set outside nature: an automaton galvanised into some simulacrum of life by covetous desires, but an automaton – that is to say, a dead man – nevertheless. My cadaverous eyes make people afraid.

Today, however, those cadaverous eyes are full of tears.

One day you will perhaps realise
The value of a heart which understands you.
The good which is found in knowing it
And what is suffered in losing it.

Paris, 25 March 1899
I re-read my journal yesterday. What stupidity! A pretty thing, the sentimental crisis of the Duc de Fréneuse! I have been tenderised by de Musset, and behold – I have the soul of a milliner now!

Why did I weep? Today, I understand the reason.

It was that conversation heard by chance through the partition-wall in that hotel-room where I ended up the other night. It was the two or three phrases exchanged between my neighbours which turned me upside-down. From the miry depths of my shaken being an old regret has climbed to the surface of the bog – and, watered by a tear, has flourished.

That flophouse in the Rue des Abbesses, with its sign lit throughout the night and *rooms for one franc* inscribed in transparent letters on the frosted glass of its lantern, that semi-slum to which I know the way, which had seen me so many times before . . .

> *On a moonless evening, two together,*
> *Sending my pain to sleep on a hazardous bed.*

(I now quote Baudelaire to excuse my worst failings . . .)

It was in that sixth-rate fleapit, where I had failed to find my road to Damascus, that I thought I heard the words of redemption.

Is that sufficiently ridiculous?

I went there with a girl who was neither ugly nor pretty, gathered up in I know not what dive, motivated far less by desire for her depraved appearance than by that craving for strong sensation which has been a bitter and mordant taste in my mouth ever since I first drank that foul wine. The setting and the atmosphere of adventure which surrounds these escapades interests me far more than the partner I select, for I have a mad hunger for danger, an addiction to low and louche locales.

Oh, the beauty of sinister promiscuity and equivocal companionship; the atrocious risks of unexpected encounters in those banal dens of vice and vagabondage, of cozenage and crime.

Anyhow, scarcely had we crossed the threshold than the girl displeased me. I paid her off – she was so very listless even in her haggling – and, laid low by fatigue, I went to bed. I lay there listening; the thin partitions between the rooms of such hotels are always replete with unforeseen lessons. Sure enough, less than ten minutes had gone by when whispering commenced in the room next door. A couple who had fallen silent when they heard us come in now resumed their discussion. A young voice whose freshness astonished me merrily burst through the rustlings of the bed-linen and the creaking of the mattress. With turtle-dove cooings, in the half-fainting manner of a happy lover, the woman spoke in a thick Parisian accent.

'You feel so good . . . you feel like ripe corn. I love you! You are as fair as corn too . . . I am so hungry for you!' I could imagine the way she was lying, the gestures of her hands: the image imposed itself on my closed eyes. The little voice, thoroughly suburban but as murmurous as a spring, was smothered by a cascade of kisses.

The couple were in love.

What manner of man was it to whom a sixteen-year-old voice spoke such intoxicating things?

'You feel like ripe corn . . . you are as fair as corn . . . I am so hungry for you . . .'

Never had such things been said to me.

That night, the couple loved one another very much. The man remained silent, and it was not until first light that I heard his voice, saying: 'How bright your eyes are, Mimi!'

My overexcited imagination once again imposed on me a vision of the gestures and smiles of awakening lovers. The girl, in her voice like a bubbling stream, replied with delectable mischievousness: 'Are my eyes bright? It is because you have looked at me, monsieur.'

Their games and their kisses resumed, extending through the room. Bare feet pursued one another hither and yon. The girl had jumped out of the bed and the boy tried to fetch her back.

From the sound of their comings and goings I deduced that they were now getting dressed. She was not a whore, nor he a pimp, for they did not intend to linger in bed all morning. They were a couple of honest lovers: he, some workman in a hurry to go to work; she, some apprentice who had to lie to her parents in order that she might spend the whole night with her lover. She must have invented an excuse: some vitally important piece of work to do at the shop, which required an all-night session . . .

They were probably both young.

I was curious to see their faces. I got up and stood behind the venetian blinds, with my bare feet on the tiles, undressed at the open window, keeping watch on the entrance of the hotel . . .

He came out first, wearing a beige overcoat and a bowler hat. He was tall and lean, of insignificant apearance – evidently some petty bureaucrat or an employee in a department store, no more than twenty-two years old. She, for the sake of prudence, did not venture out until two minutes later, but he waited for her at the end of the street.

She was charming – blonde, like him, with her hair in crazy curls, untidily gathered beneath a little black hat, which she had decorated herself with bluebells and poppies. She had a little collar of black cloth, and a thin dress of blue foulard completed her outfit. She trotted lithely away on the toes of her yellow ankle-boots. Love had made her lithe, and a little pale and hollow-eyed too. But her youthful little figure was so happy that she embodied all the joys of spring.

They had not forty years between them.

The wine-merchants and the greengrocers were beginning to put back their shutters. She rejoined him at the street-corner and there, once again, they embraced for a long time.

I spied on them from my window.

At last, they separated. After taking ten paces, she returned yet again for one last goodbye, but it was too late. He had turned the corner. She accelerated her pace, with her shoulders suddenly bowed, as if weighed down by a profound sadness, she disappeared.

Adieu: I sense that in this life
I shall never see you again!

. . . .

In losing you, I feel that I love you.

I went back to bed and promptly fell into a drunken sleep. It was a troubled sleep, shot through with incoherent and contradictory images: Thomas Welcome, Ethal's wax doll and various figures observed in the slums filed past my bedhead in turn . . . and then yet more faces: faces from my early youth, even from my chidhood; faces that I thought I had forgotten. Among others, there was the face of Jean Destreux, a farm-hand who had been run over on our estate one evening at harvest-time, after falling from a cart laden with corn. I was only eleven years old at the time.

Why has that figure reappeared to me now? I have never seen it since the accident. Thomas Welcome resembles him a little, but I was not previously aware of the resemblance. Is it the apparition of Thomas which has brought back that of Jean Destreux, or has the phantom of my childhood arisen of its own accord from my past?

I awoke with the sun shining directly on my bed, to the sound of an organ playing under the window. It was after eleven.

Outside, there was the most beautiful blue sky. It was one of those March mornings which seem more like May, which sometimes greet the Paris spring with glorious azure. On the boulevards there were barrows fully-laden with gillyflowers and tea-roses, yellow tulips and sweet and heady narcissi, all pushed along by ambulant merchants. Housekeepers standing at the edges of the pavements were buying them; working girls were putting them in their buttonholes as they passed by. Paris had already been at work for five hours and people were leaving their workplaces to swarm around a seller of fried potatoes. There was a whole flock of young and bare-headed female burnishers in black smocks, amusing themselves.

I happened upon this volume of de Musset after returning from the hotel, and my fingers began turning the pages mechanically – and, in the empty and luxurious living death of my womanless existence, discovered these verses full of tenderness and loving distress:

One day you will perhaps realise
The value of a heart which understands you.

I know now why I wept.

THE REFUGE

Paris, 28 March.

Jean Destreux has returned to me in a dream, and all my childhood with him: the childhood I spent at Fréneuse in rich and rainy Normandy.

I remember watching him working on the farm. I used to escape from the château in order to go to play with him. I had only to go through the little birch-wood on the far side of the lawn, near the entrance of the park, and open the gate to the orchard; the lazy and grassy orchard.

The farm!

The rooms at Fréneuse were so vast and high, and so very bright with their large French windows and the gleam of their polished parquet floors – but it was a sad brightness. All the melancholy of the sky, the open country and the changing seasons entered the house by way of those windows. Oh, the dry austerity of their little white curtains! How lonely I felt there; how hostile the things around me seemed to be!

There were huge pieces of furniture, in a heavy and sullen style, surmounted by the heads of lions and rams and other Imperial insignia. I was always bumping into their corners; contact with them was cold and sickening. I did not like them in the least. Nor was I any fonder of the massive mahogany chairs which seemed to be squatting in front of the wall-hangings ... and what hangings! They were glossy, full of great eagles and golden laurels – captives, one might have thought, in the dull green or crimson depths. The waxed parquets, where diamond-shaped pieces alternated with rosettes, were like an ice-field, like satin to the touch and slippery underfoot.

The great halls of Fréneuse! I shivered there even in midsummer. And the tops of the trees in the park, visible in the clear glass of the transoms, eternally agitated – as if they were filling up my childish soul with distress!

How infinitely preferable to the cold luxury of those vast empty rooms were the dairy, the barns and the byre: the endless dripping of the dairy; the dusty and odourous shadows of the barns; the suffocating tepidity of the byre where the cows were so comfortable!

I liked the dairy best of all: overpowering afternoons in the July heat; the odour of curdled milk, seemingly fresher than fresh, with its particular acidity; the musty scent of slightly-soured cream fermenting in the air currents streaming through the open casements. What a strange and powerful sense of wellbeing I had as I drank in all of that! And the red hands of the farmer on the bloated udders of the cows, the heavy fall of cow-dung in the straw . . .

And I liked the hasty search for eggs laid in hiding-places: eggs which we sometimes found in the corners of the racks when we furtively stole, on tip-toe, into the deserted stables . . . and all the mad adventures, when I galloped through the timber-framed barns with the farmer's children!

Yes, I liked all that far better than the bleak days spent in the house: the hours of study in the library, under the tuition of the abbé. I even liked it better than the few minutes of conversation I had with my mother, who was always extended on her chaise longue when I went up to greet her, every morning and every night!

My mother's room! It was always decorated with white lilacs, and there was always a fire, even in midsummer. It was scented with ether and creosote, and another odour which, as I detected it at the threshold, lifted up my heart. My mother! I can still see her long hands, heavy with rings: her diaphanous and carefully-manicured hands, where the blue of the veins stood out beneath the surface. They were gentle, caressing and sweetly-scented; they lingered upon my head, tousling my hair, digressing for a moment to straighten my tie, then lifting once again to my lips, to claim a kiss.

They were soft and delicate hands, impregnated by the finest scents: the pale, slow hands of a woman condemned to die young. And yet I hesitated to touch them. Oh, how I preferred the sweaty bodies of the farmer's children! They radiated health and strength. All that lost health, the fruits of the earth, the odour of wheat and moist leaves, haunts me still; it has brought back to me the spectre of Jean Destreux.

29 March 1899
Jean Destreux!

There was a great deal of work to be done out in the fields. On autumn evenings, when the furrows fumed in the mist and the tired horses plodded slowly back to the stables. I would slip away from the château and race madly to the edge of the little wood. There, heart hammering, I watched out for the return of the horses to the farm. I watched out especially for *his* return. He was so merry, so good to all of us – all the little children. His good spirits animated the whole farm. It was as if the very air of the place had been transformed since he had returned from his military service.

He had served in Africa. He still wore his spahi's cap while he worked. Africa! He had brought back from the Arab lands a great fund of stories, which he would act out theatrically, with laughter bubbling upon his lips and joy in his eyes. The irises of his eyes were so blue that it was as if the profundity of the sky were smiling in his ruddy face. He was tall, lean and muscular; his hair was the colour of ripe rye; the desert sun had tanned, dried and burnished him. With his bright head of hair and the fluffy moustache superimposed on his baked brown complexion, he was like a great vine-shoot ablaze in the warmth of the August days. He was indefatigable in his work, and his good example, his buffoonery and his devil-may-care attitude, motivated the other harvesters, driving out their natural indolence.

On winter evenings, when the labourers gathered together to entertain themselves, he would sometimes don his military uniform and inspect a parade of his bewildered fellow farm-hands.

As for myself, I loved him for the frankness of his great bright eyes, for his insuppressible gaiety, for the stories that he told, and for his unfailing gentleness towards us. Then again, he taught me how to handle a sabre for my amusement: 'Parry! Thrust!' And he knew such diverting songs: stirring and vigorous marching songs; the irreverent and indecent refrains of the guard-house; and yet others, chanted so monotonously and so sadly that tears would come whenever we heard them. Those, he had learned far away, in the distant countries of Africa where he had served in the army.

On Sunday, while the other farm-hands were either at the tavern or at vespers, he would stay behind to read old almanacs in the barn. Then, I would go to find him relaxing in the hay. The farmer's children would already be there. Muffled laughter would greet my arrival. Jean Destreux would read out prose and verse from the old periodicals. He had heaps of them.

The vivifying odour of the hay and the harvest; the shadowed frames of the sheds; the luminous rays falling from a skylight; scintillating dust-motes dancing in the warm air; the play of light and shadow in the granaries; the meadow-grasses gathered in; all the heavy thatched roofs . . . and Jean Destreux, with his shirt of khaki linen open at the neck, was the living incarnation of all of that.

I took little or no account of it all. I was incapable, then, of appreciating the colours, the perfumes and the forms. I experienced them powerfully, unconsciously, with an undeveloped soul, dark and burning – so happy in all my sensations as sometimes to wish that I might die – but without analysing their rewards. It was all of a piece, synthesized into a whole by the force of ignorance. That kind of ignorance is fortunate, isn't it?

Oh, the heavy labour in the open fields, and the furrows fuming in the first chilly mists of October, when men and horses came so wearily home! Every evening intoxicated me, as if I were smelling the odour of earth for the first time. I loved to sit behind an embankment, at the edge of a field, among the dead leaves, and listen delightedly to the sound of voices dying in the distance: the voices of exhausted labourers riding on a cart. I loved the odour of raked leaves too, the freshness of rain and wet branches, and my soul would lose all its strength as I watched the sun sinking towards the horizon where it would set.

O my childhood! O sad and rainy Normandy!

Is there any reason why I cannot recapture all that? After all, who can say whether that calm and melancholy might not be the cure I need? Oh, if I might wash away all the shame and all the stains of my life in the lustral water of memory! An immersion in verdure, a baptism of dew – of those November dews which harden into frost, when the vapour of furrows awakes as silver in the dawn – *that* is what is wanting in my sore and falsified soul and my broken-down imagination. That is how the sword blunted in evil combat might be sharpened again.

Yes, I must return to Fréneuse! I must escape from Paris, from the deleterious and baleful atmosphere where my sensuality is aggravated, where the hostility of beings and things engenders within me impulses which frighten me. Paris corrodes, depraves and terrifies me; in Paris my hands itch with the urge to murder; in Paris I grow ulcers; Paris has made me cowardly, libertine and cruel.

The little church of Fréneuse! There I was baptised. There, for better or for worse, I made my first communion. There I followed the funeral-procession of my mother. She rests in the village cemetery: a poor little cemetery, enclosed by a wall of dry earth, which the church shelters with its shadow.

What might I learn from that grave which I have not visited for more than six years?

> *They rest. The alarms and sorrows of sad and ardent life*
> *No longer haunt their peaceful pillow.*
> *Dawns and nightfalls bathe them with their tears,*
> *Life is a detour on the road to the tomb.*

Should I examine the shadow of that road? What do I have to offer that dead woman?

I know that this is the continuation of my sentimental crisis – but at whatever cost, I must leave. Fréneuse can be my sanctuary. I shall go without leaving a forwarding address; it will be as if I had vanished into the night. I will disappear, and no one shall prevent me; no one must know where I am, especially Ethal. His occult influence would pursue me. It is from him that I must escape. He is my evil spirit, the hand of shadow extended over my thoughts and deeds: the hand with the horrible rings; the monstrous and hairy hand whose gleaming pustules of pearl ooze poison; the predatory and agonising talon which embraces my impuissance and which – if I do not withdraw from its grip – will surely drive me to crime.

This slow suicide, and the pangs of anguish in the midst of which I struggle, are dreadful! I have had enough of agony! I want to live!

How triumphant Ethal would be if he knew what terror he inspires in me!

And yet I shall be shattering my life, repudiating an entire past and all the pleasures of that past. For that past, which I propose to discard, has had its pleasures – guilty, abominable pleasures, but pleasures nevertheless! And I propose to do this on the strength of a spectral visitation: the inanity of a dream; the bloodied image of a ploughman killed twenty years ago!

I saw him again last night, with his great beautiful, astonished and limid eyes and his suntanned face, his spahi's cap perched on his bright head of hair – and, at the corners of his lips, that red trail: the flood of lukewarm blood risen from his breast. And across his torso, on his unbuttoned and sweat-stained shirt, was the track of the wheel: a track of mud and blood, but very little blood, more like a bruise than a wound . . . the crumpling and crushing effect of the cart which passed over his body . . . the lean and muscular body of a young man of twenty-six.

It was in August. Twilight was falling. In the farmyard,

where the last rays of the sun lingered, three great carts were arriving: three heavy carts loaded with odorant harvested grain. They had run up all the slopes, jolted in all the ruts, as they had so many times before, because it was harvest-time. We were lying on top of the heap of dry grass, with the other haymakers.

We were both on the middle cart. He was standing up with a bunch of poppies attached by a thread to his waistcoat, gesticulating, cutting a dash, perhaps a little drunk – the day had been so warm! – and he was sounding with all his might the great conch-shell which, in Normandy, serves as the trumpet of the harvesters. All around him, stretched out like the hayricks, girls and boys were laughing and jostling, with the rosiness of pleasure and fatigue in their cheeks and sweat on their brows. In the midst of them, I breathed in all the joy of the life of the farm, shared in all the happy animation of that beautiful evening.

A cart-wheel sank into a rut; the entire edifice of bundled hay swayed – and the man, losing his balance, fell down, rolling on the ground. The third cart was following behind. The driver, perhaps drunk, could not contrive to halt his horses. There was one great cry, and they rushed headlong over him. The horses did not trample him with their hooves – they avoided him easily enough – but the cart-wheels continued to turn with the blindness of mere matter.

Blood trickled from his mouth; a little mud soiled his bruised breast; the great beautiful eyes, a little stupefied, were still wide open.

And it is that death which now calls me to Fréneuse! How he resembles Thomas Welcome! If I had not recognised Jean Destreux, I would dread that some evil had overtaken his double, out there in the distant Indies.

LASCIATE OGNI SPERANZA

5 April 1899. Fréneuse

I have returned here in the hope of a cure and have found nothing but *ennui*. One by one I have visited the empty rooms, the rooms I left behind twenty years ago. They have not awakened a single emotion in me. Fréneuse, which contained the whole of my childhood, now seems to be a foreign land. In every room whose doors were opened for me by the gardener the fusty odour affected my sensibilities disagreeably. Even in the room where my mother spent the last months of her life I experienced nothing but the dry and cold hostility of an old provincial dwelling examined for the first time by a chance inheritor.

The gardener's wife opened the Venetian blinds slightly; a little sunlight leaked through the interstices, awakening the dust on the marble tops of the chests of drawers. Beneath their enshrouding dust-sheets, the rigidity of the chairs retreated into shadow. In the great drawing-room I noticed that the floorboards were rotten and giving way. The pedestal table in the centre was leaning slightly, disturbing the glacial harmony of that vast rectangular space set among the green hemlocks and brocaded gold lyres of its wall-hangings.

On the first floor, a musty odour of ether still remained, tenaciously clinging to the panels of a cupboard. Mechanically, I opened a bathroom cabinet. Empty medicine-bottles were still ranged on its shelves; I read their labels. It was one of the little rooms where the sick woman liked to go, to seek solace in her suffering, far from her own chamber; this was one of the dispensaries from which she tended her sickness. In a drawer which I pulled open I found a little fan spangled with mica, resting on a bed of dried rose-petals amid faded lilac ribbons. Among these ribbons I happened upon a portrait: a yellowed photograph of a child, blurred and almost effaced. I was quite unable to recognise myself.

That evening, alone in the great dining-room ornamented with the antlers of stags and other hunting trophies,
leaning my elbows on the tablecloth before an empty cup,
I waited until nightfall for some emotion or some spectre
to surge forth from all those things which had once been
my life! I hoped that a tear might ascend to my eye, that
some fear-inducing frisson might clutch at my heart and
set it to beating a little faster.

Would the shade of Jean Destreux – whose apparition
had brought me here – come forth?

I heard the nibbling of mice in the wainscot. Perhaps
they were surprised and disappointed to find me there, in
that sad and uninhabited place, alone in the silence of the
sleeping countryside. The Unknown that I awaited did not
manifest itself. No tears came to my eyes. What kind of
man have I become? My soul has congealed and dried up,
and can never be revitalised; it is as if a hunger for
enjoyment and a thirst for suffering surrounded something
petrified and hardened.

I wished so fervently that I might be moved, or frightened! A single tear, a single pang of fear, might have
signalled a change in the direction of my life: a gateway
opening to the future! But the future was playing with me.
I felt not the lightest embrace of the smallest anguish,
merely an acute consciousness of the uselessness of my
experiment, of the childish step I had taken, of the ridicu-
lousness of my forlorn presence in that deserted château.

When the bell of the village church had sounded one
o'clock I went out on the front steps to breathe the cold
night air. A dog barked in a farmyard; the whole kennel
responded with growls. I went to the stables, unleashed
two Pont-Audemer dogs, and took them out into the park.

The great trees were quite still and skeletal – spring
comes so late to Normandy! – but the sky was so full of
fleecy clouds filtering the moonbeams that it seemed as if a
spring of luminous milk were flowing through the mist!
What tranquillity! What solitude! I could not hear the
stirring of a single leaf, but the odour of young bark and

damp moss filled the whole park with freshness. I returned by way of the kitchen-garden. The lights of the sash-windows shone gently in the moonlight, and I had a momentary desire to cool my burning forehead against the glass.

How cold its bluish lustre was! As cold as the glass in my casements when, as an adolescent enfevered by puberty, I used to rise from my bed and run barefoot to lean my head against their moist surfaces!

My desire to see the immense and tranquil sky evaporated then, like the mist. What were the ephemeral fevers of my past days, compared to the appalling erosion to which my flesh and my soul had now fallen victim?

I re-entered the house at dawn, enfeebled by fatigue and soaked with dew. I was bruised and aching, weighed down as if by a tumour by the physical lassitude of my indifference, of my dismal inability to weep and suffer!

What will it take to burst that abcess of rancour and aborted tenderness, that bloated ganglion of stifled passions and dead dolours? What atrocious forceps and clamps will have to be brought to bear in order to deliver me of that abominable and burdensome foetus which was my soul?

How shall I come by the gift of tears? I would surely be saved if I could only weep. If I could only recover the spark which reignited the fires of emotion that night in Montmartre, in that three-franc flophouse in the Rue des Abbesses . . .

Fréneuse, 6 April 1899
Today I was confronted with a lamentable and pitiful procession of farmers and local dignitaries, including the parish priest. Everyone knows everything in these bucolic holes. My arrival could not be kept secret, and the village is needy. All the avarice and guile of Normans lying in wait for a windfall has come to the château to beg and complain.

I have given five hundred francs to the priest and reduced the rents of three farmers, but I did not receive the mayor – nor the schoolmaster, who wanted to take me to visit the new school-buildings, built to the plans of a Parisian architect: some monstrous modern construction, if I may judge by the high pretentious roofs which now disfigure the left-hand side of the park.

The school! I do not even want to return to the farm. It has sufficed to listen to the manager enumerating the improvements made during my absence to meet the demands of the tenants: ditches and conduits; slate roofs to replace the thatch; improved stables and model dairies; paved swimming-baths for bathing the horses. Forty thousand francs kept back from the rents, over three years, for 'modernisation'.

No, I have not the slightest desire to return to the farm. Jean Destreux would not have been Jean Destreux under the framework of a slate roof, between the tiled walls of an English stable with pitch-pine boxes instead of the old-style stalls. People are created by their environment, and when that is destroyed, their memory is obliterated. I did not come here to exorcise a ghost, and I have been spared any such sorrow, by virtue of the fact that since my arrival at Fréneuse, all the ghosts have vanished.

How dismal the region is in April! Springtime is tremulous, harsh and hesitant here. All the showers of March are still suspended in the air, the leaves and shoots reluctant. The cultivated fields curve away to the horizon, bearing the tentative thrust of young rye and green corn. It is the childhood of the harvest, but it is a rickety and destitute childhood under the sour north wind and the menace of an eternally cloudy sky. Oh, how stony and raw Normandy skies seem at the end of March! It was their incurable distress, appearing in the transoms of the high windows of Fréneuse, which saddened my whole childhood and caused my soul to sicken with that strange desire that I have always painted over with acid sensations and other lands.

It is the same with Fréneuse itself! The rooms, which seemed so vast when I left, now seem shabby. The park I used to love, whose woods once seemed so mysterious and murmurous, is less than three hectares; it could almost be taken in my hand. At the end of every path one can see the fields. The monotony of those fields engulfs and shrivels the soul.

Being in Fréneuse is like being on an island battered by a sea of ploughed fields, and I now understand the origin of that stormy heaviness, in which I can scarcely breath, where I await I know not what miracle to tear apart the atmosphere of anguish which hangs upon those furrows and that park. I feel that I am locked up here, imprisoned as in a lighthouse, and the infinite extent of the plain gives me the same sick feeling that one sometimes suffers when looking out to sea!

The sea! The watery eyes of Jean Destreux! It is because those eyes had in them everything that I desired, everything that I have since sought and everything that I still pursue, that they have remained in my memory. They were the first revelation of an impossible good fortune: the luck of the soul! They were the pure eyes of my years of innocence; it was only after I had been depraved and corrupted by contact with men that I began madly to covet the green eyes. The obsession of those glaucous eyes is a symptom of my fall from grace. What a frightful fixity of adoration there was in my loves and my desires, when I was a child!

Perhaps the secret of good fortune is to love all creatures and all things without preferring any one!

I remember reading somewhere that every creature points towards God, but none can reveal him. Because our experience stops short, every creature turns us away from God.

Same day, nine o'clock in the evening
A little while ago, while returning from the cemetery, I made a long detour so that I would not have to pass through the village. I wanted to avoid the women gossiping on the doorsteps, the children coming out of school, and the men holding discussions outside the saddlery and the

blacksmith's forge. It seemed to me that my horrid reputation must have preceded and followed me here. Irritated by the anticipation of inane laughter and whispers, I clung to the hedgerows and made my way behind the houses.

A gypsy caravan was parked in the middle of a field near Castel-Vieux. Outside, a woman was cooking on a little cast-iron stove. Tranquilly seated on a chair, she watched the evening meal as it cooked. Damp linen was hung up to dry at the windows of the caravan. Two children – half-naked urchins with superb black eyes – were teasing a nanny-goat which must have been reckoned one of the family. Grubby little hands were avidly kneading her udders, greedy mouths trying to seize her teats.

The sky was softened by the twilight, striped near the horizon by vermilion-tinted clouds. The wind had dropped. Through the gentle warmth of the evening the silhouette of a man approached, weighed down by a sack of potatoes which he carried on his shoulder. Silently, the man kissed the woman on the forehead. Then, letting his sack fall to the ground, he untied the goat and took hold of the two little ones, hugging them enthusiatically. He was a big, lean man with a daring face, illuminated by very white teeth. His manner was dark and joyous at the same time as if the scent of broom clung to his rags in spite of the sweat and the dust. He took stock of me, insolently, and burst into nasal laughter, still greedily embracing the kids.

I stopped to look at him but I went on my way without saying anything, repeating to myself in a low voice a passage from André Gide's *The Fruits of the Earth*:

'I became a vagrant in order to make contact with other vagrants; I am tenderly enamoured of everyone who knows where to get warm, and I have a passionate love for all vagabonds.'

Presently, after dining in the solitary intimacy of my own company, I went into the library and picked out a volume at random, to relieve the tedium of waiting for bed-time. It turned out to be an Italian text of Dante's

Divine Comedy. I leafed through it idly, and fell upon the passage which begins: *Lasciate ogni speranza . . .*

Abandon all hope!

These words echo throughout Fréneuse.

A CONSIGNMENT OF
FLOWERS

Fréneuse. April 1899

My luggage is packed. In an hour I will have left Fréneuse.
In five hours, I will be in Paris. I can stand no more! I can
stand no more!

This solitude is suffocating me; the silence weighs me
down. Oh, the anguish of last night, in confrontation with
the dead tranquillity of the town and the open country! In
Paris one can at least feel the breath of a whole population
abed: so many lusts remain on watch, so many ambitions,
disquiets and hatreds! Here all humanity falls exhaustedly
into sleep as if into a hole. Oh, the lethargy of these farms,
these mute hamlets under the vast sky – the frightful
anguish of all those night-dark places, without a single
illuminating spark of life!

Leaning on my elbows at the open window, I had the
sensation of being in a cemetery. It was as if I had been
forgotten in the panic of a plague which had emptied the
province, left alone in the midst of desolation. It seemed to
me that all those villages might never wake again – and I
felt a violent and commanding need for some affirmation
of life, a lust to bite and kiss which dried out my mouth, a
rage to touch and embrace which made my fingers clench
painfully.

If I had still possessed the common knowledge of former
times, I would have gone out in search of a farm girl. In
town one always knows where to go when such frenzies
takes hold. I have experienced these atrocious hysterical
crises before. It was only two years ago that I had a similar
attack, and it only required me to come to Fréneuse to
reawaken the horrible malady. But I came here in search of
calm! I believed that this place would provide me with a
refuge! On the contrary . . .

The solitude! The silence! How strongly they excite evil instincts! *Ennui* causes the sap to rise in all the poisonous blooms of the soul. It is in the cells of monks that Evil issues its sternest challenges to consciousness.

There is just time to write these few hasty lines in my note-book, in order to establish the fact of my irreedemable fall from grace. Time marches on: the carriage-horses are pawing the ground in front of the steps; I can hear the bags being brought down. In ten minutes, we shall have departed.

April, Paris.

> *Thyrses of crêpe opened out in funereal chalices:*
> *Proud black irises, I am enamoured of your darkness.*
> *Flowers of anguish and of dreams, monstrous desire*
> *Inflates your stems of shadow and fills them with a pleasure*
> *Vibrant with the strange and heavy ferment of life.*
> *You live in a fever, eternally unsated,*
> *And the Evil within makes you stronger by far,*
> *Than other irises, the chaste and the gentle.*
> *A slow death-agony embraces your hostile hearts.*
> *You are cruel and subtle at the same time,*
> *O dolorous flowers of velvet and the moon.*
> *Aborted schemes and untamed rancours,*
> *The dismal treasons of gazes and mouths*
> *Sleep in the night of your heavy petals:*
> *The turgid blooms of a garden of tortures,*
> *You are the sisters and accomplices of my soul*
> *And of its dream obsessed by harrowing amours!*

I composed these verses in my youth, to sing the praises of black irises – like everyone else, I took to poetry for a while when I was about twenty: the apparent complexity of the game of rhyme and rhythm was bound to seduce a soul as puerile and complicated as mine, so that the barbarous child which remained within me might be amused by the conquest of its difficulties. Black irises! It had to be black irises, and all that they implied, which greeted me on my return.

Some unknown hand had caused these monstrous blooms to be distributed throughout the ground floor of my apartments in the Rue de Varenne. From the ante-chamber of the morning-room to the parlour every single room was beset by a disquieting flowering of darkness: a mute outburst of huge upstanding petals of greyish crêpe, like a host of bats set within the cups of flowers. They filled the great enamel vases in the hall, the white Sèvres urns in the drawing-room and the Satsuma pots in my study. Clumps of heady narcissi mingled with the darker flowers, like a rain of luminous and guileless stars amid all that extravagant black mourning-dress.

The hall porter explained that they had arrived two days before from Nice: a consignment of five baskets of flowers. He had taken it upon himself to unpack them and distribute them in the vases. The sender was Monsieur Ethal . . .

So Ethal was in Nice? Since when?

In addition, there was another dispatch from Ethal, conveyed by the postman. A little box had arrived eight hours before that avalanche of flowers – but the box came from London. As it was marked 'personal and fragile' on every side, in both English and French, the porter had not dared to open it, and it awaited my return in the study. There was also a pile of letters for me.

'There is one from London and one from Nice, in which Monsieur le Duc will doubtless find the explanation for these dispatches.'

It was eleven o'clock at night, and I was falling asleep, but the consignment of flowers and that mysterious box awoke my curiosity. Nerves jangling with the desire to find out what was going on, I no longer thought of sleep.

'Have someone bring the box here,' I commanded. Then, with a feverish hand, I sorted through the letters in the tray, searching for those from Claudius . . .

What a heap of correspondence! I had been at Fréneuse for a mere six days, and I found more than thirty letters awaiting my return. I knew only too well where they came from: middlemen, touts, shady hotel-proprietors and brothel-keepers. A whole venal and voracious army of inveterate vice dogged my steps like a pack of jackals; for years they had been lying in wait in my shadow, eager to excite my desire in the hope of alleviating my *ennui*. I crumpled the envelopes between my fingers, not intending to open them because I knew well enough what they contained and what offers they would extend to me. There are days when I am roused to such anger that I am tempted to send these letters to the public prosecutor, in order that society might be purged of a few of their signatories. There is Poissy and Fresnes and Saint-Lazare . . .

But, after all, it is certainly true that everyone must live. I know too well, from bitter experience, how false the claims of these spicily amorous advertisements for 'fresh meat' really are, and the kind of trafficking in bodies and souls which they represent. All the same, the juxtaposition of the calm and the dispiriting silence of Fréneuse, the return to Paris amid Ethal's black irises, and the workings of the Stock Exchange of all the prostitution of the city, seems significant and appropriate. It is the *Mene, Mene, Tekel, Upharsin* which was inscribed in letters of fire on the wall of Belshazzar's palace. Dante's *Lasciate ogni speranza* . . . is not only to be seen at Fréneuse.

That hostile night-watch of sinister flowers upon my threshold – these flowers that I used to love, in times of fever and confusion, these monsters whose praises I once sang – and that shameful correspondence from all those brokers and brokeresses of *amour* . . .

I drag the burden of my life with me, wherever I go. What a punishment!

There is, however, one note of relief in all this disgust: the news that Ethal is not here. His absence is reassuring.

His two letters, whose envelopes I tore open almost simultaneously, confirmed my deliverance. I read them at random.

My dear friend,

I have left London. The divorce of Lady Kerneby has been decided in my favour. I have heard as much from her solicitor. English hypocrisy – from which I have so often suffered – has worked to my advantage this time, against the imbecility of Lord Edward. I have benefited from his condemnation as an adulterer. The court has dismissed his claims in respect of my portrait. You know that of all my works this is the picture which I prize most highly: so far as my aesthetic sensibilities are concerned. The Marchioness Eddy Kerneby is perhaps the prettiest creature who ever lived in the kingdom. I have further idealised her, exaggerating her morbid and slightly funereal grace. It is this portrait – on which I worked for nearly six months – that Lord Edward did not want to give me, and for which he only paid half the fee. The outcome of the lawsuit has settled everything: it is now the property of the Marchioness. Lady Kerneby is here in Nice, dying of consumption! The poor creature has always been ill, but the vicissitudes of these last six months have advanced her illness considerably. If you only knew how beautiful she is, having been refined by that slow death-agony for two years – the span left to her will be far too brief. I see her every day, and spend most of my evenings by her side. I have joined her here because I am counting on the fact that she will decide to return the portrait to me. You may not know that Lady Kerneby is the sister of Sir Thomas Welcome. Welcome is illegitimate, but she has always had the most tender affection for her brother, and if I manage to obtain from her the portrait that I covet it will be on the express condition that I give it to Sir Thomas on his return from Benares, which is where he ought to be at this moment. How complicated these English families are! If this picture is returned to me, I shall take up my brushes again, and you shall see at last the painting of yourself.

CLAUDIUS.

P.S. The marchioness, to whom I have spoken of you, has allowed me to ransack her garden and her conservatories in your honour. I address to you, on her behalf and mine also, a whole harvest of narcissi and black irises. I know that you like them, although you have never told me so. These are particularly beautiful, as if they are bloated with horrid black blood: true flowers of the battlefield. I address them less to you than to the little idol which I sent you eight days ago – I still await your news, and am still disturbed by your departure. It would be a pity if she went astray en route, for – quite apart from the fact that she is unique and of an exceedingly rare material – she has a story attached to her, which you have heard. Her emerald eyes have seen the climax of a dreadful drama. She alone knows the conclusion of the story – the conclusion which she might perhaps reveal to you, if you render her the worship which she requires and show her sufficiently fervent adoration.

I promise that she will love the form and the perfume of those irises very much . . .

I shall remain here until circumstances change – somewhat in the position of a vulture lying in wait for a cadaver.

Flowers for an idol? A lawsuit won? I had opened the second letter before the first; I should have begun with the one which bore a London postmark.

My dear friend,

I have left Paris abruptly, without taking leave of you, summoned here by a matter of great importance. The great scandal of the Kerneby divorce offers me an opportunity to reopen and win my suit against Lord Edward. You know that the vile husband has illegally retained in his possession the portrait that I made of his wife. The Marchioness Eddy should now obtain her divorce from the Marquis, reclaiming all rights in respect of her fortune and her personal possessions. My picture ought to be among the objects due to her; her solicitor, who is also mine, has striven to persuade the judges of this: hence the urgency – more, the necessity – of my presence here. There are a thousand and one personal things I must attend to, but if the portrait comes back into my possession, I feel that the painter I used to be will be reawakened, and that the revitalization of my work will make a new man of me, so that my taste for light and colour will return. Pray to the good and evil spirits alike that I might succeed.

I have rediscovered, among a heap of curios and forgotten items, a little statuette that will interest you: the little Astarté of onyx at whose feet Monsieur de Burdhes was found strangled in the house in Woolwich; the idol with emerald eyes of whose religion he desired to be the founder, and whose worship – somewhat tainted with blood – has enriched our friend Thomas Welcome with the millions which now permit him to travel the world. When de Burdhes' effects were auctioned, I bid dearly for her against the antique-dealers of the City. I remember how my description of her appeared to fascinate you, that evening when I described to you the final tragedy of poor de Burdhes.

This little Far-Eastern idol has a rather pretty halo of mystery. Welcome knew her, perhaps adored her – who knows whether she herself might not have suggested the idea of the murder? For the Astarté of Carthage and Tyre is also known, in the forests of India, as the goddess Kali. The incarnation of the embraces of love, she also symbolises the murderous embraces and through the medium of the sect of Thugs, she is a strangler. The Thugs – the famous brahmin stranglers of Delhi – are her most fanatical devotees. For nearly ten years she has been mine, and I reckon her a dear friend. Permit me, therefore, to offer her to you to remind you of Welcome and of me. She will be one more link in the invisible but strong chain which unites the three of us.

I know not when I shall be able to return to Paris: I am rather afraid that I may be forced to go to Nice to rejoin Lady Kerneby, who has been receiving treatment there since the begining of winter.

Have you been to see Gustav Moreau's old studio in the Rue La Rochefoucauld? I can thoroughly recommend it to you. You will see strange gazes there, limpid and fixed: hallucinatory eyes with divine expressions. Compare them to the eyes of emerald embedded in the onyx of the idol. See how intense they become, especially at night, by candlelight.

The porter had put the little box in the hall. I opened it

with three blows of a hammer, removed the straw and gently unwound the delicate silken wrappings. The blind and androgynous statue was revealed. It is indeed the little idol featured in Claudius's story. Here is the full torso, the frail and gleaming arms, the receding hips. Hieratic and demonic, her body of pure black onyx attracts and reflects the glow of candlelight. Her firm round breasts thrust forward, gleaming above the shadowed abdomen: the narrow and flat abdomen which swells out at the place where the sexual organs should be, in the form of a tiny death's-head.

The mocking, menacing, triumphant death's head, symbolic of motherhood and of ancestry!

Beneath her low forehead there is the blind gaze of two green eyes: two profoundly dead eyes which see nothing . . .

In the half-light of the antechamber, the black irises and the narcissi stand erect, the blacker silhouettes within the shadows alternating with whiteness; their solemn vigil extends throughout the entire suite of rooms. It seems as if the whole apartment is being guarded by flower-phantoms.

Outside, carriages roll towards the Boulevard Saint-Germain. The scent of all the flowers, stronger by night, makes the atmosphere heavy and unbreathable. The little idol is silently mocking, and I am oppressed by anguish and stupor!

THE CITY OF GOLD

18 April 1898

Yesterday evening, on my return to Paris, there was the strange reception of all those black flowers and the little onyx Astarté: the enigmatic idol of the Woolwich sanctuary, introduced to my home by courtesy of Ethal. All these presences suddenly served to remind me of Thomas Welcome, whose natural sister was at that very moment aproaching her final agony in Nice – watched over by the same Ethal. In the midst of all these funereal things, there arrived for me, this very morning, a letter from Benares. The envelope, bearing the stamps of British India, contained eight long pages, written in an unfamiliar hand – which was Thomas Welcome's!

Can this be pure chance? Or are these two men, bound together by I know not what obscure past, acting in concert according to some prearranged plan? Have not the simultaneous arrival of these flowers, that statuette and that letter combined to strike me a considerable blow?

And yet, how stimulating – and how very different from the depressing counsels of Ethal – the long and luminous epistle of Thomas Welcome is! What an appeal to the cause of my health and my deliverance! No, this man wishes me no evil.

Benares, 19 March 1899.

Why did you not listen to me, my dear friend? Why have you not followed me into this marvellous land of dazzling visions and consoling legends, into the depths of the mysterious India of the Vedas? Why have you not followed me – as I asked you to, as I almost begged you to – to this holy city of ecstasy and light: Benares? Am I to understand that you are staying in Europe, beneath the narrow sky of our cities, in spite of that tortuous want of expansion which is in you, that thirst for life which is your sickness? Will you remain a prisoner of the inhuman laws of our civilization?

Here you would have found a sure remedy: here, in this atmosphere of immense fervour, this permanent exaltation of a crowd in prayer, beseeching by day and by night a divinity which is almost visible in the sublimity of the landscape and the sky.

Benares! The mosque of Aureng-Zeb; the ceaseless flow of the Ganges crawling with the boats of pilgrims; the pilings of temples at the 'Ghat of Five Rivers'. It is a place of palaces, mosques and domes, all bathing in the river by virtue of their innumerable staircases which descend step by step, with their escorts of statues, into the moving gold of the water!

Everything is golden in this holy city. Golden: the heavens of apotheosis into which the gold-clad domes and the pink cones of minarets are forever reaching. Golden: the squares, the pillars, the roofs of sanctuaries, and the images of apsaras and musicians springing forth, all in the attitude of distracted flight, the cornices and the entablatures of temples. Golden: the nudity of beggars, crushed by the crowds on the bank of the river. Golden: the immobility of fakirs in trance. Golden: the great vases held between the hands of the worshipful priests moving in procession on the high terraces. Golden also: the mass of the faithful prostrate, step by step and column by column, in mute adoration of the Ganges: 'Ganga Djaï', mother Ganges; the sacred stream; the holy river which flows through the holy city, to which they dedicate all their vows.

The whole of Buddhist India converges at this point, in the exaltation of the light and the infinite thirst for certain well-being, visionary, adoring and happy: happy in their fervour and in their faith. Fervour! The whole secret of human well-being is there: love with fervour; be passionately interested in things; encounter God everywhere and love Him madly in each encounter, amorously desiring everything that is natural, beings and things alike, without stopping at mere possession, devoting oneself to unbridled desire for the external world without pausing to worry whether the desire is good or evil. For all sensation is a presence, and the splendour of things derives entirely from the ardour that we have for them. The importance is in the beholding and not in the thing beheld. What does it matter where ecstasy comes from, so long as ecstasy comes? All emotions are like so many doors opened towards a wondrous tomorrow: becoming is the essence of religion. The things of the past are already dead; why tarry over a corpse? Everything possessed is already corrupted, and whenever we regret something, we are already carrying a seed of death within us.

To enrich oneself with desires: total fervour is there, and fervour is a delicious attrition of love.

Benares, century after century, agonises and mortifies itself in an intense fervour: it is that very fervour – the hallucinatory ecstasy of all India – which makes it live and sustains it.

Oh, the golden temple: the holy of holies of the holy city; the displays of idols, lingams and amorous charms in its little narrow steets; their descent towards the river; the infinite succession of palaces and temples; the dreadful promiscuity, puerile and charming at the same time, of the brahmins, the beggars, the idols and the beasts: all received and respected with the same soft and loving gentleness by the religious soul of the crowds!

Priests slowly wheel around a great bull of red stone, which is the emblem of Siva. A woman devotedly sprinkles a lingam of sandstone with lustral water, and crowns it with marigolds. Cows descend towards the river, nonchalantly chewing flowers. The cow-dung and the fresh leaves are slippery. A beggar implores an image to inform him as to the position of the planet Saturn. At intervals, from loggia to loggia, gongs and enormous tambours ring out; a great rumbling which imparts a dolorous and ardent vibration to the heavy air. Heavy miasmas ascend from the founts of knowledge where the gods reside: the musty smell of decay of the innumerable vegetable offerings accumulated there.

In the wild sky, above the domes clad in gold, emerald parakeets wheel about the gleaming ellipses, joining up in pairs to chatter in the forecourts of the temples. The whole place is haunted by the stink of corpses and fermentation; the disturbing soul of the founts of wisdom, which contain life and death.

The boatmen are the masters of the river, the refrain of 'Ganga Djaī!' always on their black lips as their large sluggish

221

boats surmounted by terraces, where entire families live and die, slide towards the horizon, rocked by the divine current. 'Ganga! Ganga Djaï!' The guttural refrain seems to encapsulate all the mystery of the different human races. 'Ganga! Ganga Djaï!' is also the echo of the holy city, and the echo of the centuries; it is the shadowy voice of dark idols and mysterious temples: the very soul of that impenetrable land which is India.

The palaces built by Hindu princes stretch in infinite succession, each one known by name. There is the palace of the Rajah of Indore, with balconies painted with blue-tinted floral designs which might be Louis XV; then there is the palace of the Maharajah of Udaipur, with its crenellated walls and its door flanked by two towers like a citadel . . .

Here are dogs, big turtles in the water, flames around a pyre, three rigid silhouettes clad in linen, a silent group of people: in Benares the dead are burned. The ashes are put into the river, and because the despised Untouchables who have the sole right to tend such fires make their clients pay dearly, poor people go badly-burnt into the stream. Thousands of men bathe themselves daily in the Ganges, and drink its waters without hesitation; thus the unique substance of life and death is naturally recycled.

Here are yet more terraces, more crowds swarming on the long staircases. There an observatory opens its elegant watch-towers over the river; gigantic instruments loom within. Here a dark alleyway abruptly descends to the river, where an immobile ascetic sits entranced while grey monkeys and bluish pigeons fight over a grain of corn fallen between his feet.

Further away, a ghat broken at the edges has allowed a temple to slide into the river. The columns and sculptures project from the water; stylite fakirs display their thinness upon them, and the backwash of boats rocks floating marigolds in their shadow. Near-naked bodies girdled by shreds of material swarm about the jumble of wherries and bamboo platforms. Among the stray dogs and prostrate worshippers there is a mad flowering of straw parasols, of every possible shade of yellow. They stand up at all angles, fixed in every wall, some thrusting like golden mushrooms above street-stalls, others flat, set beside doorways like so many shields.

*A thousand changing visions, continually renewed. The sink-
ing sun sets them alight. And there is the atmosphere, always
conspicuous and triumphant, full of all the disquieting effluvia of
the river: the sour odour of scorched flesh and the fragrances of
spices, the odours of cinnamon, gum benzoin, withered marigold
and cattle-sheds. And always the haunting and spasmodic 'Ganga!
Ganga Djaï!'*

*All this is dominated by the outbursts of bell-turrets and
domes, the produce of improbable edifices of stone, some of them
reminiscent of flames, others of enormous lotuses: a diverse
architecture of reverent ambition reaching for the sky, moving in
the heat-haze, crackling with sparks in the magnificence of the
evenings.*

*To describe such an evening would require the molten-metal
style of a Villiers de l'Isle-Adam or the gemmed palette of a
Gustave Moreau.*

The Triumph of Alexander . . .

*Do you know the little museum in the Rue la Rochefoucauld?
There and there alone, among the treasures of a unique body of
work, you will be able to hypnotise yourself so as to come to
know the inflamed splendour and transcendental atmosphere of a
March evening in Benares. Benares! I have already been here for
fifty days and yet every day, at twilight, the religious emotion of
an entire city in ecstasy permits me to watch the sunset as if the
daylight were indeed dying.*

*When a spectacle attains grandiosity in its beauty, it seems
that it ought never to disappear. In our European climates,
similar emotions cannot be experienced twice. That is why I
want you here, why I am sending you this last appeal. With a
loving and liquid heart, full to overflowing, you would blossom
here in the plenitude of all your desires. That can only happen
here, in the exaltation of the light, where every creature and
every object is the vibration of a metal and the nuance of a
flower. You will be born again into a new Heaven, with a new
being, surrounded by things completely renewed. You will learn
to carry your good fortune with you, and not to demand it of the
past. The past is a decaying carcase; it is that which poisons your
whole self. In Benares you will live in impassioned stupefaction,*

*in the midst of architectural, racial and climatic magnificence,
where every minute will bring you the savour of an unexpected
and perfect encounter.*

*It is to these encounters that I invite you. It is because I have
done all this myself that I say to you: 'Come.' Here, life is that
which it was intended to be: an intoxicated dizziness. The eagle
is intoxicated by its flight; the nightingale by summer nights; the
plain trembles in the heat, and the dawn reddens with joy as the
moon pales with voluptuousness. It is civilization which has
deformed life. Among young peoples, all emotion is intoxication
and all joy becomes religious.*

*Buddhism, which prostrates its crowds at the edge of the
Ganges, is the compassionate and enraptured recognition which
an entire race extends towards its gods. And the race remains
youthful, although it is a thousand years old, because it is
voluptuously consumed by its fervour. Nothing is fixed but its
future; it is utterly careless of tasting the stagnant waters of the
past. 'Inspired by hope, it isolates itself in its vison, absorbed in
the contemplation of nature and indifferent to immediate contingen-
cies. The agitation of others surrounding it only serves to
augment the sentiments of its own life.*

*The fakir does not rub shoulders with others; the possibility
does not exist. Oh, how far away we are, here, from ancient Europe!*

*Come to join me, as quickly as you can, my dear Duc. India
will be a delicious convalescence for you. Here you will breathe
the odour of the eternal lotus, as in the sonnet of Ary Renan,
whose lines I have recalled during these last few days in Benares,
and which embodies the spirit of Hinduism:*

> *The Brahmins say to me: 'Ponder the Sutras!*
> *The way to Great Peace is open in Dreams.'*
> *The mitred ones whose robes are long*
> *Offer me pleasure in opening their arms.*
>
> *Then the noblemen say to me: 'Follow us. Choose*
> *The caste which pleases you and the drapery*
> *Which suits you.' In the leper-hospital I hear*
> *The chandala singing: 'Love and you shall suffer.'*

224

I have chosen to love and to suffer in the shadow.
I forget my sins. They are probably numberless,
But Wisdom and Gold have not dried up my heart.

Marching under an anathema, draped in heresy,
I breathe the scent of the eternal lotus
And in my wooden cup I have tasted ambrosia.

THE TRAP

April.

Have you been to see Gustav Moreau's old studio in the Rue La Rochefoucauld? I can throroughly recommend it to you. You will see strange gazes there, limpid and fixed: hallucinatory eyes with divine expressions. Compare them to the eyes of emeralds embedded in the onyx of the idol. See how intense they become, especially at night, by candlelight.

ETHAL.

The Triumph of Alexander . . .
Do you know the little museum in the Rue la Rochefoucauld? There and there alone, among the treasures of a unique body of work, you will be able to hypnotise yourself so as to come to know the inflamed splendour and transcendental atmosphere of a March evening in Benares.

WELCOME.

Gustave Moreau! Ethal and Welcome direct me to the work of this painter as if to a good doctor. Without acting in concert, these two men between whom I sense some irreparable enmity, and who detest one another (of that I am sure) both send me advice – one from Benares and the other from Nice – to the effect that I should go to Rue La Rochefoucauld as if to some marvellous apothecary. And yet Welcome wishes to save me, while Claudius aspires only to aggravate my sickness.

Gustave Moreau: the painter of svelte Salomés streaming with precious stones, of Muses bearing severed heads, and of Helens in robes woven in living gold, posing with lilies in their hands – similar to huge blooming lilies themselves – on dungheaps of bleeding corpses! Gustave Moreau: the manipulator of symbols and the perversities of ancient theogonies; the poet of charnel-houses, battlefields and sphinxes; the painter of Dolour, Ecstasy and Mystery; the one artist, out of all modern painters, who has most closely approached Divinity – and in the course of that approach has discovered so many murderesses: Salomé; Helen; the *femme fatale* Ennoïa; the Sirens, bane of seafaring men!

Gustave Moreau; the painter and philosopher whose art has always troubled me more than any other! Has any other man been so haunted by the symbolic cruelty of defunct religions and the divine debauchery that was once adored in long-lost lands? A visionary without compare, he is the acknowledged master of the realm of dreams, but insofar as his works embody an uneasy frisson of anguish and desperation, he has cast a spell on his era. The master sorcerer has bewitched his contemporaries, contaminating the entire *fin de siècle* of bankers and stockbrokers with a morbid and mystical ideal. An entire generation of young men has been bathed by the radiance of his paintings, becoming dolorous and languid, their eyes obstinately turned towards the splendour and magic of former ages: a whole generation – its writers and poets in particular – nostalgically enamoured, like him, of the long naked bodies, the fearful eyes and the morbid voluptuousness of his dream-enchantresses.

For there *is* sorcery in the pale and silent heroines of his water-colours.

His princesses, armoured in their nakedness by gold-smiths and jewellers, communicate ecstasy and are themselves ecstatic. Lethargic as they are – as though half-asleep – and so distant as to be almost spectral, they only serve to stir the senses all the more vigorously, and to subdue the will all the more certainly. Their charm is like that of great passive and venereal flowers brought to us from sacrilegious centuries – still in full bloom – by the occult power of damnable memories.

Moreau! This is a painter who can boast of having forced the threshold of mystery, and claim the glory of having troubled an entire century! This man, with the subtle art of the lapidary and enameller, has given powerful aid to the forces of decay which afflict my whole being. He has given to me, as to a whole modern generation of sick visionary artists, a dangerous erotic fascination with dead women and their set and empty expressions: the hallucinatory, long-dead women of yesteryear, resuscitated by him in the mirror of time.

> *Under the pearly frissons of an ardent and sad sky*
> *Flourished, a hymn adorable in its melancholy,*
> > *The song of the sirens.*
> *An incurable ennui swims in the amethyst*
> *Of their deep eyes; the ennui of the god who marooned them*
> > *On those serene shores.*

The sirens, bedecked with diadems of pearls and madrepores, of the famous water-colour: the sad and implacable sirens, grouped like some monstrous white coral reef whose branches are both dead and living . . . !

And it is to this morbid oeuvre, to this perilous and disturbing art, that Ethal and Welcome urge me to return; it is in this oeuvre, which has already entered into me so deeply as to augment my suffering, that they assure me I will find my cure.

And that little idol with the emerald eyes, which mocks me . . . for although she is made of mute matter, I can still hear her unseen laughter in the night.

Paris, 30 April
I have been there, and the same evening . . .

For shame! If this is what they wanted, they ought to be fully satisfied, for the trial has succeeded, beyond all expectations.

I went there right away. Without stopping in the first room, I asked to be directed to the *Triumph of Alexander* on the second floor, and I stood before it, utterly absorbed, for a long time. I found it incomparable, one of the most beautiful of his masterpieces.

It depicts a crowd moving through a setting whose

splendid and grandiose architecture evokes all the magic of ancient India: a sumptuous procession of human figures, chariots and palanquins, and elephants presenting a frieze of tusks – and incessant trumpetings. The whole crowd is adoring the figure of a man seated on an inaccessible throne decorated with all manner of chimerical designs – dragons, sphinxes and enormous lotuses – like some kind of monumental altar constructed from monsters and flowers. Flowers are strewn around a mosaic floor; in the background, there is the cold blue of the stagnant waters of marble fish-ponds which duplicate by reflection the images of pagodas and temples carved out of porphyry, onyx and precious stones. This doubled image gives the impression of a high, steep cliff whose epic dimensions are entrancing and terrifying. This magical scenery is bathed from the sky above by an indescribable atmosphere, a yellow and blue dust which seems to be compounded of fluid gold and iris-petals. The ambiance created by all the nuances of this ensemble, and all its details, give rise to such a gentle charm and such a drunken joy of life as to generate a poignant regret that one never knew that epoch and that crowd – and at the same time, a disgust for our own time and our own civilization so profound that one might easily die of it.

The Triumph of Alexander! According to Welcome's letter, this is the atmosphere of Benares!

All around me in the high room – a true museum of the master's works, which cram the walls from the ceiling to the skirting-board – were the dangerous phantoms with which I was already familiar: the images of Salomé dancing before Herod, with her hair encircled by sardonyx, and the hieratic gesture of her fully extended arms; the dream-cathedrals with cupolas of bright amber which serve as settings for that immemorial scene of lust and murder; variations on the theme – repeated as many as ten times – of the tragic and bejewelled group of Sirens gathered upon the seemingly-foaming rocks; representations of Helen wandering with half-closed eyes on the walls of Troy . . .

And everywhere – in the images of Helen as in the images of Salomé; in representations of Messalina at Subura as in depictions of Hercules in the house of the daughters of Thespius or in the marches of Lerna – the same obsession with ancient myths is manifest. Those elements which are the most sinister and the most cruel are perpetually on display: the purulent charnel-house of the corpses slain by the Sphinx; the bleached bones of the victims of the Hydra; the heaps of wounded, agonised and dying, dominated by the placid and silent figure of Ennoïa; the bleeding heads of John the Baptist and Orpheus; the final convulsions of Semele, consumed by lightning on the knees of an impassive Zeus . . .

I wandered about, unsteadily, in an atmosphere of massacre and murder; it was as though an odour of blood floated in the air of that hall. I recalled what Ethal had said to me, boastfully, one evening in his studio in the Rue Servandoni, about the atmosphere of beauty and of dread which always envelops the man who has killed.

I went down the stairs.

The body-count there were no fewer dead bodies on display than there were in the upper hall.

From a heap of putrefying corpses an enormous lily-stem sprung forth, standing up straight, virile and lissom – and in the giant petals of its flower was the seated figure of a mystic princess. She was young and slender, haloed like a saint. In one hand she held the globe and in the other a cross. It is from the pus and the putrid blood of the charnel-house that the miraculous flower grows; the produce of all these murders is the angelic figure of a woman.

She too had the empty and fixed expression of the Helens and the Salomés.

I left the corner of the hall where that dangerous symbol glorified the uselessness of martyrdom, and I had already set foot upon the staircase which led down to the street – to the fresh air and the reality of the world outside – when my attention was captured by a large composition at the very end of the vast room.

Between the colonnades of a temple or Greek palace were a host of godlike young men, some in groups, others standing alone, some crowned with flowers, others bejewelled like women, but all striking tragic and impassioned poses. Their refined and barbarous attire served only to emphasize the near-nakedness of their bodies and the tortured convulsions moulded in their flesh. It was a banquet scene, but the banquet had been interrupted, for the amphoras and the metal plates were strewn about the foreground. There they mingled with corpses, for this was also a scene of murder. Extended on the flagstones, the superb bodies spread their limbs, flung outwards by the violence of their falls and stiffened by death. The painting depicted the slaying of the suitors in Penelope's palace after the return of Ulysses. The hero was visible in the background, standing in the embrasure of a huge bronze door, while Minerva, the Pallas Athene of the *Odyssey*, appeared as a vertiginously fluttering swallow in a nimbus of flames, guiding the arrows in their flight.

Many had already found their mark, for the palace was full of dead men.

For effect, the painter had represented all the suitors as adolescents, hardly more than children, thus giving to all their death-agonies a voluptuous and cruel sensuality. It was a hecatomb of youth worthy of Tiberius or Nero.

In the centre, a whole group of frightened men jostled one another furiously, around the couches of three more intrepid heroes, who continued to drink while awaiting death. They had not even left their cushions. Nonchalantly lying down, cup in hand, they seemed scornful of the agonised howling and desperation of their companions. I was seized by a great admiration for such calm and such disdain, in the midst of that terror-stricken mob.

Among all these divine figures clad in silks and jewels, two in particular attracted me, not so much by the purity of their features as by the imperious charm of their expressions. They were faces full of resolution and anguish, whose hallucinatory eyes were intoxicating.

One, who had brought himself upright with a single bound, had torn open his clothing the better to receive the fatal arrows. With his chest bared, drawing back the bluish draperies to offer up all his young flesh, he seemed to be cursing the gods and inviting death.

It was adolescence flinging itself into the abyss, with the thirst of the martyr: the offering of a young and heroic soul to death!

The other, seated in a corner of the hall, leaning against a pillar with capitals of green bronze, was slowly lifting a cup to his lips and, with a superb profundity in his two eyes, calmly drinking death – for the cup was poisoned. A poppy, half-stripped of its petals, floated on the surface of the draught. Defying the serene gravity of the gesture, the tragic illumination of his eyes proclaimed the surpreme determination of that lover to yield nothing but a cadaver to the avenging arrows of the husband.

What I could not fail to recognise, and what moved me so profoundly, was the expression in the eyes: the inexpressible eyes of those two death-agonies! In what violet had the painter steeped them? In what livid green had he found their surrounding rings? They were living, those eyes: like two phosphorescent gleams, like the corollas of two flowers.

Ethal had not deceived me. These were most certainly the eyes of my dream, the eyes of my obsession, the eyes of anguish and dread which he had predicted that I would encounter: gazes more beautiful than all expressions of love by virtue of having become decisive, supernatural, and – in the final analysis – *themselves* in the anguish of the last moment of life. Ethal's theory appeared to me to be proved at last, by the talent and genius of the painter. I understood, at last, the beauty of murder: the supreme make-up that is dread; the ineffable empire of eyes which desire to die.

THOU SHALT GO NO FURTHER

April 1899

And for the obsession of those eyes, I nearly killed that girl. Yes, it has come to that; I go forth to intoxicate myself, to hypnotise myself with beauty before the work of Gustave Moreau – and I bring back the soul of an assassin! What ignominy! All day, I exalt and hallucinate myself before the terrible phosphorescence of a picture painted by a poet and enameller – and that same evening I find myself yet again in a slum, caught between the horror of an under-age whore and the menacing mockery of her pimp.

It was the presence of the man which saved me. Without him, without his abrupt intervention, I would have continued to close around that frail neck the hideous hands of a strangler – for they have become hideous, my hands! Now, having at last returned home, I look at them coolly, under the glow of the lamp, they appear to me deformed. I did not suspect that my narrow hands, with their long and slender fingers, had such power in their enveloping suppleness . . .

Now that I have felt in their grip an agonising desire to frighten and to demand satisfaction they seem to have turned into claws. How long my thumbs are! I have never noticed it before.

On due reflection, however, I can only conclude that it was the haunting memory of the inexpressible eyes of the suitors which guided me in my descent. When I took hold of the neck of that frightened litle girl in the hotel room it was certainly the anguish of the last moment of life that I sought in her eyes – but how did she come to have that form and that quality in her eyes?

I will always remember that moment. I felt myself

overcome by such a vertiginous rush of sensations and such emptiness that I believed I was becoming a god – that a second self was emerging within me, and that I had taken hold of the unknowable at last.

But what a pitiful and banal adventure it was!

That hellish excursion into that suburban fairground; the reek of burnt fat, of the sweaty and dirty rags of labourers after work, gathered beneath the already dirty trees of that avenue; the weary dawdling of the gawkers in the alley-ways between the booths ... the beat walked by that gamine ...

She was scarcely seventeen years old, showing just a glimpse of tender and very pale flesh at the open neck of a loose jacket. The nape of her neck was gilded and her sunburnt cheeks were ripely pink, of a different shade from the throat and neck. She looked like a country girl, still innocent in spite of the livery of prostitution which she wore.

In an unready manner, as though reluctantly harnessed to the task, she strolled back and forth in the fairground, stubborn and lazy at the same time. Not pretty to start with, she seemed worse by virtue of her surly virgin manner and the awkward way she had of lifting up her dress to expose the red cloth of her underskirt. It stood out a mile that she was a debutante: some poor debauched good girl sent forth into the night, watched over from some near vantage-point by some frightful bully-boy.

Twice she passed close by me, mumbling some ill-bred obscenities in an indistinct voice, then threw a rapid side-ways wink at a policeman before setting forth again on the hunt. She was evidently choked by terror, and sadly inexpe-rienced in the vocation of streetwalking. Her awkwardness interested me, and – more out of pity than depravity – I set out to follow her. I fell into step with her, and she became aware of my intention. At the corner of the street she turned around abruptly, lifting her big eyes towards me at last, and looked me in the face.

'Buy a girl a drink? I ain't 'alf thirsty!' she said, using the vile conventional jargon of such suburban encounters.

Her eyes? The irises were at the same time blue and violet, iridescent and changing – and their expression was so sad, so utterly timorous . . . ! She was a mere kid! I was immediately overcome – by pity much more than desire. I took her to dinner – I, the Duc de Fréneuse, took that little prostitute from Vaugirard to dinner at a restaurant near the railway station. She was scared and bewildered, hardly able to believe in her good fortune – dinner in a restaurant with a well-set-up client! The people with whom she normally did business were presumably more expeditious. I talked to her gently, asking what she liked with reference to the menu.

Until that moment I had not observed that her eyes, with all the charms of their deep and indefinable hue, had already acquired the delicious relish of terror – for it was terror that I inspired in her. My amiability, my little caring gestures and my gentleness only served to redouble her anxieties. The man who lived off her must have followed us, and must have been watching us from outside. Her only replies to my courtesies were starts and recoils; with her large, staring eyes, she gave the impression of a little creature in danger, trembling as she suppressed the impulse to cry out for help. I felt a mounting sexual excitement; her anxieties were bringing out the beast in me.

Nero must have felt something similar as he delightedly drank the tears of martyrs. It was akin to the sinister voluptuousness of the Augustans delivering up to the Praetorian Guard the modesty and fear of Christian virgins; akin to the frantic and ferocious joy which filled the infamous Circus even before the bloodier games commenced, when young girls were twice delivered to the beasts – first the man, and then the tiger!

It was the cruel and iconoclastic pleasure of crushing something frail, of breaking a stem: the triumphant ignominy of the power to please oneself in pulverising everything that is fragile! It was all that filth and fever which was buzzing in my head and causing my fingers to clench when, once we were in the hotel-room, the child with the

235

great sad eyes refused to undress. She had not the time, she said, I had to get it over with quickly; she was staying with her parents; they would have missed her at the evening meal; her father was brutal; she would get into trouble because of me ... and all the other excuses which false novices usually make, in similar cases.

The truth is that she was afraid – afraid of me, and of the expression in my eyes, which was becoming strange and blazing. She had sat down on the bed and had crossed her hands before her bosom, with the instinctive gesture of a victim, as I tried to unbutton her jacket. There was a frightful fever in my fingertips and I became brutally insistent. She got up again, moved by fright and perhaps by rebellion.

'I want the money now!' she announced, in a harsh voice – and, as slippery as an eel, she slid out of my embrace and took refuge in a corner. Her horror of me was manifest.

I saw red. I was sorely annoyed by the thought that this little trollop was refusing herself to me – me, the Duc de Fréneuse, the some-time lover of Willie Stephenson and Izé Kranile, whose caprices were appreciated and whose presence was implored in the house of every trafficker in flesh in London and Paris! Her violet eyes, which had now become immense, fascinated me and drew me forward. I was maddened by a furnace-like heat; I was suffocating, strangled by rage and desire. I felt the need to seize that shivering and timorous body, to force it back, to pound it and knead it ...

And my two hands seized the gamine by the throat, stetching her out at full length on the bed; with all my strength I bore down on her, crushing my lips against hers and staring into her eyes.

'Fool!' I hissed between my teeth. 'Little fool!'

And while my fingers dug slowly into her flesh, I watched entranced as the blue of her eyes gradually darkened. I felt her breasts palpitating beneath me.

'Mathias! Mathias!' she croaked, hoarsely.

The door was broken in by the blow of a shoulder. A hand grabbed me by the back of the neck, lifted me by the collar of my jacket and brought me to my feet on the carpet.

'Here! What's going on? What're you after? What're you trying to do to the kid?'

The man was not young, and had not shaved for three days; he was wearing the loose neckerchief of a labourer – probably some wretched zinc-worker. He looked me up and down with his little bulging eyes: the restless and disquieting eyes of a wild beast. Then, the examination complete, he twirled his moustache around one finger and thrust the other hand deep in the pocket of his velvet tunic. 'Well, Toinette, what's monsieur up to?'

Then, favouring me with a knowing wink of the eye, he added: 'Go on then, get on with it.'

It was a set-up. I liked nothing better. Within the pocket of my coat I took hold of the revolver which I always carried there. I cocked it, and with my free left hand I plucked a few coins out of my waistcoat.

'The show must go on?' I replied, using the same jargon. 'Not with me – I already know the tune. The little one is a minor, isn't she? But she was soliciting when I picked her up. That game won't work on me. I could have you both banged up, but it isn't worth the trouble. Go on, get out! Get back to where you belong or *this* little darling will be doing the talking.' I showed him the revolver.

The man listened to me complaisantly. My argot interested him, and so did the coins I was holding – and the rings on my fingers even more, for his eyes never left my hands. He mimicked a dancer's bow, and put on a thoroughly obsequious manner: 'Monsieur is one of the gentry, but we have to work for a living. Yes, the little one is my cooking-pot, but we're honest tradesmen. Toinette would have done a trick for a five franc piece – maybe ten for you, as you're so well-heeled – but what were you trying to do to her? She's only a kid – you frightened her so much that she cried out. Some dirty toff's trick! Come on, Toinette, show a little life! What was monsieur doing to you? Let's give her a chance to explain, shall we?'

The frightened little girl, cowering against her protector, stammered out an account of the encounter and the following scene, illustrated with grand gestures. The man listened; his eyes lit up and his sinister face was shining. He looked upon me with apparent benevolence.

'Go on,' he said, sweeping up the three twenty-france pieces that I had put on the table, 'I see what's what. We understand one another well enough. Go on, greenhorn, hop it. Outside! Clear the deck, spoilsport! You must excuse her, monsieur; she's young, doesn't know what it's all about – there are such funny people around; she was scared. Go on, wait for me in the wine-merchants downstairs – ask for Nénest, the little printer, the apprentice who's been with Big Marie for ten years, the kid who lodges with her . . . come on, are you dense, or what?' He raised his hand to the little girl 'Big Marie – from the corner at the crossroads on the Rue Lecourbe. Tell her that she has to come with Nénest – bring them both to the wine-merchants. I'll come down with monsieur. Take this, for a drink!' He threw five francs at the girl.

When the unhappy girl had gone he repeated: 'We understand one another well enough. If monsieur had explained . . . me, I'm wise to all that. I'm not thick. I see things quickly, me. Monsieur had only to say, and what he requires can easily be found. I can do business with you.'

He stood aside to let me precede him through the open door.

'If you would be so kind . . . '

To have come to this! To carry imprinted on my features such a mask that they come forth to whisper to me, in Grenelle and in Vaugirard, the kind of propositions that are murmured in the streets of Cairo and the quays of Naples!

And it was before the painting of Gustave Moreau that my soul put on this mask. My God, what have I come to?

I did not even kill the person who dared to speak to me thus! Has Ethal, then, abolished everything that was within me?

THE LILIES

Paris, 15 May

Nice.

My lawsuit is won. The portrait of Marchioness Eddy and some others left London five days ago; a telegram from Rothner informs me that they arrived yesterday at the railway station. I shall take delivery myself; they will all be unpacked and on show in my studio tomorrow evening. Come, therefore, to make the acquaintance of the exquisite Lady Kerneby, whose divorce will give me back to my brushes. She still continues to die slowly in the blue and gold spring of the Riviera; her agony has given her complexion a new shade . . . I make haste to return to Paris to make some slight alterations to my canvas. This consumptive little marchioness will have provided me, unawares, with a masterpiece. I began it when she was already ill; by the time I have completed it she will be moribund. It will be something more, I believe, than one more variation on a woman's face . . . She and my bust of wax, based on the little Neapolitan model, will represent the two great emotions of my life . . . purely artistic emotions, you understand – but they are the most poignant and the richest of all complex sensations. You are only a dilettante yourself, my dear Duc, but you will understand my joy and my pride in standing before the portrait of tomorrow.

You will also see, in the Rue Servandoni, how much the Marchioness Eddy resembles her brother, and you will discover some other works by yours truly. There is my ink-drawing of the Duchess of Searley, the poor little peeress who died so unhappily some days after the completion of her portrait. There is also my pastel of the Marchioness of Beacoscome, the most neurasthenic of those Americans who are wedded to London, who was so exhausted by her sittings that I was never able to finish it . . . in the end, she was forbidden to visit my studio by order of her doctors. Be reassured – the Marchioness of Beacoscome is

240

not dead, although she ought to be. By this time, she will be in
China; the Marquis has been appointed ambassador to Peking.
So the affair to which I am inviting you is not entirely a ball of
victims.
Until tomorrow, then. My entire London studio has now been
transferrd to my Paris home. Come about seven o'clock: seven
o'clock is an admirable time, in May.

Yours
CLAUDIUS ETHAL

The letter is dated the 14th. It is this evening, therefore,
at seven o'clock, that Claudius invites me to contemplate
the morally dubious beauties of languor and death-agony
exhibited by these famous cases of murder.

The Duchess of Searley, the Marchioness of Beacoscome . . .

I recalled to mind all that Pierre de Tairamond had told
me during the conversation we had when he visited me
last August – less than a a year ago.

'He has in his house certain carefully-prepared cigarettes
which provoke the worst debauchery. The young Duchess
of Searley was dead in six months, in consequence having
breathed the scent of certain strange and heady flowers
during her sittings.

'As regards the Marchioness of Beacoscome, she has
ceased, by order of her doctors, to pose for Ethal. Her
neurasthenia was exasperated in the atmosphere of the
studio, which was eternally crowded with amaryllids and
lilies; she felt that she was dying there.

'These flowers have the peculiar property of giving a
pearly lustre to the skin and delectable rings around the
eyes of those who breathe their scent, but in awakening the
touching rings and the marvellous pallors, such flowers let
loose a lethal miasma. For love of beauty – a fervour for
deep, drowned expressions and delicate flesh-tints – Claudius Ethal poisons his models; the man cultivates languor
and sows mortal agonies.'

Yes, these were certainly the names Tairamond had

mentioned in discussing the redoubtable legend which had grown up around the painter: the clamour of clubland; the echo of London.

Bluebeard has invited me to come and visit his dead women this evening.

Paris, 16 May, four o'clock in the morning
I have killed Ethal!

There was nothing else I could do! Life had become odious, the air unbreathable. I have killed. I am delivered and I am a deliverer – for, in putting down that man, I am conscious that I have saved others! What I have eliminated is an element of corruption; a germ of death lying in wait; a watchful larva with hands of shadow extended towards all that which is youthful, towards all weakness and all ignorance. I have liberated Welcome – of that much I am certain – and I might perhaps have saved that gentle Marchioness Eddy, whose soul he stole and whose death-agony he imposed. I might possibly have broken the frightful curse which he has put on the Marchioness of Beacoscome. For that man was more than a poisoner: he was also a sorcerer. In poisoning him with his own hand I have been an unconscious and just instrument of fate; I have been the arm lifted by a will more powerful than my own; I have completed the gesture with which he menaced the world at large, and I have secured his destiny.

And the enchanter is dead of his enchantment . . .

And I have saved myself . . .

I acted out of fear too, from the instinct of legitimate self-defence. I have killed him in order that I might not be killed – for it is to suicide and perhaps worse that this Ethal was guiding me – and in excusing myself I demand the respect of others . . .

But when I smashed the frightful emerald against his teeth I was not thinking of others; I was only thinking of myself. So I am only a common murderer – not even an impassioned assassin, who kills for the pleasure of killing, let alone the assassin of sensuality that I might have been able to become — no better than the bewildered bourgeois who tremulously shoots the burglar denounced by falling furniture.

I have killed Ethal! How could I do such a thing? I detested him, to be sure, but I was no longer afraid of him. I am still trying to collect my thoughts, here in the glow of these two candelabras in the silence of the sleeping household, and I am not afraid! *I am not afraid!* Words and images run into one another in my poor empty head, where that dolourous thing which is my liquefied and mortified brain stirs restlessly; my temples are buzzing; my skin is dry and I have a bitter taste in my mouth. Behind the closed shutters, it is already broad daylight.

No one has seen me re-enter my apartments; I did not ask the concierge to let me in; I opened the door myself, with my own key, and slipped through the shadows like a thief . . . no, like an assassin.

Welcome also has killed, according to Ethal. We are two of a kind now. Yes, we can clasp one another by the hand. I remember that he said to me that I would kill one day, when I came to it. Did he know, then? If I were sure that he suspected me, I should do away with him too; I do not want to be known as an assassin — not I, not the Duc de Fréneuse!

If I could only sleep! I need, before doing anything else, to relive that moment — to write a minute-by-minute account of how I did it, and how I was led . . . Oh, I am ill! . . . Let it go . . . An injection of morphine, and I shall fall into sleep as if into a hole . . .

I will regain possession of myself tomorrow.

Same day, ten o'clock in the morning
It happened very simply. He said to me: 'Come at seven o'clock'; at seven o'clock I was with him. He greeted me with an enthusiastic and vigorous handshake; his embrace was vice-like. He was wearing all his rings: the monstrous

livid pearls like pustules of nacre and – on the middle finger – the glaucous gem clasped by a silver claw, the ring of Philip II himself, modelled on the one in the Escorial. It was to that green gleam that my gaze immediately went as I entered his home last evening.

'The ball of victims!' he cried, recalling the odious pleasantry of his letter. 'It has all gone well. Make yourself at home, my dear Duc – you seem a little younger. Let's go – come and see how pretty they are.'

What a showman! His studio was full of amaryllids and huge lilies, mounted high and low. All the white and heady flowers with which he had poisoned the sittings of his models Ethal now wanted to set around the portraits, perhaps in order to make clearer their hidden resemblance to those women, or – who can say? – to make a greater impression on me and bind me more tightly to him. He knew perfectly well that I could not be ignorant of the legend attached to the portraits.

That Ethal! He read me like an open book.

'How about this for a wake for dead women?' he joked, indicating the flowers. 'Are they not three beautiful lilies themselves: three delectably tormented lilies; three great white lilies in the process of withering away?

> '*A strange and heart-rending grace*
> '*Is in the white mortality of lilies.*

'The Duchess of Searley: complete nobility deserves all honour. There is nothing metaphorical about that case: the duchess is really dead. I'm not here for nothing you know – my sole purpose is to cultivate a legend, in both London and Paris: it's the only way one can obtain due recognition of one's genius.

> '*She loved flowers too much, that is what has killed her.*'

His lips were drawn back in a carnivorous smile, which displayed all his strong teeth.

'See how virginal she seems!' he continued. 'One would not think she had had as many as three lovers. Look at that frankness – and those eyes especially: the great blue eyes, of such a liquid purity in the shadow of the eyelashes . . . and the delicacy of the nose. You can almost feel the nostrils vibrating, can't you? She was mother of pearl incarnate . . . and yet it's only a sketch!'

In a tall frame of polished oak, there was a large unbleached canvas, of which only the middle seemed alive. From a cascade of muslin and buckram, such as one sees in portraits by Reynolds, emerged the frail figure of a young woman – hardly more than a girl – tenderly haloed in golden light. How had Ethal achieved the chiaroscuro effect of that enveloping aura?

The face and the throat of the young duchess seemed to be emanating like some kind of a perfume from the monotonous grey-brown background of the scarcely-prepared canvas. It was, so to speak, a *psychic* painting – for the fragility of that figure beneath the flight of the buckram, and the narrowed oval of that face, seemed more like the image of a soul than a flower.

The Duchess of Searley! She had the slimness of a stem and the transparence of a white iris bathed in soft light: an unreal creature, graceful and aristocratic; already distant, like an apparition, irredeemably consecrated to death. Oh, the astonishing profundity of her great eyes, fresh as a mountain spring! I could never grow weary of looking at her. To the extent that an English noblewoman could resemble a courtesan, Claudius's sketch reminded me painfully of Willie Stephenson. There was, to be sure, the same frail and white neck, crying out for strangulation or the axe: a nape of snow and amber, made for the scaffold. Hers was the kind of beauty, formulated by luxury and ancestry, whose delicacy dazzles and exasperates: an atavistic challenge; one of those rare and precious specimens of humanity which attracts emotion, lightning, and death.

'*Charmante, n'est ce pas?*' said Ethal, in a heavy mock-Parisian accent. 'A Caligula would have had her raped in the circus, to the rapturous applause of the entire Roman rabble. As I told you, a true lily.

> '*Suffering makes them divine:*
> '*Their elegance and their pallor*
> '*In the great Venetian vase*
> '*A seeming martyr among flowers.*

'Better than charming: touching. Now, that little angel had her own income of three hundred thousand francs, and Tommy Sternett - the great sleeping partner in the firm of Humphrey & Son – settled all her racecourse wagers for the year, which included the follies of Epsom on Derby Day . . . a trifle of eighty thousand pounds sterling at the lowest estimate; the girl loved a flutter. That granted Sternett access to her table and her bed. Yes, that very same ideal . . . And he was not the only one, my dear Fréneuse – there were two others. If I can remember them, I'll tell you their names . . .'

The man with the rings on his hands continued to drool over the lilies.

THE MURDER

It was the turn of the others now.

The Marchioness of Beacoscome was rendered in pastel, but there was a singular energy in the portrait, as if some kind of frenzy had crushed and done violence to the colours. Her full bosom sprung forth in brief and jerky strokes, zebra-stripes of grey and white indicating fragments of material: the dappled folds of a satin dress. Ethal must have painted it in haste, and in a fever: glistening pearls, outlined as if in chalk, flowed in the folds. It was a proud and confident product, almost slapdash in the disdain of its details, like an Antonio Moro or a Goya.

Antonio Moro! I could not refrain from glancing stealthily at Claudius. He was certainly the frightening double of the cowled gnome of the Flemish master. Beneath the disguise of his dinner-jacket – we were supposed to be dining together – his likeness to my memory of the portrait in the Louvre was crying out. It was all there: the enormous head; the thickened neck; the trunk which was too long on the legs which were too short; all the crookedness and obliqueness that Antonio Moro had put into his dwarf. Those bushy eyebrows and that sniffling nose were those of the Duc D'Albe's jester, and above all else there was the jester's malice, lying in ambush beneath the heavy eyelids. I am sure that it was that malice, attentive to my examination, which made him adopt the same pose as the portrait – stiffly upright, powerful and pretentious, with his fist on his hip – while he detailed the beauties of the Marchioness of Beacoscome, pointing them out to me with his horrible hand.

'The most beautiful of the three!' declared the painter, indicating the hauteur of her lips with the nacreous pallor of his enormous rings. 'Look at the splendour of that flesh! It is the triumph of a healthy complexion, the parvenu flesh which cannot acquire the impoverishment of a decadent ancestral line: the soft, purplish-blue and greenish tones as dear to Van Dyck as Velasquez. The blood of fur-trappers and virile seamen still flourishes under the skin of the millionairess – but she had such a devout desire and determination to fall, to recapture by her own efforts the lost aristocracy of her remotest ancestors! Snobbery was her vocation. She was as enthusiastic for ether, morphine and long insomniac nights as others are for the produce of their couturiers. I had persuaded her that a nacreous tint refined and exquisitely faded the cheeks and the eyes, and she yearned with all her heart to lose her freshness. What a fool! She was cold enough to make a Parisian's fingers tingle in August, but she would have made love to the ugliest Irish dock-worker as calmly as the most handsome of horse-guards. She took me for the ultimate arbiter of elegance, and her whole apartments in Piccadilly reeked of amaryllids and lilies, because she had seen them in my house. She was totally stupid. Oh, the heavy hours of those sittings when she came to pose! I always hoped that she would end up ill and becoming feeble in that studio crammed with flowers, but she had the constitution of a horse. Nothing became pale but her eyes; her complexion stubbornly remained that shade of pink, like the petals of camellias. Ah, she bored me so! It was her doctors who forbade her my studio. As you can see, though, devoid of mystery and charm as they may be, her eyes are a rather beautiful violet colour. She is a big pearl without orient, which only achieves purity as she approaches death. She is a superb lily grown out in the open, in a world which only loves the produce of the hothouse.

'To think that she is now boring the Chinese!

'Ah, she had not the attractiveness of this little bust!'

Negligently, he placed his dry and claw-like hand upon the waxen face of Angelotto, whose bust he had brought out of its recess, and which I had not previously noticed.

Angelotto was his pride and his triumph. There was an ultimate agony in that work. He had sculpted it with a knowingly prolonged pleasure in slow suffering and frightful terror. Beneath his fingers, tearful with enormous pearls, the pain-filled face of the little consumptive model seemed to screw itself up and become paler still.

'This one is another thing altogether,' said Ethal, decisively taking back his hand. 'What do you think of this physiognomy?'

It was a tall, slender canvas framed in silver, like certain pictures to be found in Potsdam and the royal museums of Germany. The setting gave the impression of being overrun by shadows whose gloom was alleviated by the light of some invisible vent, like the interior of a crypt or funereal bedroom. Seated on a stretched couch of ice-blue satin, encased in a satin sheath the colour of honesty, was the enigmatic figure of a woman. She was like the Empress Josephine in her First Empire robe, her hair gathered in a chignon, starred with turquoises. She sat perfectly still, and the bare flesh of arms and shoulders had the morbid and cold brilliancy of a water-lily. An enamelled collar supported the high throat and her hair was brown; her stiff and ecstatic face was illuminated by two large and radiant eyes whose immense irises were a liquid and dark blue. This woman of the night had the exquisite oval face of a nymph, the inspired pallor of a sybil and the magnified gaze of a priestess who sees God.

Oh, the wondrous harmony of that pose, with the two widely-spaced arms resting their hands on the couch; the hallucinated anguish of that whole attentive figure; the slender design of her fingers and the slow curve, like that of a swan's neck, of her frail arms; the strange hypnotic character of that little Diana of the Consulate!

'Isn't she delectably lunary and nocturnal in all that blue luminosity?' whispered a fervent voice close beside me. 'It's certainly the setting she requires – pompous and icy at the same time, not sinister, but funereal. A little nymph of Erebus! Have you noticed the curve of her mouth? Well, this Hecate of the three faces, this little priestess of Artemis of the Taurians, this Iphigenia of Glück's operas, is the sister of Thomas Welcome, the Marchioness Eddy in person. Do you not see the resemblance? Look at her eyes.'

Ethal's words echoed loudly in my soul. It was my own thought that he was articulating. Now that he had formally introduced me to the portrait, what infamies would he relate to me concerning the sitter? I recalled the hallucinatory opium-smoking session held in that same studio, and the frightful stories complaisantly and droolingly told about all those invited to that memorable evening. Not one of them had found favour; from the incense of Maud White to the venal past of the Duchess of Althorneyshare, all their ignominies and all their lusts had been slowly stirred by the abominable Englishman, as he spattered them one by one: the Marquise Naydorff; the Princess of Seiryman-Frileuse; Olga Myrianinska . . .

From the women encountered in his home that evening, he had let loose so many frightening silhouettes: the almost genial caricatures of a visionary observer. And at a given moment, in the middle of a congregation of ghouls and larvae conjured up by his own imagination, he had been able – without overmuch risk of disbelief, so certain was he of the nightmarish atmosphere – to breathe into my ear: 'We are at the Sabbat!'

That evening at Ethal's, the males had been evaluated just as the females were, and found equally wanting. The herd of Freddy Schappman and the well-scrubbed gardenia-sporting Englishmen, all more-or-less refugees from London, had nothing to envy the trio of foreign *grandes dames* in terms of reputation. The Comte de Muzarett and the Princess of Frileuse were able to offer their hands to one another. On that evening, however, the odious whispers had been justified by the demeanour of the people and the notoriety of their defects. Were it not for their names and high social standing – the titles of some and the fortunes of others – a police raid on Ethal's establishment would have been entirely appropriate. What guests! I had only needed to look at them to understand how accurately Claudius had spoken when he invited me to come and see some monsters. In any case, he must have whispered in their ears, according to the same formula, some such account of me: I was part of the collection myself. We were all old acquaintances; or, worse, were destined to make one another's acquaintance within the dizzy and – alas! – so narrow heights of our cycle of infamy.

But all the members of the menagerie which Claudius brought together that night were well able to defend themselves with beak and claw. I know well enough that civilization is the taming of wild beasts by fear or by self-interest, that human faces don masks of hypocrisy as the mouths of dogs are muzzled; that night, vanity might have cast off their shackles and muzzles, and left them free to bite, had their tamer not been so close at hand. I had tolerated Ethal in the role of animal-trainer then, for those monsters were alive.

It was to contemplate the images of phantoms that Claudius had invited me now, in the fluid gold light of the end of a beautiful day in May: three portraits of women; almost three portraits of dead women, given that one was already defunct and another dying. The setting was the same, and in that studio illuminated by white flowers, Ethal recommenced and continued his work of destruction. He soiled and defiled as he pleased the memory and the reputation of those women! With an iconoclastic joy, he muddied their future by piling up the mire of their past. It was as if the litter of the streets were being shovelled on to a bed of lilies; as if blows of a pick-axe were rained down on precious fragile things, impeccable and white; as if each act of speech shattered, polluted, crumbled to dust . . .

Oh, that massacrer of souls and flowers, that revealer of defects, that killer of dreams, that sower of doubts, that agitator of despairs . . . what would he say to me about Lady Kerneby? With what stigmata would he mark that gentle and fatal face, whose large eyes reminded me so painfully of those of Thomas Welcome?

Such was my dread of hearing something irreparable that I said to myself, imploringly: 'Not that one! No, for the love of God, let that one alone!'

He had kept her for last, like some choice morsel of prey. Sure of his effect, an artist accommodating and preparing his public, he sat down on a sofa, signalling to me to take my place beside him. His manner was business-like, and there was a pause before he began.

'That one,' he said, in a measured voice, his words echoing strangely in the silence, as though they were being stamped out, 'is the worthy sister of our dear friend Welcome.'

Beneath the heavy eyelids his little eyes shone, laughing with a ferocious joy. He sensed that he was making me ill, and the whole of his gnome-like face was lit up. He savoured my anguish and paused again before continuing.

'I have already told you, haven't I, that Thomas is her illegitimate brother? They have the same mother – it's quite a story. The pregnancy of Georgina Melldon was one of the greatest scandals English society has seen these last thirty years. A young Irish farmer was responsible for it. It is very warm in August in Ireland, and Georgina's family was spending the summer on their estate. There could be no question of her marrying a farmer: the young girl was sent to Scotland the following spring, in order to give birth. Thomas Welcome is Irish by descent but Scottish by birth. The Marchioness Eddy, on the other hand, is the entirely legitimate daughter of Count Reginald Sussex. That Georgina was so beautiful! It is very necessary that I explain these atavisms to you . . . '

I was not listening. While he was speaking, lolling back on the cushions of the sofa, Ethal had extended his arms. One hand had come to rest, mechanically, on the painted wax hair of the Italian bust, which was enthroned on a small pedestal some distance away. I could no longer see anything except that hand.

Decorated with metal and mother of pearl, the fingers were clenched like claws, kneading the bulging forehead of Angelotto. It was the talon of a vulture descending upon the effigy of the poor child. In the midst of all those pearls the poisoned emerald gleamed like an eye, and it seemed to me that within the grip of that cruel hand the dolorous face slowly convulsed with suffering.

Ethal was still reciting his catalogue of infamies. What was he saying? I no longer knew ... but in the dark shadow of some kind of hallucination, I saw, between those fingers of will and fever, a succession of other familiar faces wither and blanch.

There was the thinned oval and the great forget-me-not eyes of the little duchess; and there was the splendour of the rosy flesh of Lady Beacoscome; and, finally, there was the pallid face and ecstatic eyes of the Marchioness Eddy ...

The poisoner's hand closed yet again on all those bruised and dolorous temples! A ghastly whiteness seemed to flow along the rings, dampened by some uncanny sweat – and when I saw within that armature of livid jewels, coming into view after so many agonised faces, the exhausted face and scarified eyes of Thomas himself, I came abruptly to my feet. Brought upright by a somersault of horror – horror and hatred – and moved by a will foreign to my own, not knowing what I was doing or why, I threw myself on Ethal.

His was now the brow gripped and thrust back by a single hand, his the hair and cranium cruelly kneaded in its turn. With my other hand I seized his horrible hand with the even more horrible rings, and shoved it violently into his mouth: that foul mouth full of the names of Thomas and Eddy. It was my turn to be entranced by the sight of his little eyes magnified by terror.

I brutally rammed the stones of his rings against the enamel of his teeth. It required three blows to shatter the venomous emerald.

Ethal, buttressed behind, strove to lift himself up, and tried to bite. The wretch bit nothing but his own fingers! His free hand seized me by the neck and exerted such force as it could to strangle me, but still I held his head back and forced him to drink ...

The broken gem was empty. The grip of Ethal's hand

became feeble; a heavy sweat beaded his face, and his breast rose and fell like bellows. His two vitreous eyeballs rolled up, like two billiard-balls, towards the suddenly-creased temples – then they capsized beneath the eyelids which no longer contained anything but whiteness, and his whole body lost its rigidity, becoming slack.

'*Actum est.*' The deed was done.

The white and funereal night-watch of the flowers was all around me.

The head lay inert on the shoulder, the mouth hideously open. The hand with the rings had slid down on to his breast; I placed it at his side, on a cushion. The Duchess of Searley smiled in her frame, Lady Beacoscome drew herself up haughtily, above the zebra-stripes of fabric. The gaze of Thomas Welcome followed me, through the eyes of the Marchioness Eddy, astounded and complicit at the same time. I regretted nothing.

I smoothed down my shirt, calmly adjusted my cravat, opened the door of the ante-chamber, and descended the flight of stairs.

THE GODDESS

I have just left Ethal's studio. There I was confronted with
his corpse. I say confronted, but that is too dramatic a
word, since not the slightest shadow of suspicion has
touched me. I was summoned there as a friend of the dead
man, invited by the commissaire of police in the hope that
I might shed some light on the case by giving evidence as
to the hypothetical causes of this mysterious suicide – for
the whole world believes that there has been a suicide. The
broken stone of the ring testifies to that effect; the doctors
have declared the cause of death to be poisoning by curare.
Even the decoration of the studio – that apotheosis of
amaryllids and lilies accumulated around the body, as if for
a wake – has been taken as an indication of premeditation
by the commissaire.

In the eyes of the law today, and in the eyes of all Paris
tomorrow, that splenetic Englishman and artist of the
bizarre, Claudius Ethal, has voluntarily delivered himself
to death by drinking the contents of a poisoned ring. The
deliberate piling up of rare flowers and the presence in the
studio of three portraits which the painter prized most
highly will corroborate in the public mind the verdict of
suicide . . .

As for myself, the murderer, the one and only perpetra-
tor of the crime – I have not even been questioned,
although I have taken no steps to establish an alibi. At the
least suspicion, at the least equivocation, I would have
confessed. I would have proclaimed my act loudly: my act
which, since it is not punished, is just. I am an instrument
of justice.

Ethal deserves to be dead. He had filled the cup to
overflowing; the proof of it is the quasi-somnambulistic
cold-bloodedness with which I have accomplished the act,
almost without doubting myself.

Same day, eleven o'clock at night.

I have re-read my manuscript. How I exonerate myself in my own eyes! What pains I take to excuse my act: my act which *is* a crime, seeing that since this morning I have composed my attitude and my gestures like an actor, misleading to the best of my ability the opinion of the law, in the cause of remaining at liberty! As to that verdict of suicide, it is I myself who have established it, by letting it be understood that Ethal had despaired of ever being able to take up his brushes again. To lend credence to the account of a painter who did not wish to survive his talent, have I not shown the commissaire the letter in which Claudius invited me to come to admire his portraits?

It is that foolish letter – let us be perfectly clear about this: foolish from the viewpoint of a commissaire of police, not from that of an artist – which has secured the conclusion of suicide: another folly!

I soon realised how useful that letter might be. When that policeman presented himself at my apartments at ten o'clock, asking me to follow him to the Rue Servandoni, I was very careful to take it with me. I had the intention of furnishing myself with proof. Calmly, I put it in the pocket of my coat – and then, coolly, I followed the man, without questioning him further as to the purpose of his visit or the reason why my presence was required in the Rue Servandoni. It was not until we arrived in front of Claudius' house that I displayed any emotion.

'Has something happened to Monsieur Ethal?' I asked – and when the man remained silent I hurried up into the studio. The door was open. I bumped into a policeman in the ante-chamber, and rushed past him into the studio.

Nothing had been moved. The position of the cadaver had likewise been respected. The mouth, still wide open, was lightly blackened, the mucous membranes had become bluish, and under the heavy, swollen eyelids there was a gleam as of burnished silver. The tautly clenched hand lay inertly upon a cushion, in the place where I had placed it. The commissaire, a group of policemen and two doctors all got up as I entered. The portrait of the Duchess of Searley was behind them.

Then, carefully calculating the effect of my actions, I stopped in my tracks, strangled a cry, and – after quickly greeting the assembled people with a stammered 'Messieurs, Messieurs,' – ran to Claudius and took him in my arms. I swiftly searched his hand with my eyes, seized it with my own, and displayed the ring! Then, with a grand gesture of despondency, I let the hand fall again.

'You were due to pass the evening together, I believe, monsieur?' the commissaire asked me. 'Did you not come yesterday, at about six o'clock, to this studio?'

'But of course, monsieur. Ethal had arrived that same morning from Nice, and had given me notice by letter. I believe that I have it on me.' (I pretended to search for it.) 'Ethal was desirous that I should see these portraits: he had just won a lawsuit which made them his property. For a whole year Ethal had painted nothing, because the great troubles he had experienced in London had disheartened him – in brief, it was a great joy for him to recover possession of his works. He attached enormous importance to them. If only I had his letter ... Hence the childish decor of flowers; yesterday, a fête was held in this studio.'

It was all a cunning web of lies, an intricate combination of convincing plausibilities, recited with a coolness which made me marvel at myself. It was as if I were split in two. I seemed to be a helpful witness in a judicial drama whose intrigue – all the scenes and the gestures of the actors – I was also directing. The commissaire and the doctors seemed to be speaking words for which the replies were already scripted. When the interrogator reiterated the question: 'Were you not due to dine together?' I immediately responded: 'Certainly. He is still dressed for it. We were to have spent the evening together but just as we were going out Ethal declared that he was tired. He had spent the night on a train, and perhaps the odour of these flowers ... the great emotion of having recovered his pictures at last ... in brief, he begged me to excuse him, and to leave him alone. We were due to meet again, this evening.'

'There was nothing then, which might have enabled you to foresee the action taken by your friend?'

'Nothing, absolutely nothing. I am astounded, dumb-founded by it.'

'Did you not speak of a letter?'

'Indeed, the letter in which Ethal invited me to come to see his pictures. I have left it at home, but I will place it at your disposal.'

'We would be obliged to you if you could give us sight of it, monsieur. Forgive us for disturbing you, but you alone are able to give us vital information about the dead man. You may go now.'

And that was all.

In the hallway, Ethal's manservant William, who had arrived that same night from Nice, threw himself in front of me.

'Ah, monsieur, who could have foreseen this? To think that I found him thus on coming from the station. If only I had taken the same train, none of this would have happened.'

'Should I send for a nun to sit beside him, William?'

'No, I will watch over him myself; Madame will doubt-less arrive in due course.'

'Madame?'

'Yes – Monsieur Ethal's mother. We sent her a telegram only this morning.'

Madame! Ethal had a mother! He had never mentioned her to me. And I had deprived that mother of her son! That was the day's one moment of emotion. I said some comforting words to William, and left.

I can no longer recognise myself. My sensibility is utterly annihilated. Never have I been so calm. Is it the murder which has ripened within me this power of cold-blooded-ness and this singular energy? As yet I have felt not a pang of regret – on the contrary, my conscience becomes more certain with every passing hour that an act of justice has been done.

Where was I? Whence came those stumps of porticoes and those tall stone columns rising up into infinity? My God, what ruins! And those ancient mutilated statues and those plinths in the sand . . . it was as if they really existed, as if they were actually there! Where, then, have I seen that ruined city before? And not a blade of grass, not a spring of ivy . . . just sand and more sand.

It was such a strange solitude. Not a bird in the air. And what silence! And how soft the air was! How I loved that dead moonlit city, and the immaterial purity of that night. The porphyry of its columns had such limpid reflections, and nothing shifted in the shadows. It was such a delicious and enervating calm. The steles, pilasters, pylons and porticos extended into the distance . . .

By and by, I heard the faint rustle of feathers somewhere close at hand. It astonished me without frightening me. Where could the sound have come from, given that the city was dead and that there were no birds there? At the same time, glaucous gemstones seemed to gleam in the shadows, and I thought they might be stars reflected in pools of water . . . but there was no more water in that desert than there were stars in the sky . . .

Scarcely audible, murmurous words were whispered in my ears, spelling out phrases like caresses, in some unknown language. I loved those incomprehensible whispers: the consonants attenuated, the vowels so very gentle . . .

All of a sudden, the porticos and the steles were alive with people. Were they caryatids coming to life? Never had I seen such gentle female faces. They formed a circle all around me, drawing closer – and suddenly stopped still. They were the colour of ash, and their heads were decked with tapering tiaras like the priestesses of India. I was not afraid, and yet I shivered; it was a voluptuous shiver, piercing but not alarming. I had seen these figures before, somewhere . . . yes, I had seen those heavy hemmed eyelids and those triangular smiles before. Where? Somnolent and ironic, they were now swaying all around me. What I had taken for the sound of wings was the clicking of long pendants of metal and emeralds brushing their silken tunics. Their half-naked bodies were cuirassed in jewels; rings of enamel encased their ankles, breast-plates of gems their breasts.

Suddenly, unexpected phosphorescences were lit within their eyes; each face was transfigured by sublime profundity; each tiara illuminated – and then they vanished, each and every one! But I knew now who they resembled. They were a host of 'dancing Salomés' – the Salomé of the famous water colour by Gustave Moreau. As for their luminous gazes, their phosphorescent irises, they were the emerald eyes of the idol of onyx: the little Astarté from the house in Woolwich, now lodged in my apartments.

Never had I had such a lovely dream.

Paris, 5 June 1899

For three days I have been subjected to the ignominy of articles and leaders on the subject of Ethal. All the dirt has been stirred up, all the wretchedness of his life exhumed, exposed to the light of day like so much jetsam: the entire stock of anecdotes, true and false, and all the legends hawked around these last five years concerning the painter and the man. Even his talent has been called into question – and there I detect the hand of his contemporaries. Women are included in these stories, with only the merest gesture towards the perservation of their incognito; initials serve to denounce those who sat for portraits whose fashionability is unpardoned. In some of these articles my own name is mentioned; I am cited as a friend of the deceased – and all the scandals brought back to life about the dead man also rebound on me.

What a pack of human hyenas! He had every reason to despise them, to scourge them with his sarcasms and to defy them with all his eccentric follies – these starveling prowlers of cemeteries who, with the coffin scarcely closed, come to sniff out and devour the still-fresh bodies.

This has been, as one imbecile described it, a 'very Parisian' suicide.

They are imbeciles all, cowardly scandal-mongers and miserable wretches. What necrological articles have they in reserve for me? They will not have the pleasure of writing them. I have had enough of the Paris of snobs and the whole of Europe: ancient, corrupt and stuck in a rut. The murder of Ethal has liberated me and cleared my sight. I am in control of myself again, and I am wholly myself. Welcome was right: I must become a voyager, in order to live with fervour a life of passion and of adventure, to vanish into the thin air of the unknown, to lose myself in the infinite, in the energy of virile peoples, the beauty of unalterable races and the sublimity of instincts . . .

I shall meet my business agents and instruct them to liquidate everything. I shall quit Paris. I shall leave it all behind!

Paris, 9 June
There is no denying that what I experienced last night was nothing less than a vision: some unknown entity, from the invisible and the intangible, manifested itself to me.

I was in bed, but definitely not asleep. I had gone to bed early, having following the recommendations of Corbin by taking a long walk, testing my muscles to the limit in order to cultivate a healthy fatigue. The lamp on my bedside table was lit, I had a book open before me; therefore, I was not asleep.

She has appeared to me.

She took the form of a nude figure, not large – rather small by human standards, but of an incomparable purity of line. She was at the foot of my bed, her head slightly tilted back, as if she were floating in mid-air; her toes were not touching the ground. She appeared to be asleep.

Her eyelids were lowered, her lips were half-open, her naked body was offered up, abandoned and chaste. Her bare arms, joined at the back of her neck, supported her ecstatic head. She was slim at the waist, and her armpits were dotted as if with rust.

It was a delirious vision. Her flesh had the transparency

of jade, but from the diadem of emeralds about her forehead ran a flowing veil of black gauze: a vapour of crêpe, which coiled around her hips, hiding the sexual organs, and terminated in a fetter-like knot about her two ankles, embellishing the pale apparition with mystery.

I would have loved to be able to see the gaze hidden beneath her closed eyelids. Some secret presentiment informed me that this lethargic naked form held the key to my cure. The ecstatic figure of that succubus was the living incarnation of my secret.

These words sighed in my ear: 'Astarté, Acté, Alexandria.'

And the figure vanished.

Astarté is the name of the Syrian Venus; Acté is the name of a liberated slave; Alexandria is the city of the Ptolemies, of courtesans and philosophers. Astarté is also the name of a demon!

Paris, 28 July
I leave for Egypt tomorrow.

Thus ends the manuscript of Monsieur de Phocas.

AFTERWORD

Some Observations on
Monsieur de Phocas

Monsieur de Phocas is a kind of portmanteau text gathering together Jean Lorrain's ideas about the darker side of his life in that *fin de siècle* Paris which a posthumous collection of his articles dubbed *la ville empoisonnée*: the Poisoned City. The manuscript left behind by the eponymous anti-hero as he sets off for the mysterious East is a catalogue of all the Poisoned City's horrors and ignominies, and a testament to the darkly seductive magnetism of its suburban low-life, as experienced by a nobly-born, fabulously rich, contemptuously aloof and direly neurasthenic character – a character who is in some strange sense the spectre (or 'larva') which Jean Lorrain occasionally glimpsed when he looked at himself in a mirror, lurking behind the painted and powdered mask which was his face.

Like Huysmans' *À rebours*, the novel is cast as a first-person account of the adventures of a nobleman who supposedly embodies the entire *malaise* of an epoch – an epoch whose reality repels him while certain aspects of its art entrances him. Both authors were aware that they had a cause in common, but they were both fully aware that their two central characters – fantastic extrapolations of their contrasting personalities – could hardly have been more different.

Jean Des Esseintes – Huysmans' noble *alter ego* in *À rebours* – is eccentric and neurasthenic, but he is also very methodical. His opposition to the values of the world from which he is trying to isolate himself may be exaggerated to the point of grotesquerie, but it is closely reasoned and it is underpinned by an articulate and ingenious philosophy.

His adventure in the construction of a private world, drawing on the resources of all available artifice, is meticulously planned; he has a blueprint for an ideal existence which he sets out to actualise with the utmost care. It is, to be sure, an impossible project for which he is constitutionally unsuited, and which he has in the end to abandon, but his endeavours are both constructive and heroic, and the subversive moral homilies which spice his account are as deft and as witty as they are eloquent.

The Duc de Fréneuse, who eventually elects to become the humble Monsieur de Phocas, does not at first glance look like any kind of ideal self-projection, although the fact that the author chooses to distance himself from the narrative by posing as its editor hardly constitutes a convincing deception. Fréneuse is quite clearly as mad as a hatter; lest anyone should fail to notice this, the sole 'editorial interjection' within the body of his manuscript calls the reader's attention to the fact that the dates do not make sense. This underlines the claim that the various contradictions in the manuscript are deliberate on the part of its true author if not on the part of its notional author. Fréneuse's alienation from his contemporaries is entirely negative; he is horrified, terrified, inconsistent and sick, and he has neither a philosophy to underpin his situation nor a plan to help him deal with it. He is prone to outbursts of moral rage – aimed as often as not at himself – but there is little trace of wit or deftness in his commentary. Instead of making plans of his own, he looks to others for salvation, and then agonises helplessly over the merits of their advice.

At first sight, these contrasts might be taken as evidence that *Monsieur de Phocas* is simply a less careful, less original and less worthwhile book than *À rebours* – as, indeed, the world at large considers it to be – but the matter is not quite as simple as that. The disordered nature of the manuscript which forms the bulk of *Monsieur de Phocas* may be a convenient artefact, but it is an artefact nevertheless; it has a particular significance.

The difference between the two books reflects a difference between the two men. It seems that Huysmans really did think that some solution to his existential predicament might be found if he could only figure it out, whereas Lorrain appears to have given up any such hope almost before his career got under way. Despite what Edmond Goncourt seems to have thought, it was probably not the accident of his doomed infatuation with Judith Gautier which ruined him, but something much more deep-seated which he came to believe unalterable and ineradicable. It ought to be noted that in this matter Huysmans was probably wrong and Lorrain was probably right. Huysmans ultimately tried to find the kind of salvation via religion which he had mockingly advocated in the climax of *À rebours*, but a reconciliation with a worn-out faith on the part of one who has supposedly seen through the sham of his decadent era is an ignominious confession of abject failure. Lorrain's early recognition that he was never going to be accepted by the social élite, and his bitter acknowledgement of the horrific absurdity of his sexual inclinations – which were not merely homosexual but ran very definitely to what would now be called 'rough trade' – were accurate and honest, however depressing.

So far as we know, Lorrain never sought sexual partners among his own friends or in his own social class; he went slumming instead, and if the evidence of *Monsieur de Phocas* is reliable, it seems that he despised himself for it. Given his awkward sexual tastes and his craving for acceptance by the *haut monde* to which Robert de Montesquiou and Sarah Bernhardt belonged, the possibility of his ever discovering a half-way satisfactory relationship or a contented way of life was probably ruled out *a priori*. If ever a man was damned, it was he, and the fact that contemporary Paris could hold up a mirror in which he could readily perceive the relative success of others slightly more blessed undoubtedly increased his chagrin. It is not surprising that the darkest of all his fabular *contes* – which became increasingly dark as his career advanced – is a bizarrely transfigured and inverted version of the myth of Narcissus: *Narkiss*, first published in 1898, in book form 1909. Nor is it surprising that his archetypal image of the Decadent personality should be a man fatally and irredeemably obsessed by a mirage. Given that he was not only narcissistic but proud, it is understandable that in his darker moods he would flirt with self-hatred, and with the notion – both direly horrible and perversely comforting – that he might be mad.

We must remember too that Jean Lorrain knew full well – although many readers apparently overlook the fact – that *À rebours* is first and foremost a black comedy. Although it contains fewer jokes, *Monsieur de Phocas* is also a black comedy; its grotesquerie is calculated and its irony cuts much deeper than may initially be apparent. The conclusion at which the Duc de Fréneuse ultimately arrives is, of course, no redemption at all; it is best regarded as the blackly ironic climax of a *conte cruel*.

Monsieur de Phocas was a long time in gestation. Lorrain produced a kind of prototype for it in the title story of his collection *Un démoniaque* (1895), in which one M. de Burdhe (to whom acknowledgement is wryly and obliquely made in the text of the novel) offers an account of his similar obsession with a certain elusive gaze. The subject-matter of several other short stories and articles is also absorbed into the text – for instance, 'L'homme aux têtes de cire' from *Buveurs d'âmes*. What is new, however, is the way in which the contending forces surrounding the Duc, pulling him forcibly in different directions with scant regard for the authority of his own vacillating will, are incarnated as actual persons (or, at least, as the images of persons). The most powerful and the most problematic among these forces – and hence the most interesting – is materialised as the odious Englishman Claudius Ethal.

Several commentators – including Lorrain's biographer Philippe Julian and the only English commentator to have writen extensively about Lorrain's work, Jennifer Burkett – have suggested that Ethal is based on Oscar Wilde. This identification is undoubtedly encouraged by the fact that Ethal arrives in Paris having exiled himself to Paris in the wake of a lawsuit involving one 'Lord Kerneby' but it would probably be a mistake to take it too seriously. Lorrain was an admirer of Wilde, and used one of his 'Pall-Malls' to launch a searing attack on the English hypocrisy which had condemned Wilde to hard labour and wrecked his career. Lorrain met Wilde in the early 1890s, when his friend Marcel Schwob – also a writer of supernatural vignettes and wryly dark *contes* – brought Wilde to dine at his house; Lorrain thought that occasion sufficiently auspicious to invite Anatole France as well. Although Lorrain seems not to have renewed this acquaintance when Wilde came to Paris after serving his sentence, there is no reason to suppose that his attitude to the English writer was such as to licence the kind of parody that would have been involved in transforming him into Ethal. We need not accept the Duc de Fréneuse's view that Ethal is an archetype of evil – he gives a rather different account of himself, which is rather more convincing than the Duc's paranoid and rumour-based fantasies – in order to recognise that if Ethal were based on any real person the characterisation would be horribly unflattering.

The text itself gives us a different account of the manner in which the character of Ethal might have been inspired. He is explicitly linked to a painting by Antonio Moro of the dwarf kept as a jester by the Duc D'Albe, and he does indeed function as a kind of jester, whose malicious buffoonery masks an all-too-perceptive wisdom. Ethal's rival within the plot, Thomas Welcome – who has a very different notion of how the Duc's existential malaise can be cured – is likewise associated with a painting, but this time a purely hypothetical image produced by Ethal himself. Welcome thus becomes a kind of 'secondary creation' – the better aspect of the equivocally threatening Ethal (the text is always telling us how inextricably bound together they are).

The most useful key to the decoding of these symbols is undoubtedly the names attached to the characters. Lorrain rarely gave his characters realistic names and was fond of sometimes convoluted wordplay. To an English reader there is nothing in the least abstruse about 'Welcome', but French readers would probably have found the other two names more obvious in their implication. 'Fréneuse' is an adjectival modification of *frénésie* (the actual adjective is *frénétique*), straightforwardly translatable as 'frenzied'. 'Ethal' is superficially reminiscent of *étal* (a butcher's meat-stall; *étalage* refers more generally to window-dressing and vulgar ostentation) but if that name too is regarded as a calculatedly-botched adjective then the noun from which it comes is surely *éther*.

Ethal's role in the plot – he is a 'thought-reader' who gets inside the Duc's head and feeds his fantasies, all the while pretending to be working towards a cure for all his ills – might easily be regarded as a phantasmagorical extrapolation of the role played in Lorrain's life by ether. If we elect to interpret things according to this pattern, then Thomas Welcome's alternative cure – although studiously couched in terms of the familiar Decadent rhetoric regarding the virtues of culture unspoiled by civilization – becomes suspiciously akin to the kind of cure by climate which was the nineteenth century's most hopeful treatment for tuberculosis. The fact that Welcome's travel brochure – according to Ethal, at least – deceptively neglects the forces of 'base prostitution' may be taken to reflect the awareness (which no Decadent was without) that the sun can do nothing at all for syphilis. It is no coincidence that the figurine of Astarté which features in the plot has a death's-head superimposed on her genitals, nor that Fréneuse suspects at one point that the 'mouth of shadow' whispering ideas of murder in his ear might be the voice of this death's-head.

If it is seen in this light, the Duc de Fréneuse's struggle is essentially an internal one, and given that we are conscientiously reminded that his account has gaping logical flaws – the most striking of which are the nonsensical dating of the last few entries and the curious business of the letter which is supposed to provide an 'alibi' – we may be entitled to wonder whether Claudius Ethal has any existence outside the feverish brain of the Duc de Fréneuse. Perhaps he is a mere hallucination conjured up by stress: the externalisation of an enemy within. The 'murder' would thus become one more fantastic vision, one more desperate gyration in the Duc's frenzied but hopeless quest to find someone or something to turn to. .

If the names of the characters really are so vital within the symbolic scheme of the novel, much must hang on the explanation of the one name which seems to have no obvious function save to be symbolic. There must, after all, be some reason why the Duc de Fréneuse opts to become Monsieur de Phocas, and why the author thinks this move sufficiently important to generate the title of the story. It is probably not significant that the word 'phocas' actually exists in English, even though Jean Lorrain probably knew that *Phoca* was the Latin name applied in the Linnaean classification to the genus of seals, and might conceivably have known that Spenser had used 'phoca' as a trivial noun referring to a kind of sea-monster. Perhaps the Duc's change of name and new-found sense of purpose could be metaphorically linked to that of a group of mammals which reverted to the sea and thus to a more 'primitive' way of life, but the more obvious play is phonetic: the Duc de Fréneuse changes his name because he has got his life, and his predicament, 'in focus' (*focus* itself was not commonly used in French at the turn of the century, but the adjectives *focal* and *focaux* were fairly familiar in technical discourse).

The Duc de Fréneuse was probably not the first character in French literary history to put matters into clearer focus by virtue of an act of murder, and he was most certainly not the last; he is an obvious literary ancestor of Mersault, the alienated central character of Albert Camus' existentialist classic *L'étranger* (1942; tr. as *The Outsider*) with the one vital difference that Camus took the idea far more seriously. Had Colin Wilson known of the existence of *Monsieur de Phocas* when he wrote *The Outsider* (1956), his celebrated study of *angst*-ridden literary anti-heroes who seek solutions in behavioural extremes, he might well have used the text as his starting-point instead of *L'Enfer* (1908; tr. as *The Inferno*) by journalist-turned-novelist Henri Barbusse. Barbusse must, of course, have been familiar with Jean Lorrain's work, although he was born too late to be a Decadent himself.

We know, of course, that whether the writer of the enigmatic manuscript which forms the major part of Lorrain's novel joins Thomas Welcome in Benares or not, he has no hope whatsoever of making any kind of satisfactory contact with the magical gaze which fascinates him. He might have brought his vision of Astarté into sharper focus (although that is dubious, given that her genital region is carefully screened from view in the final vision) but she is and will remain as elusive as ever. Whatever 'fervour' the virile races of the un-Decadent East might possess, and whatever effect that fervour might have on the way they live, it is not something that can be shared by the Duc de Fréneuse, nor even by Monsieur de Phocas. Ethal or no Ethal, Welcome or no Welcome, the author of the manuscript is damned.

All the honest Decadents knew, at least by the time they found out what had actually happened to Arthur Rimbaud when he put an end to his *saison en enfer* by going to the East and hurling himself into a very different way of life, that there was no way out of their particular blind alley. All of them had mixed feelings about this, but in general they were ironically content to accept the verdict – Huysmans was something of a traitor to the cause. There was no escape from the Poisoned City, once its poison had been absorbed; the only consolation to be found was in palliative measures: all those art-works, comforts and petty luxuries which could transform the horrors of life just as the paints and powders which so fascinated Jean Lorrain could illuminate ravaged faces.

Alas, as Jean Lorrain unfortunately found out, even palliative measures can be fatal.

Francis Amery

APPENDIX

The Works of Jean Lorrain

Sang des dieux (1882) [poetry]
La Forêt bleue (1883) [poetry]
Modernités (1885) [poetry]
Viviane (1885) [drama]
Les Lépillier (1885) [novel]
Très Russe (1886). [novel]
Les Griseries (1887) [poetry]
Dans l'oratoire (1888) [articles]
Sonyeuse (1891) [stories]
Buveurs d'âmes (1893). [stories]
Yanthis (1894) [drama]
Sensations et souvenirs (1895) [stories]
Un démoniaque (1895) [stories]
La Petite Classe (1895) [articles]
La princesse sous verre (1896) [conte]
Une femme par jour (1896) [articles].
Poussières de Paris (1896) [articles]
Ames d'automne (1897) [stories]
Contes pour lire à la chandelle (1897) [contes]
Lorelei (1897) [conte]
L'Ombre ardente (1897) [poetry]
Monsieur de Bougrelon (1897) [novel]
Ma petite ville (1898) [stories]
Princesse d'Italie (1898) [conte]
La Dame turque (1898) [novel]
Heures d'Afrique (1899) [travel book]
Madame Baringhel (1899) [articles]
Vingt femmes (1900) [stories]
Histoires de masques (1900) [stories]
Monsieur de Phocas (1901) [novel]
Poussières de Paris (second series 1902) [articles]

Princesses d'ivoire et d'ivresse (1902) [contes]
Le Vice errant (1902) [novel]
Quelques hommes (1903) [stories]
La Mandragore (1903) [conte]
Fards et poisons (1904) [stories]
Propos d'âmes simples (1904) [stories]
La Maison Philibert (1904) [novel]
Le Crime des riches (1905) [stories]
L'École des vieilles femmes (1905) [stories]
Heures de Corse (1905) [travel book]
Madame Monpalou (1906) [novel]
Ellen (1906) [novel]
Théâtre (1906) [drama]
Le Tréteau (1906) [novel]
L'Aryenne (1907) [novel]
Maison pour dames (1908) [novel]
Narkiss (1909) [conte]
Les Pelléastres (1910) [stories]
Correspondance I. Lettres, suivies des articles condamnées (1929)
La Ville empoisonnée: Pall-Mall Paris (1930) [articles]
Femmes de 1900 (1932) [articles]